FATAL MISTAKE

A Brooks' Family Values Novel

Printed in the United States of America

ISBN- 978-0-9913426-3-1

Library of Congress Control Number: 2015905401

SIRI ENTERPRISES
RICHMOND, VIRGINIA
www.sirient.com

www.irisbolling.net

Prologue

Isaac Singleton sat in the modest tri-level home of Felecia Kennedy. It was nice...not his taste, but nice. There were pictures of her son around the room in various stages of life. The woman had aged well; she didn't look a day over fifty and he knew for a fact she had just turned seventy-five. Yes, he knew all about the whore his father had dared to have a bastard child with. He watched her under his eyelashes as she poured the tea. Dressed in tan slacks and a green cardigan sweater and shell, Felecia Kennedy was a very attractive woman and had to have been a beauty in her day.

"Would you care for sugar or cream?"

"No, thank you, Mrs. Kennedy. Please have a seat."

Felecia sat on the sofa across from the Queen Anne chair Isaac occupied. "I have to say, I was surprised when I opened the door and you were standing there. For a moment, I thought you were your father. But we both know that's not possible."

"Unfortunately, he is no longer with us. Dad left long before his body departed this earth." Isaac sat the teacup down, it was a domestic brew and not of his liking. "His death and my mother's deteriorating health is one of the reasons I decided to reach out." Nodding his head in a sincere motion, he stated, "It's time for me to get to know my brother. I regret his presence is only coming to light now. I can only believe my mother was doing what she thought was best."

"I regret William's and my deception. I'm certain it was a difficult topic for your mother to come to grips with. It was for me as well. When she came for a visit I wasn't certain what her reasons were. Yet I found her to be understanding and forgiving. At my age you can't ask for much more than that."

That was the opening he was waiting for. "My mother came here to see you?" he asked in mock surprise.

"Yes, I thought that's why you were here. To discuss the will."

"What will?"

A confused Felecia sat forward. "Her will. She brought over a copy for me to have so Bobby will be recognized."

Isaac smiled. "That's why I came." He moved to the sofa next to her and took her hand. "I know it is much later than it should have been. But I feel all of my father's children should live in the fashion he worked so hard for." He looked around, then back at Felecia and smiled. "It seems you provided well for your family. I'm sure they were very happy here. However, my father accumulated quite a portfolio. I could never live long enough to spend all he acquired. For so long I thought I was the only one. Now that we are aware of Bobby" —he nodded— "well, I believe financial arrangements should be made for him. It's what my father would have wanted." A tear dropped down Felecia's cheek. "I'm sorry. I did not mean to upset you."

Felecia waved him off. "Nonsense, you did not offend me. Your generosity and thoughtfulness overwhelm me. I did not tell Bobby about the will because I had no idea how you felt about your mother giving away what you thought would be your inheritance."

"Our inheritance. The family is just a little larger than we anticipated. In fact, I think I'll speak to my mother to have it adjusted. Half of the estate should go to Bobby, after all he is my brother."

"What an unselfish gesture."

"You haven't taken it to your attorney yet...have you?"

"Oh, no." Felecia put her hand to her chest. "I have it right upstairs in the file cabinet, with all my other important papers."

"Good." Isaac stood. "Keep it there. It should only take a few days for my attorney to make the changes." He walked towards the door. "I will bring the new will back to you and then you can share it with Bobby."

"We should do it together, Isaac."

"No, that moment should be between you and your son. Bobby and I can meet on a different day."

"You are a good man, Isaac Singleton."

"Thank you for being a good mother to my brother."

With that, Isaac walked down the sidewalk in smooth even strides as he contemplated just how he would get his hands on that will.

Two nights later, Felecia Kennedy had fallen asleep dreaming of the life her son would have before him. Her daughter would never experience what came so easy for Bobby because she was always scheming. Using her body and good looks to prey on unsuspecting men. Not her Bobby. No, Bobby had worked hard for what he had and this, this inheritance from his father, would lighten the load. Thank God for Isaac Singleton was the last thought she had before a cloth soaked in chloroform covered her face. In less than three minutes, she was out. The search for the document took less time to find. One read-through to ensure it was the correct document and then a lighter opened. The document was left on the table, with the gas oven turned on. Within minutes the man dressed in all black raised the back bedroom window and climbed out.

Monday was Estelle Singleton's housekeeper's day off. Isaac knew because he'd set it up that way. At precisely nine o'clock in the morning Estelle was sitting in the sunroom of her estate as she did each day. This morning would be her last.

Isaac entered through the side door of the kitchen, then quietly walked up the back stairs to his parents' bedroom. He walked into what had been his father's closet, straight to the back wall. He removed the picture of the old house and set it on the floor. Using the combination, he opened the safe and sorted through a few documents until he came to the handwritten will. He grinned as he read through the document. Once he was finished, Isaac placed the document in his suit pocket, closed the safe and replaced the picture.

He walked out of the room, thinking all was right with the world once again. When his mother died, all would come to him. The mansion, the land, all the properties, the stocks, the bonds, and the biggest prize of all, the billion-dollar asset of Singleton Enterprises. It would all belong to him.

"What are you doing here?"

A surprised, but calm, Isaac looked up to see his mother coming up the grand staircase. He tilted his head to the side and grinned. "Good morning, Mother. I thought I would come by and check out the old home front."

"How did you get in without me seeing you? I was right downstairs."

"I came up the back staircase."

Estelle took the last step as regally as her eighty-year-old body would allow. "Why are you sneaking around my house?"

"It is my home too, Mother."

"No, Isaac, you have a million dollar home in Atlanta that you purchased with the NBA money you ran through instead of investing like your father advised."

"Father built this estate for his family. That includes me."

"Your father wanted no parts of you after the way you shot that young man and showed no remorse."

"I did my time."

"Three years, Isaac. For a young man's life, you did three years." Estelle shook her head. "He had a wife and children."

"I did my time, I said," he snarled. "I'm not going to keep hearing about it from you. The judge did what he thought was right. Who are you to question that?"

"Your mother," she yelled back. "The one who has made amends for all the things you and your father did to people who got in your way." Estelle grabbed her chest. "I'm not feeling well Isaac. I don't want to do this with you today."

"I need a check for five-hundred thousand and I'm gone. You can stay here in the grand old house and be rid of me."

"Until next month. No, Isaac. No more." Estelle took a stop to go around him, but he blocked her. She lost her balance and began falling backwards. She reached out for Isaac's hand. He started to reach out to catch her, then suddenly pulled his hand back. Isaac stood at the top of the stairs and watched his mother fall to her death. He looked over the railing without touching anything.

"Huh. Looks dead to me." He walked down the steps, over his mother's body and out the door without looking back.

Three weeks later he was sitting in the corporate offices of Singleton Enterprises. His parents' attorneys were there reading the will.

"Gentlemen, time is of the essence; get on with it. I have a business to run now." Isaac sat at the end of the twenty-seat conference table with four attorneys, two on each side.

"Mr. Singleton," the oldest gentleman spoke as he pulled out an envelope. "There was an addendum made by your father some thirty-odd-years ago." He put the envelope on the table. "The letter was sealed. As you can see, the signature of all partners of our firm at that time is across the seal."

"And?" Isaac asked. "What is inside the envelope?"

"A letter written by your father. The message to us was not to unseal it until both William and Estelle had expired."

"They have reached that requirement. Isaac glared at the man. "I am the only child. My father left the majority of his estate to my mother and she was the trustee over what he left to me. That now reverts to me."

"That is correct. However, what is inside this envelope trumps everything."

Isaac's eyes narrowed on the man. "Open the letter."

"Very well." The other attorneys sat up as the letter was unsealed. The oldest member of the firm read the letter.

To Whom It May Concern:

This is an addendum to my last will and testimony. The signatures on the outside of the envelope are proof that I am of sound mind and body.

I am not a perfect man, however, I did what I could to make a perfect son. Isaac Singleton fell short. I don't hold him responsible. It was due to my bad decisions that he rebelled against us. This addendum is my humble attempt to correct that mistake. At the age of eighteen, Isaac fathered a child by a young girl named Gwendolyn Spivey. I forced him to abandon the girl and the child. I never knew what happened to the young girl; however, I am hereby ordering the law firm of Benet and Edmonds to search for this woman and the child. If located, the child is to receive one half the value of my total estate at the time of Estelle and my deaths. There are two conditions to be met.

1. The child must be of good moral character. This is to be determined by public standards. For things that are not acceptable in my day and time may very well be the way of things after my death.
2. The firm must locate said child and make a determination within a five-year time span from our deaths. If the child is not located, then my entire estate reverts to my son.

The man closed the envelope and looked up at Isaac. "Do you know the whereabouts of this child?"

Isaac's fist closed and opened under the table. Each time, the blood seemed to pump vigorously through his veins. "No," he finally replied as all eyes were upon him.

"As you know, this is a sizable estate. Since your mother was the trustee and you are her heir, the control of the estate goes to you. One half of the market value of the estate at the time of your mother's death will be put in escrow until the child is located or the five-year time period expires."

Isaac nodded, keeping his fist under the table and his facial expression concealed. "Since I am the trustee, all information regarding the search for my child will come to me. I, alone will be the one to explain the contents of this letter." He reached for the letter. The attorney picked it up.

"This remains in the hands of the firm until which time the child, who would be in their late thirties now, is found."

The attorneys stood. "I believe that concludes our discussion."

Isaac watched as the men left the room. The moment the door closed, his nostrils flared, his eyes became hard as he stood pushing the chair back with a force that sent it crashing into the wall. He looked around the room, his eyes bulging.

"No one is going to take what's mine. I don't care how many people I have to kill."

His jaw muscles tightened as he paced the room, thinking. His pace slowed as the words of the addendum came to him. A plan began to form in his mind. His heart rate decreased. His lips curved into a cynical smile. He had a head start on the firm. Isaac knew exactly where his child, a son, was and who raised him. It should prove to be entertaining watching one of the most prominent families in the country fall from grace.

Chapter 1

Nicolas Brooks stood in the mirror adjusting the tie to his tuxedo. This was his night. All the dedication, the long hours, the many doors that were closed in his face, all led to this night. With a lot of help from a man he admired, he believed he would now get the one thing he longed for...his father's respect.

From the moment he'd told his father of his decision to go into sports agency instead of litigation, he had been treated as a leper. As if he had abandoned the family in some way. The law was the family business. Every adult in the family was a lawyer. Not just lawyers, they all excelled in whatever field of law they applied. Starting with his father, Avery Brooks, who just happened to be the go-to lawyer for civil rights cases around the country. He'd had so many unlawful arrest and detainment cases overturned that when appeal judges would see his name on a docket, they would immediately close the courtroom so they would not be embarrassed. It was well known that Avery Brooks would not ever take a case to court without the means to win. *"People's lives are placed in my hands. It's my duty to not let them down."* That was his father's motto. Then, there was his oldest brother, Vernon Brooks...the attorney's attorney. He was known as the attorney to the rich, famous, and wealthy. He was the one who was called to handle criminal situations for those who could afford to pay the big dollars to keep themselves or their children out of jail, when jail time was a guarantee. Vernon played hardball and did not mind getting his hands a little dirty to keep his clients out of jail. *"The bigger the case...the bigger the paycheck."* The middle son to Avery, and his second brother, outdid them all. James Brooks made presidents. He'd taken a relatively unknown man and made him President of The United States of America in as little as ten years. Now he was the advisor to the President. *"The people of this country deserve the best. It's my duty to develop and deliver the man to them."*

Nick pulled the tie loose as he thought, *How in the hell am I supposed to compete with them?* He placed both hands on the Italian-marble sink top, lowered his head, and shook off the doubts.

He glanced at himself in the mirror. He was not only the baby boy to Avery and Gwendolyn Brooks, he was their youngest son, beating his twin sister Nicole by a mere, four minutes. He began to work on his tie again as he thought about his fearless twin sister. Nicole tackled everything head on, sometimes too directly. All through high school, Nicole battled with dyslexia. She was teased terribly by some of the girls. Instead of her turning the cheek, she would turn the other girls' cheek by using her fists. Whenever there was a game, Nick would hear the adventures of Nikki in the locker room. "Man we are going to rename your sister Laila, with the stinging right hook. You should take a few pointers from her." Nick would always smile and reply, "I'm a lover, not a fighter."

And he was right. As the point guard and leading scorer of the high school basketball team, Nick had no problems getting girls. His problem was getting rid of girls. To this day no girl had ever broken up with Nick Brooks— ever. Any of his ex-girlfriends from high school or college would tell you Nick was the sweetest guy, but when he was ready to move on, that door was closed. When he moved on there was never any drama, no immediate new girl in his life or anything to belittle or disrespect the previous girlfriend. Nick always believed in allowing himself time to transition from one to another. To this day Nick could call anyone of his former girlfriends to talk or hangout. He respected them and they all respected him.

"Nick, what is taking you so long?" Nick turned just as his twin sister Nicole walked through the door. "I flew in from New York for this event," she said as she knocked his hand away from the tie. "I have no intention of spending half the night in here with you." She began adjusting the tie. It was clear he was nervous about tonight, but she knew something else was bothering him. Her usually direct, take-no-prisoners approach would put him in a funk and that was the last thing she wanted to do. "Will Mother and Poppa be there?" she asked as she pulled the bow tie tight, then patted his chest.

"I'm not sure. They didn't say." Nick shrugged off the question as he studied the tie in the mirror. "Good job." He smiled at Nicole.

"Well, I can't wait to see the presentation. You've been raving about it for two months." She walked out of the bathroom, grabbed her purse off the bed, then turned to him as he came out. "If it's half as good as my opening, you will be set."

They walked out of the bedroom, down the long hallway to the foyer. "You're referring to the little get-together you had for Brook's International?" He waved her off as he opened the door. "You are comparing the governor's mansion to Buckingham Palace. Not even in the same neighborhood."

"Oh, you got jokes." Nicole smirked. "That was a red carpet event."

"A red carpet joke." He laughed as the limo driver opened the car door.

She turned and kissed him on the cheek before getting in. "I'm so proud of you, little brother."

"I'm older than you by four minutes and twenty-two seconds."

"Still, my little brother," she smiled as she slid onto the backseat of the limo with Nick following.

Nicole had to concede, stepping on the red carpet at the Brooks-Pendleton event was amazing. "I want your planner," she whispered as they stepped into the rooftop of the prestigious Club Enticement. Every corner of the room had huge monitors with the *Brooks–Pendleton* logo in lights. The ceiling was covered with gold and blue balloons, with corresponding ribbons hanging from the bottoms and though many in the room were six-five or taller, they could not reach the ribbons.

Every man was in a tuxedo and every woman was dressed to snag any one of them that gave a hint they were available.

"The women are on the prowl tonight, Nick. You better watch yourself, you are the man of the hour."

"One of the men of the hour."

"Tyrone, with his fine self, is married and his wife Kiki don't play," —Nicole laughed— "leaving you as Mr. Available. They are after you tonight."

"No worries, sis. I know you have my back."

"You know it."

"Nicolas Brooks, don't you look like chocolate-boom pop I could lick all night." A tall blonde kissed him on the cheek.

"Save me a dance." Nick smiled as he hugged her and continued walking through the crowd.

"Chocolate-boom pop..." They both were laughing when they reached their table. "Hey Vernon, Nick's a chocolate-boom pop."

"Is that so?" Their oldest brother Vernon Brooks stood and shook his youngest brother's hand. "Congratulations Nick, you have a packed house. You should be proud."

Nick looked around. "Looks like everyone

made it."

Vernon's wife Constance stood and hugged Nick. "Congratulations Nicolas." Nick returned the hug as he noticed the other seats at the table were empty. There was no time to think about it as two of Nick's clients hit him on the shoulder.

"Nick, Nick. What's up man? Do you see all the honeys in here? Man, a brother could get hurt." Derrick "Switch" Richards, a center in the NBA, stared down at Nicole's legs. "Is that all you, girl?"

Nick and Vernon both stood "Don't go there, Switch, that's my sister." Nick stared up at the man.

Switch threw his hands up in surrender. "All right, all right man. You should cover your sister up." He said as he walked away.

Nick turned to Nicole. "Stay here with Vernon. I need to find Ty so we can get started."

Tyrone Pendleton, the six-two, one hundred and ninety-five pound, dark chocolate, bow-legged suave owner of The Pendleton Agency, turned heads in whatever room he was in. Tonight his magnetism was multiplied as half-owner of the merger about to be announced. If his looks and bank account didn't draw the women, his family sure did. His stepbrothers were Eric "Silk" Davies, sexy Grammy award winning R&B singer, and his manager Jason Davies. His mother was renowned, sultry, jazz singer Miriam Davies. His agency's clientele list was the who's who of entertainment. His representation of his clients was copied by other agents throughout the industry.

Ty, as he was known, was talking with a few of the performers in the green room as Nick walked in.

"Brooks, Brooks," a few men yelled. Nick held up a hand, speaking as he continued towards Ty. He shook hands, kissed a few cheeks and finally reached Ty as a scantily clothed actress approached them. Ty excused himself from the group and turned to the woman.

"Tyrone," she whined as she swirled around. "I'm practically coming out of this dress." She pouted over her shoulder at him.

Nick stood next to Ty with a slight frown. "Haley Santana is going to be very upset if she wears that dress." He shook his head as he watched the woman in the dress that was designed to do exactly what it was doing...draw attention.

"We wouldn't want to upset Haley." Ty frowned at Nick. "Maybe you should change."

"Do you really think she would be upset?"

Nick nodded. "I do."

The woman smirked, "Well, if you think it will, I'll keep it on." She walked away, then glanced back over her shoulder to ensure both men were looking.

They were. "Thank God I'm a married man," Ty said as he stared.

"Trouble with a capital T." Nick laughed as he turned to Ty. "Are we ready?"

"I've been ready." Ty grinned. "After tonight, Bryson, Hylton and Whitfield are all yours."

"I've met with Whitfield's parents. I don't see any issues."

"No issues, one concern." Nick looked up. "Your niece, Taylor. She is too talented to be an opening act for someone like Snake."

Nick was shaking his head in agreement. "I agree. However, her mother is her manager, we only handled the contracts. The good news is that contract ends when Taylor turns twenty-one. I want you to change the direction of her career."

Ty nodded. "We'll start working on a new path for her. If we find an opening to pull her contract before it's up, we'll step in."

"Please do." Nick paused. "Listen, before we step on stage there is something I need to say. You could have picked any agency to merge with. You chose Brooks. This could have easily been a takeover. Instead you made it a partnership. I appreciate the opportunity you've given me."

"Let's be clear, Nick. I didn't give this to you. You earned it by the way you protected your clients. You put them first, while others put their pockets first. We, you and I, have a hell of an opportunity before us. I say we grab it and show the world what two brothers can do." The two shook hands then walked onto the stage.

The lights went down as a single spotlight took center stage. The announcer spoke.

"Ladies and gentlemen." A hush came over the crowd as all eyes turned to the stage. "Please welcome Nicolas Brooks and Tyrone Pendleton."

The crowd erupted in applause as excitement could be felt around the room. People moved forward to get a better view of the two men walking through the drawn curtain with microphones in their hands.

"Good evening, I am Tyrone Pendleton," Ty spoke.

"Good evening, I'm Nicolas Brooks."

"I'm a man of few words," Ty spoke from center stage at the luxurious Club Enticement on the top floor of the Black Tower in downtown Richmond, Virginia. The largest gathering of entertainers and sports figures in recent times had congregated for this announcement that would impact their lives and bank accounts.

"So we are keeping this short and to the point. While The Pendleton Agency holds the number one spot in entertainment management, there is a firm who rivals us in sports management, Brooks and Associates. We both come from proud families who believe in taking care of each other. It is on that basis we have run our respective agencies, like a family."

"We value family," Nick spoke. "Tonight we are merging The Pendleton Agency with the Brooks Agency."

The crowd erupted with cat calls, whistles, applause and cheers. Nick held up his hand to quiet the room as he continued to speak.

"Everyone in this room is a star in their respective fields. You deserve nothing less than the elite in representation. Under The Pendleton Agency, you have the best in entertainment representation. With The Brooks Agency, you have the best in sports representation. Tonight, you all have become a part of an organization that will provide you with superior representation, with a touch of elegance."

Nick and Ty stepped back as the curtain behind them opened revealing a television monitor that covered the entire wall. Appearing in gold lettering was the name, The Brooks-Pendleton Agency. A ten-minute presentation featuring top clients from both agencies played, to roars of laughter, and cheers filling the room.

As the presentation ended, R&B sensation Taylor Brooks, also known as Lil Tay, along with baseball mega star Jarrett Bryson stepped through the curtains as if they were stepping onto the stage from the monitor. Lil Tay was dressed in a one shoulder, red, A-line gown with a thigh-high split in the front. Jarrett complimented her outfit by sporting a black tuxedo with a red bow tie. He took her hand and twirled her to reveal a low cut back, which drew, whistles and catcalls from the men in the audience.

Lil Tay raised her microphone. "Welcome to Brooks-Pendleton. The Agency for the elite athlete and entertainer."

Jarrett raised his microphone. "As clients. we have the combined talent of Nicolas Brooks, Tyrone Pendleton and their associates in multiple locations, across the country."

Justin Hylton, quarterback in the NFL, currently holding three Super Bowl rings and Haley Santana, an A-list actress, appeared on stage. The crowd erupted in applause.

"The goal is to provide you, the client, with the utmost in service," Justin added.

"You've been viewing the presentation all night. Now tell me..." Haley's sultry voice rang out as she seductively ran her hand over her body. "Do you like what you see?"

The music exploded in the room and the celebration was on. The two men were immediately surrounded by the crowd, including clients, potential clients and team owners or representatives, each trying to have a moment with the men of the hour.

It took Ty and Nick a while to make it back to their tables. Ty's wife, literary agent, Kiki Simons and his brothers, Eric and Jason and their wives, award-winning author Siri Austin and photographer TeKaya, greeted them.

Nick was happy to see his parents Avery and Gwendolyn Brooks, and his brother James with his wife Ashley by his side.

"Nick." James shook his brother's hand as he patted him on the back. "This is outstanding."

"You think I could meet Jarrett Bryson," Ashley asked. "He is so fine." James and Nick stared at her. "What? He is. I don't want to take him home. I just want to look at him." She laughed.

"I'll see what I can do." Nick laughed as Ashley kissed him on the cheek.

"What a turnout." Gwen stood and hugged her son. "Nicolas, I am so very proud of you. All of these people are here to celebrate your accomplishment. This is wonderful."

Nick kissed his mom on the cheek, "Thank you, Mother." He glanced at his father, not certain what his reaction would be. The others around the table looked on as well. Nick glanced at Nicole. She sent her encouraging wink and a nod his way. Vernon gave a slight tilt of his head. Nick held his hand out to his father.

"Hey Pop. I'm glad you could make it."

"Son," Avery spoke with that deep baritone voice. "These people are depending on you. You have their livelihood in your hands. They couldn't be better protected."

Pride, so strong it caused Nick's chest to expand, filled him. He held his father's eyes and knew he meant what he said. "I appreciate that, Pop. I appreciate that." His father pulled him into a bear hug and held his son. He never understood why Nick felt he loved him any less than the rest of his children. No he wasn't happy when Nick decided to go into sports management rather than civil law. But it was his life, his choice and Avery understood that.

"Mr. Brooks." Ty stood behind Nick with his hand held out. "I would like to thank you for sending Nick my way. You were right. He is the best damn sports agent in the country."

"I believe I said the world, son."

"Indeed you did, sir." Ty laughed, as Nick looked on stunned.

"Am I missing something?" Nick asked.

Ty looked from father to son. "I never told you how I came across your name to help out with Jason Whitfield?"

"No."

"Remind me to tell you the story sometime. At the moment, we have a number of owners to meet with."

They walked away as Nicole stood, hugged her father and kissed his cheek. "You were rooting for him all the time."

"Of course I was. He's my son and he's damn good at what he does."

"I think you should tell him that, Pop, at least once." Vernon stood. "I'm going to mingle."

"I'll do the same." Nicole stood and walked towards Ty's table.

"Nicole, would you get Siri Austin's autograph for me?" Constance asked.

"Come meet her. You ask for yourself."

"I'm not going to ask anyone for their autograph like some kind of groupie," Constance replied in a huff.

"Then you don't want her autograph," Nicole replied as she continued on her path. She reached the table just as a woman approached Ty's table from the other side.

"Excuse me," she said anxiously, "which one of those men is Tyrone?"

The three women at the table all looked at each other, before Kiki, Ty's wife stood. "The tall, dark-chocolate one. "

The woman smiled and licked her lips. She adjusted her dress to show more cleavage, if that was possible. "This is going to be fun."

"He's a married man," Kiki snarled.

"I don't want him for keeps, just long enough to get what I need." She was about to walk off when Kiki snatched her by her weave. "Heifer, I said...he's married. See this..." Kiki held up her hand and wagged her finger. "One-point-two-million solitaire says married...damnit...married." She twisted her hand tighter in the woman's hair. "Now, back the hell up." She let the woman go.

The woman grabbed at her hair and backed away from the table.

TeKaya stepped in front of the woman. "I believe you were leaving." She raised an eyebrow.

The woman glared at TeKaya and thought better of it, then turned and ran away.

Nicole's eyes widened and her lips parted as she watched the woman in red walk away. She turned back to Kiki, laughing so hard tears were forming in her eyes. "I'm through....I'm so done."

"I don't play when it comes to my man. I know who he is and what he has to offer. These skeezers don't care that he's happily married. They will strut up on him with me standing next to him."

"You have to let them know," TeKaya nodded in agreement. "You don't play." She looked around the room. "Look at them, checking the NFL salary site to see who has the biggest contract."

"Both of you should stop." Siri langhed. "Ty nor Jason is going anywhere."

"Oh, I'm not worried about him going anywhere. I'm concerned about the heifers parting the red sea as temptation." Kiki gave TeKaya a high-five as they laughed.

"Been there, played the game, not doing it again," Siri huffed.

"They are definitely on their A-game tonight," Nicole added.

"Oh yes." Kiki pointed. "See the one in the green dress?"

"Nice dress," Nicole commented.

"Yes it is." Kiki took a drink. "She's been

following and watching your brother all evening."

Nicole's eyes narrowed. "What?"

Kiki nodded as TeKaya spoke. "Jason noticed her earlier. He thought Ty was her target until he walked away and she followed Nick."

"I think she is about to make her move."

Nicole watched the woman.

"Look, she walked by Nick," Siri said. "You two should stop."

"That's a ruse. She's good," Kiki said.

"What are you talking about?" Nicole asked.

"Just watch." Kiki nodded.

The ladies stood back, listened and watched.

"She's going to flirt a little with Stretch. As soon as he flirts back, she's going to pretend he offended her."

The woman in green did exactly what Kiki stated.

"Now she's going to drop something...oh wait, no it's the accidental bump."

Sure enough the woman bumped into Nick.

"Excuse me. The woman looked behind her and frowned at Stretch, then turned back to Nick with a half-smile on her face. "I'm afraid I wasn't looking. Please forgive me."

"Not an issue," Nick replied. "Are you all right?"

She looked down at her dress, smoothly ran her hands over her curves, then looked up, contritely. "I'm fine. Again, please forgive me," she said, taking one last long irritated glare at Stretch.

Nick narrowed his eyes as he turned to

Stretch.

"She your sister, too?" Stretch laughed as he took a drink.

"No, but she is a lady and a guest. You may want to take a minute, clear your mind." Nick tilted his head toward the drink in Stretch's hand. "Find another way to enjoy the rest of the night."

Stretch stepped towards them, with his hand on his crotch. "That I can do, my friend." Nick stepped between the woman and Stretch while motioning to one of the security team members.

Stretch laughed as his friend pulled him away.

Nick turned back to the woman. "Please excuse him. He's enjoying the evening a little too much it seems."

"You shouldn't make excuses for ill-mannered athletes who think they own the world."

"That's a harsh generalization. Maybe a bit unfair since you were flirting with him." The woman parted her lips to speak, but Nick gently touched her elbow as he smiled. "Allow me to get you a drink and try to make it up to you."

The woman frowned. "A friendly smile and hello does not constitute flirting. "Thank you for the offer of a drink, but I think I'll pass. Who knows, a drink with you may constitute an agreement to have sex," she replied as she raised an eyebrow.

Nick nodded, "Touché. At the very least allow me to escort you out. We wouldn't want anyone else to offend you on your way to the door." His lips curled at the ends as he extended his arm.

The woman gave a faint smile and nodded, "Okay," as she took his arm.

"Ding, Ding, Ding, Ding. And the winner is," Kiki announced. "The woman in green." She turned to Nicole. "That my dear is called the fake-out."

TeKaya huffed. "At a glance it seems she isn't interested, but our Nicolas is that woman's target."

"You don't know that, for sure," Siri exclaimed. "It could all be a coincidence and quite innocent.

Kiki and TeKaya turned to Siri with an incredulous look. "Does the name LaToya Wright bring back any memories for you?"

Nicole was no longer listening to the women. Her eyes were on her brother walking out of the room with a gold digger.

Nick walked to the foyer with the woman in green, not sure why he felt compelled to. He knew the game. Recognized it from the moment she walked into the room. With the first inconspicuous glance from her, the ball was in play. Any other time he would walk in a different direction. But the woman peaked his curiosity. Whatever she was after he might be willing to give. Not because she was beautiful, nor because she had the body of any man's fantasy. No, it was none of those things that captured him, it was the thigh that caught him and would not let him go. Yes, a single beautiful chocolate thigh peeking from under the green gown that hugged her body. Every time she made her way into his line of sight throughout the night, he caught a glance of that thigh. She was smooth with her subtle moves. But as the youngest male in the Brooks clan, he was used to women pulling all the stunts in the world to get next to the men who were born into millions and had been granted even more at the age of twenty-one. They could live very well off of the interest from the trust fund left to them by their grandparents. They were not first generation rich. They were generational wealth and most women in the country knew who each of them were and pulled unimaginable stunts to get their attention. Putting his heritage aside, it was his job to spot and keep these types of women away from his clients. Nick was very good at his job, that's how the woman first hit his radar. He thought one of his clients was her target until he was the recipient of the slow bend and even slower rise, with the sideward glance to ensure he was watching. He should have shut the game down. Instead, he allowed the play to continue.

Nick raised a hand to one of the attendants. "I'll have valet bring your vehicle around."

"That's not necessary." She reached into her purse. "I'll call my driver."

Nick nodded. "Before you do, please accept my apology for any actions on my guest's behalf that may have offended you." He pulled out his card. "My name is Nicolas Brooks." He gave her the card. "Use the number on the back to give me the opportunity to make this up to you Ms....?"

"Edmonds, Ericka Edmonds." She put her hand out.

The moment their fingers touched, the

game changed. Nick felt the jolt that raced through them just as she did. Nick knew then and there that the lovely Ms. Ericka may have begun the evening with him as a target, but it was now she who needed an escape.

Nick held her fingers, firmly within his hand as he kissed her knuckles. "I look forward to hearing from you."

When the attendant he'd motioned for a moment ago reached them, Nick whispered something in his ear, then turned to the woman.

"The gentleman will see you to your vehicle. Enjoy the remainder of your evening." He gave a slight bow, then walked away.

Still caught up in his touch, Ericka watched as the wide shoulders, slim waist with the indention of a firm behind dressed in a tuxedo, walked away. By the time she regained her senses Nick Brooks was walking back into the party. She looked around wondering what in the hell just happened. "That is not how the game is played." She said out loud, speaking to no one in particular.

"He tends to make his own rules."

Ericka turned to see a female with bouncy curls loosely flowing around her face. She gave the woman a once-over then raised an eyebrow. "And you are?"

"Very happy Nick did not fall for your act." Nicole stepped from the shadows with arms folded across her chest. She stopped, bracing herself for any possible backlash from the heifer.

Ericka smirked as she turned away from the woman to give her valet ticket to the attendant, then turned back to the woman. "That was only round one." She stepped closer. "I always get my man." She flipped her hair across her shoulder, put the card Nick gave her inside her purse, then held it up and clicked it closed in the woman's face. "That one is mine." Her car pulled up. The attendant held the door open as she walked towards him. "Find your own gold mine."

"Mines have a tendency to collapse. Tread too deep and I promise you, the walls of hell will tumble around you."

Ericka got into her vehicle and Nicole watched as she drove off.

Chapter 2

Monday morning Brooks-Pendleton was buzzing. With some of the clients still in town, many stopped by to check out the offices and meet new staff members. With all the activity, Nick was to find his top investigator in his office when he arrived at seven.

"Rene Naverone," Nick said, as he stood in the doorway to this plush office. "If I didn't think you would kick my ass around the room, I would comment on your legs," he stated, as he reviewed his messages while walking to his desk. "A little early for a problem, isn't it?"

Naverone, the stunning five-six, one-hundred thirty pound ex-Secret Service agent, who worked exclusively for The Pendleton Agency, was now the head of security for Brooks-Pendleton. She had a devastating team of four women who handled investigative as well as protection services for their clients. It was hard to determine which was more dangerous when it came to Naverone, her very feminine style of dress, which included her trademark four-inch spike heel boots, or the fact, that with the right rifle, she could take out a person nine hundred feet away with precision.

"I'll just throw you across your desk and have my way with you."

Nick looked up. "In that case, your legs get longer and more intriguing with every dress you wear in here. Any chance of an exploration?" He sat behind his desk while drinking the cup of coffee, which he knew would be waiting for him.

She smiled, which added to the mystique of her beauty. "Not a chance in hell."

Nick shrugged. "Well at least we know where we stand." He laughed. "Which one of the clients has you in the office so early in the morning?"

"You have that honor this morning." She put a file on his desk. "Ty asked us to use face recognition to identify the woman in green from the kickoff event."

Nick picked up the file. "Don't tell me, her name isn't Ericka Edmonds?"

"Close. Twenty-eight year old Ericka Kennedy. She has a number of cons under her belt. Nothing with any of our clients to date. Her targets are usually corporate types who are too embarrassed to press charges."

"Ever been married or any children?"

"Why is that important?"

Nick looked up. "Because I asked."

Naverone nodded her head. "Okay, no,

never married. No children." She stood. "But a dangerous woman for the profession you are in. Did it ever occur to you she may be targeting you to gain an opening to your client list?" She shrugged her shoulders as she walked towards the door. "Or better yet...their bank accounts. Just a thought."

"Ericka Kennedy is an intriguing woman." Nick sat back in his chair. "On the other hand, that walk of yours borders on harassment."

"Flattery, Mr. Brooks, gets you nowhere with me." She walked out the door, then peeked back in. "But it is nice to hear." She winked, then closed the door behind her.

The warning from Naverone was clear. Ericka Kennedy was not a trustworthy woman. Was that enough to stop him from pursuing the only woman to capture his attention in...years? Should he walk away from the woman who made him wonder...what if? He stared at the picture in the file.

"Good morning Nicolas." Sylvia Perry interrupted his thoughts. "Mr. Hylton, your eight o'clock, is here. You have a ten with Jason Whitfield and a twelve o'clock lunch with Mr. Bryson." She walked behind him, reached across his shoulder, closed the file he was looking at, and turned on his computer. She then moved to the conference area of his office with other files in her hand as she spoke, "It would be in your best interest to take your secretary to that particular luncheon."

He glanced up from the document on his computer she'd pulled up. "Why?"

Sylvia Perry was a sophisticated, confident, organizing genius. They'd attended undergrad together and it was Sylvia who helped him start his sports agency. It had been a two-person operation for three years as they attended games, talked to parents, knocked on doors and did whatever it took to get clients. She became his administrative assistant and now was his personal secretary. Nothing or no one fazed her. She treated everyone with the same respect and strong arm. That's why he hired her. He knew the client's arrogant attitude would not faze her nor would the looks and potential income.

She turned to him in a mock huff. "Well, for one, lunch is the least you can do given that I haven't received a raise since my workload doubled due to the merger. Two, you don't take good notes and I have to guess at things all the time. And third, but definitely more important than the other reasons, I will be pissed if you don't allow me to meet Jarrett Bryson."

Her reaction surprised him. "What is it about Jarrett Bryson that causes women to lose their minds?" he asked, while shrugging and turning back to his computer.

She was clearly perplexed as she glared at him with her hand on her hip. "Look at me."

He did and was at a loss as to what he was looking for, however, he knew better than to say that. "Okay...?"

"I am a beautiful, single, twenty-nine and holding..." —She put her finger up to keep him from saying she was the same age he was,— "woman. Jarrett Bryson is a FINE single man. Need I say more?"

"I'll take no for a hundred on that Alex."

Sylvia grinned. "I'm serious Nick. I want to

go."

"All right, all right. You can go."

She placed the files on the conference table and ran over and kissed Nick on the cheek. "Thank you. When Whitfield and his parents come in, I'll be leaving for a few minutes." She hurried towards the door.

"What? Why?"

The incredulous look she gave him, again, threw him off guard. "I have to change clothes for the lunch date." Nick frowned. "Straighten your face before I bring Mr. Hylton in." She left the office before he could say anything further.

Nick shook his head, then turned back to the file on the new acquisitions. It was time to get women off his mind and focus on work.

Due to the merger, he received ten notable clients, three with the top salaries in their respective sports. This added to the twenty-two clients they already had, giving them a total of thirty-two sports clients he now had the responsibility of representing. The majority of the clients would go to other agents within the firm. However, the top three, Justin Hylton, Jason Whitfield and Jarrett Bryson all fell under his umbrella. Jarrett Bryson was a no-brainer. He was a walking billboard with his good looks, impeccable business sense and down-home southern hospitality. He was in negotiations for his second contract with the New York Knights baseball team. The owners were giving a little pushback on the numbers, but Nick wasn't concerned. The ball was really in Bryson's glove. Bryson earned more from endorsements than he did from the game. Justin Hylton was a different story. He was going into his last years in the NFL. The Atlanta team was looking at starting the number one draft pick. The problem was Hylton still had that unbeatable arm and the knack for seeing the entire field before shooting a rocket to one of their receivers. The new kid had better movement in the pocket and could run, but the accuracy in the arm was nowhere near Hylton's. Therein lay the problem for Atlanta. To add salt to their wound, Hylton was a fan favorite. They were sure to anger fans if they benched Hylton. It was Nick's job to get him the best contract he could that would end his career on a high note and to navigate his future after retirement. Then there was the most exciting case for Nick, Jason Whitfield. With him, Nick had the opportunity to shape the NBA star's future from nearly the beginning. Ty had negotiated the initial contract with the Washington team. There were one or two hiccups. Jason was a young natural talent who'd just come from a blue-collar environment into the champagne life. It was going to take some adjustments and long hours to guide him in the direction of longevity in the industry, but Nick was excited about the unlimited possibilities.

Nick closed out the report Sylvia hadn't missed a detail on. He picked up his coffee cup and walked over to the files she'd placed on the conference table. The door to the office opened.

"Nick." Sylvia stepped inside. "Mr. Hylton."

Nick extended his hand. "Come on in Justin."

Sylvia walked to the credenza next to the wall. She poured coffee for Justin and sat a platter of danish pastries on the table. "Will there be anything else Mr. Brooks?"

Nick turned to Sylvia. "No interruptions. Thank you Sylvia."

"Yes, sir," Sylvia replied as she stepped out of the office.

Nick pointed to the table. "Have a seat, Justin." He unbuttoned his suit jacket before taking his seat. "There are a few issues I want to bring to your attention before we discuss endorsements and job offers."

Justin sat at the table and clasped his hands together. "Before we do, I have a delicate situation I need you to discreetly check into."

Nick closed the folder, sat back, raising one leg to rest on the other. "Haley Santana?"

Justin sat back and nodded. "Something happened this weekend, but I can't tell you what."

"Anything you say to me is in confidence, Justin. Just as with Ty, I represent you."

Justin held up his hand. "It's not that. I can't tell you what happened because I don't remember." He hit the table and pushed his seat back, standing then pacing. "Hell man I don't even remember her in my room."

"Hold on." Nick motioned for Justin to sit down. "Start at the beginning."

Justin sat back down. "I don't know the beginning. I can tell you the end. I woke up in my hotel room naked and there was a note from Haley stating 'thank you for a memorable night.'"

Nick cleared his throat. "How did she get into your room?"

"No freakin' idea!" His hand slammed on

the table.

"Were you drinking?"

"Of course, we all were." He shrugged his shoulder. "But I can hold my liquor, man. I never get to the point where I black out or lose track of time. I know my limit and three drinks of Hennessy does not have an impact on me. When I entered my hotel room, I was alone."

Nick could see the frustration on Justin's face. "Man, I love my wife. We've been married for twelve years and I have never...ever cheated on her. And if I did...it would not be with someone like Haley Santana."

"We'll get in front of this before anyone gets wind of anything." Nick pushed a button on the conference table phone. "Sylvia, ask Naverone to step into my office, please." He looked at Justin. "Listen, we have a top notch investigation team. The first thing I'm going to do is have her test you for any foreign substance in your body."

"You think someone drugged me and put a beautiful woman in my bed?" Justin's expression made Nick think twice.

"Did you put her in your bed?"

"Hell no."

"Then someone did, without you detecting it. "

Naverone knocked on the door, then walked in. Nick stood. "Naverone, thank you for coming."

"So your idea is to put another beautiful woman in front of my wife to tell her this shit didn't happen?"

"Not exactly." Nick grinned.

Two hours later, Nick's simple morning

turned more complicated with the arrival of Jason Whitfield without his parents, but he also did not have the entourage, Ty had mentioned with him. When Jason arrived, Naverone was still in his office wrapping up her notes on the Justin Hylton situation.

Jason took a step back when he spotted her. Nick saw the reaction and raised an eyebrow at Naverone.

Naverone winked at him. "Hello Mr. Whitfield." She stood and walked towards him.

Jason stepped back. He remembered the last time he'd seen the woman. She had taken one of his boys down in a club and pulled a Glock on him when he called her a bitch. "Look, I don't have no beef with you." Jason put his hand up and put some distance between them. He backed up so far he bumped into Nick. Jason looked over his shoulder. "Sorry about that Mr. Brooks."

"We're good Jason." He looked between Naverone and the young man. "You two know each other?"

"We've met. So, you're a new client of Nick's?"

"Yes. I mean yes ma'am."

"Naverone is good."

"Okay, Ms. Naverone."

Nick had to grin. What could Naverone have done to make a six-foot, six-inch forward in the NBA fearful of her, he wondered.

"Just Naverone." She smiled. "I'm your protection now Jason. When things hop off and you need help, I'm your first call."

He glanced at Nick then back to Naverone. "You work for me now?"

"No, I work for Nick. Since you are someone he represents, that means you are under my protection now."

Jason half smiled. "For real?"

Naverone nodded. "For real," she almost laughed.

"Well..." Jason hesitated, then took a step towards her. "Can you find people?"

Naverone shrugged. "Sure I can."

"You need help with something, Jason," Nick asked, concerned.

"Well, kind of."

"Let's take a seat at the table. Who do you need to find?" Nick asked once all of them were seated.

"Umm...it's a girl."

Nick and Naverone glanced at each other. "A girl, Jason?" Nick asked.

"She's hot, Nick. I mean man, she's bam...bam..bam." motioned in the air with his hands the outline of a woman's body. "And she got the face, you know, the kind in magazines and shit."

"Watch your language," Naverone cautioned.

"Oh, sorry." He lowered his eyes.

Nick grinned. The kid Ty called "terror on wheels" was actually a pretty decent young man.

"And she can sing...man she got a sweet rap, but the other night I heard her singing. Man, she should trash that rap and just sing, you know what I mean"

Naverone tried to hide her smile as Nick spoke. "You like this girl?"

"Man, she got it like that."

"Okay, well, what's her name," Nick prompted. "Maybe we can arrange an introduction."

The young man who was sitting and still felt like he was standing looked at Nick with wonder in his eyes. "You think you can do that...for real?"

The excitement in the young man's eyes made Nick feel good. It was like experiencing puppy love all over again. "Tell us her name and we'll see what we can do."

"Lil Tay, from the other night. Man, if I could get a chance with that, I swear I'll never give you any trouble Nick."

Jason was so excited he never saw Nick's face drop at the mention of his niece.

Naverone was doing all she could to keep Jason's eyes on her until Nick could straighten his face. She kicked him under the table, but it wasn't Nick legs she kicked, it was Jason's.

When he looked down, she motioned for Nick to change his expression.

"You know, I think I'll work on that for you Jason." Naverone stood to leave before she actually laughed out loud. "In fact I'll work on it while you meet with Nick."

Nick glared at Naverone as if he could kill her. "You know Lil Tay is probably out of the country on tour," he said more to Naverone than to Jason.

"Awe man," Jason slumped, "It's all good. I'll wait on that. She's worth it."

"We'll see," Naverone said, as she walked out of the office laughing.

"You think she will do it?" Jason asked Nick.

Nick walked over and picked up the young man's file. "I'm sure she will try. I thought your parents were coming with you today."

"They felt I could handle the information on the endorsements."

"Are you ready for that responsibility?"

"With your guidance, I'm sure I can make the right decisions."

The young man was well mannered. However, Taylor was his niece and ballers had a reputation. "Well, let's get your mind on business, what do you say?"

"Okay Nick, show me what you got?"

It turned out Jason, the one he expected to bring drama, was the easiest of the day. His lunch with Jarrett Bryson brought on a new dimension to the meaning of celebrity. They'd reserved the private room at one of Nick's favorite restaurants, The Rendezvous, so they could discuss the upcoming year and contract negotiations. However, getting to the private room was a journey. The existence of Twitter and instant messaging was turning out to not be their friend.

Nick and Sylvia stepped out of the car to a crowd of about twenty women standing outside the door. Garland Simmons, the owner, was doing his best to control the crowd. Sylvia pulled out her cell and pushed a button as Nick made his way through the crowd. When he reached Jarrett, he was patiently signing a woman's arm with a black marker.

"Excuse me, ladies. Thank you all for stopping by to see Jarrett. I'm afraid I have to pull him away now."

There were moans as the crowd began to

move forward. Sylvia stood between the women and the two men. "Mr. Bryson will be happy to take a picture with the first five people willing to give us your email address or number to text. We also have two tickets and after-game passes to the next game for a lucky winner. Follow me." They ran behind Sylvia like children after candy. Nick guided Jarrett.

"She's a keeper." Jarrett smiled as he followed Nick and Garland into the private room.

"You better know it." Nick smiled as he looked over his shoulder at the crowd. "She's worth her weight in gold."

"Mr. Brooks." Garland seated the men on the balcony, which overlooked the entire restaurant. "I apologize for the inconvenience. The moment Mr. Bryson stepped out of his car, he was recognized. One call led to another and another and it was on after that."

"You handled it well," Jarrett praised the young man.

"I appreciate you saying that. May I get you gentlemen something from the bar?"

"Water for me," Jarrett replied.

"Same here." Nick nodded. "And a sweet tea for the lady."

Garland nodded. "Casey will be your waitress. She will be right out with your drinks."

"Thank you." Nick nodded, then looked up at Jarrett, who appeared to be unfazed by what had just occurred. "You realize the crowd is going to double within the hour. We can leave out the back if you like."

"It's not a problem. I believe your assistant

stated I would take pictures with some of them." He shrugged. "It shouldn't take long."

Nick liked the cool demeanor of the man and wondered if anything ever got to him. "When do you head back to New York?"

"I'm making a detour to Miami for a few days, then I'll go back."

The waitress appeared with the water and took their orders. Nick thanked her and turned his attention back to Jarrett. "What do you want in this contract?"

"To play ball. Give the fans a few more years. Close my career out with the team."

Nick nodded. "Ten years, guaranteed base, signing bonus, award bonuses for each milestone, perks." He shrugged his shoulder. "Sounds like a good starting point."

"Do they have good burgers in this place?"

"The best." Nick grinned. "You take the works?"

Jarrett smiled. "The only way to do it."

In that moment Nick learned something about Jarrett Bryson. He was a humble man. Talking money made him uncomfortable. "Casey, we will have number two with the works and a salad for the lady."

"Got you covered," came the reply.

Nick closed the electronic tablet he traveled with and decided the best way to connect with this man was to simply have a conversation. "How's the family?" The relief on the man's face was clear. Nick listened as he talked about family, then a little politics. By the time the food came, the topic eventually turned to women. "How do you handle all the attention?" Nick asked as he bit into his burger.

"I try to keep things simple," Jarrett replied as he shook his head while eating a fry. "I don't deal well with drama or the crazy antics." He took a drink. "The other night at the hotel, I walk in my room and there's a woman butt naked in the bed."

"What?" Nick wiped his mouth with a napkin as he laughed at Jarrett. "What did you do?"

Jarrett huffed. "Turn around, walked out of the room, and closed the door behind me. I hung out with Justin for the rest of the night."

"Justin Hylton?"

"Yeah, we go way back."

"What night was that?"

"Saturday. We had a few beers, laughs. I stretched out on his pull-out."

Nick nodded, taking in the information and storing it for later. "I met with him this morning. He's good people."

"One of the best in the game." Jarrett nodded. "The man loves his wife. I envy the man. I've seen him shut down beautiful women at the drop of a hat. He leaves no door open and lets them know his wife is his life." Jarrett looked down at the crowd. "What he has is real. That, down there, is not."

"You have to know what real looks like so when you find it, you know to grab it and hold on for life."

Jarrett looked at Nick and smiled. "You probably will not get ten years from the GM. If he bucks, I'm good with five."

"If he bucks, I'll get him to seven, but there will be a price to pay in incentives."

Jarrett nodded. "Send me the specs when

you put them together."

Nick nodded. "So does your nephew play ball?" And just like that Nick had won over Jarrett Bryson.

By the time Nick arrived home, it was well after midnight. He pulled onto his street which consisted of three homes, his, his brother James' and a few miles down, the personal home of the President of the United States, JD Harrison. His end of the estate did not have the guarded gate with the Secret Service ready to greet you. However, there was a security gate, which opened when his vehicle was within a certain range. Once he drove through the gate, it would close and lock behind him. He was tired and did not bother to drive around to the garage. He parked in the circular driveway and entered his home through the front door.

Outside the gate, a respectable distance from the entrance, Ericka sat inside her vehicle watching and making mental notes about the property. She stayed out of range of the agents posted only a few miles down the road. Once Nick returned to his office after his lunch and photo session with Jarrett Bryson, she came here and parked. The success of her plan depended on research. Isaac Singleton may not understand the intricacy of a con, but she did. And she simply did not know enough about Nick Brooks. Today she learned a little more by watching him from the time he arrived at his office that morning. People seemed to genuinely like the man. She saw him walking three major clients out to the black sedan he had transporting them to the office. Of the three, she believed the most volatile was the

kid, Jason Whitfield. Both Bryson and Hylton
had more money than God. If a couple of
millions disappeared, they probably would not
notice. But a young kid just coming into money
would count every dollar. According to
Cannon, if Singleton wanted a public spectacle,
it would come from the kid.

With her plan in place, it was time to make
contact.

Chapter 3

Ericka dressed carefully for today. This was going to be her first official connection with Nicolas Brooks. From what she could gather, he liked his women sweet and sassy, which meant she didn't have to change much. Well, she had to admit she wasn't exactly sweet. That disappeared at fourteen, when her first boyfriend decided to share their one sexual encounter with the entire school via video. Her mother deemed her a whore and shipped her off to California to live with her aunt...a distant aunt. From that point on, she would be the first to admit she was a bitch. Her aunt taught her everything there was about looks. If you were pretty, you could get just about anything you wanted. She used the knowledge to the fullest

Exotic was what her first producer boyfriend called her. She was the product of an African-American mother and a wealthy Italian father who also happened to be married and was a real estate investor. She couldn't help but be captivating. From her mother she acquired a body that stopped traffic and from her father the warm olive-tone skin coloring, that made it look as if the sun kissed her. She had his coal black eyes and from both a hair texture that allowed her the luxury of going natural when she wanted, or simply flat-ironing it to take it straight. The producer boyfriend brought her a Mercedes Coupe at the age of sixteen. Oh, high school boys couldn't do anything for her. If you wanted to take a ride with her, you had to have a bank account, in your name only, with seven figures or more.

After a few years, producers became boring and she moved up to movie stars. While their pockets were deep, their vanity was unbearable. No one or nothing could be more beautiful than them. When she walked in the room on the arm of a star and received more compliments than he...well that was generally all she wrote. But hell, she couldn't help it..it was what it was...deal with it.

After getting smacked around a few times for being more beautiful, she decided, men with no looks, no talent, but enough brains to buy the ones with looks and talent were a better choice. What she found was a gold mine. With them, she didn't even have to sleep with them. All she had to do was be on their arms so they could tell the other old men they called friends, that's my side. Ericka would smile, wave or give a kiss on the cheek and then sit back and watch her bank account grow.

'Like mother, like daughter', she told her mother once when she came for a visit and her mother criticized her lifestyle in front of her little brother. They were having dinner when her mother asked if she had found a respectable job. Ericka replied she was doing okay. Sleeping around waiting for a man to give some of his hard earned money is not doing okay, her mother said. Ericka watched as Bobby bowed his head as if the food on the plate had suddenly burst into action.

"You slept with my father who was a wealthy executive and got pregnant with me. When that well ran dry, you did it again with Bobby's father. At least, I'm not bringing home any bastard children." With that, her mother threw her out and told her she was never to return. She didn't, but she kept in touch with Bobby.

Bobby was a good kid. He did things the right way. He got shafted when it came to his father. Mother never told him who his father was, but Ericka knew. She'd always wondered how mother paid for the house, kept food on the table, and them in nice clothes. William Singleton paid for it all. They didn't live like his real family, but Bobby did okay. He never questioned Mother, although he brought it up with Ericka a number of times. But, like or dislike her mother, she would never tell what was not her business. The answer would come out one day...it always did. Until then, she would be there for her brother no matter what. If what Cannon suspected was right, she was not going to allow anyone to take what was legally Bobby's. Not even the great Isaac Singleton.

Ericka pulled into the parking space behind the Brooks-Pendleton offices. A glance in the mirror confirmed she had the look she needed to get in the door. The clean, professional, if she ever had to do a nine-to-five, look. Little makeup, hair pulled back into a stylish bun, a black and white sheath dress that revealed little skin, but fit just right to get attention. Four-inch heels and a classic black and white clutch finished the look. She stepped out of the vehicle with her game plan in mind. Just moved to town from Atlanta. Don't really know too many people. Since she had been treated poorly at the event this would be a perfect opportunity for him to make it up to her. Every woman needs a big strong man to show her around. That usually pulled the corporate type. Yes, she had her game plan in mind.

Ericka's walk from the parking lot to the front of the building proved she had on the right outfit. The appreciative second glances made her smile. She opened the door and stepped into the spacious long foyer that had burgundy and tan Persian carpeting, and white columns strategically placed throughout. On the wall to the right in the shape of an arch was the name 'Brooks–Pendleton'. Ericka walked in that direction and stopped at the double doors. Under the arch were framed pictures of their current clientele, from the ceiling to the floor. Perusing the display, it was clear Brooks-Pendleton's client were a virtual who's who in sports. Her eyes settled on the young man she planned to use to get Singleton what he wanted. "Get the money," she said as she opened the door and walked through.

A receptionist sat at an oval-shaped desk with the name of the agency engraved on the wall behind her. Nothing could be seen from the foyer. To the right, there was a door with the name 'Pendleton' above the opening and to the left was a door with the name 'Brooks' above it. Each had a key-code bar for entry. The office was a little more secure than what she imagined. She made a mental note. Most of her dealings with Nicolas Brooks would have to take place at his home.

"Good morning." Ericka smiled as she greeted the receptionist. "I'm here to see Nicolas Brooks."

"Good morning," the very attractive brunette replied. "Do you have an appointment with Mr. Brooks?"

"I do not. Please give this to him. I'm certain he will see me."

The woman smiled as she picked up the telephone. "Your name?"

"Ericka Edmonds."

"Ms. Edmonds, please have a seat. I will see if Mr. Brooks is free."

Ericka stepped into the reception waiting area, which offered an assortment of coffee, tea, drinks, water or snacks behind a bar with four stools around it forming a semi-circle. To the left were two large leather chairs that would easily accommodate the larger frame of a male athlete. On the monitor above the bar ESPN was on with the latest scores from the games the night before. She placed her purse on the bar and prepared a cup of tea. Taking a seat at the bar stool on the end, she crossed her legs and slightly turned her body away from the

door as she waited for Nick Brooks' secretary to
arrive.

"Ms. Edmonds," the rich voice echoed
through her as she turned to find Nicolas
Brooks in all his fine glory standing before her.
Normally a tuxedo adds to a man's mystique in
a James Bondish kind of way. Saturday night
with all its glitz and glamour took away from
this man's charm. Nicolas Brooks, dressed in
black slacks, loafers, and a crisp white shirt
with his sleeves rolled up, had a down-home,
Southern charm and wholesome good looks.
*Were those brown eyes that bright, his skin
that smooth, his lips that thick before?* Ericka
thought as she looked up at the man. Stop it,
her mind raced. This is a target, just like any
other.

Ericka set the cup down on the bar. "Mr.
Brooks. I hope I'm not disturbing your
morning."

"Of course you are." Nick tilted his head
and smiled. "A nice disruption."

Ericka smiled back. The two remained
frozen in place and time for a moment longer
than either should have.

Nick was the first to recover. "I'm in the
middle of a meeting. If you have the time, I
would love an opportunity to make up for
Saturday."

He was making this too easy. "I have time."

Nick held out his arm. "Join me."

The two walked through the office to the
glances of staff along the way. The tall, dark,
handsome, six-two, one hundred ninety-five
pound man with long powerful arms and the
five-eight, olive-toned, body of a goddess, face

of an angel beauty walking next to each other. They could have been runway models.

Nick approached his office, stopping at Sylvia's desk. "Sylvia, this is Ericka Edmonds. You think you could find something to keep her occupied until I wrap up with Sergio?"

Sylvia stood. "I'm certain I can."

Nick turned to Ericka. "I shouldn't be too long."

"I'll wait." Ericka took a seat in the lounge area next to Sylvia's desk.

Nick glanced at her and then at Sylvia before walking back into his office.

Sylvia smiled at Ericka. "Ms. Edmonds may I get you any refreshments?"

"No thank you." Ericka looked around as Sylvia sat back down. "You've worked with Nick long?"

"We started all of this together in a two-bedroom house that was smaller than Nick's office."

"Really?" Ericka was surprised. "Why? It's not like Nick doesn't have means. Even back then he certainly would have had the means for an office building."

"He did. But Nick..." Sylvia hesitated as she shook her head back and forth. "Nick's a special type of person. He believes in making it on his own. See, his father wasn't too happy with his decision to become a sports agent. So Nick, in all his wisdom, did not want to use his trust fund to start the business. So for about six months, he did a few gigs to pay the rent on a two-bedroom house. We had a kitchen, one bathroom, the living room was the reception area, one bedroom was the filing room and the other bedroom was his office."

Ericka was fascinated by the story. The more she learned about Nick, the easier she knew it would be to get next to him. She moved and sat on the edge of Sylvia's desk as she continued with their meager beginnings. "What kind of gigs?"

"Ah, what people don't know is Nick is quite the musician. He could have easily had a music career like his niece, Lil Tay."

"Lil Tay, the singer? That's his niece?"

"Yes."

"And Nicolas is a singer?"

"He was." Sylvia turned to the documents on her desk and continued preparing the file. "As I said before, Nick is a very special person. We love him around here. You should keep that warning in mind." She sent a sideward glance Ericka's way just as Nick and his client Sergio Martinez, the catcher for the New York Knights walked out of the office.

"I'll have a talk with the front office," Nick said as he patted Serg on the shoulder.

"I know I'm not one of your big-time clients but Jarrett said you wouldn't care. You would treat me just like you treat him."

"You're a client Serg. Your status isn't important. You deserve the best we have to give."

Sergio was no longer paying any attention to Nick. His eyes had wandered to Ericka, who was sitting on the side of the desk with gorgeous thighs exposed. He reached out and took her hand. "Sergio Martinez at your service." He kissed her fingers then smiled up at her.

"The pleasure is all mine," Ericka replied.

"Sergio this is Ericka Edmonds."

"In that case, may I interest you in lunch?" Sergio asked with a sexy accent.

"Hmm a tempting offer, but I'm afraid I must decline. I'm spoken for" she glanced at Nick. "at least for the day."

Sergio looked from Nick to Ericka. "Man, the dark skin brothers have all the luck." They all laughed.

Sylvia pulled her purse from the bottom desk drawer. "Come on Sergio, I'm free for lunch." She took his arm and strolled off.

Nick turned. "Would the lovely Ericka like to step into my office before another one of my clients tries to pick you up?"

Ericka nodded and followed him inside. The office was nice, not overbearing as some she had visited.

"Nice spacious office," Ericka stated as she glanced around. "Tastefully decorated with a touch of class." She looked up at Nick standing behind his desk. The thought occurred to her that she could watch him there for hours and never get tired. She shook the thought quickly from her mind.

"Thank you," Nick replied as he unrolled his sleeves while watching her. He took his jacket from the back of his chair and put it on. After adjusting his collar, he met and held her gaze. "Before we go down what I think is uncharted road for both of us. Let's determine how we want to deal with fact versus fiction."

"What do you mean?" Ericka braced herself not sure what was coming next.

Nick walked over and stood close enough to touch her lips with his. "You clearly want something from me. Whatever it is will be revealed in time." He took a slow gaze over every inch of her face as if branding it to his memory, then he stared into her eyes. "Let's hope the depth of your deception will not interfere in what I believe could be an intriguing relationship."

His eyes unsettled her. It was as if he could read her mind and knew what she was up to. She started to speak, but he held up his hand. "Fact or fiction?"

"You're asking if I'm about to lie to you?"

"Yes."

"You don't know me and you are labeling me a liar?"

"No. I'm giving you the opportunity to get to know me. Once you do, you will think twice before you do whatever you have planned."

"If you think I'm targeting you, why even consider allowing me in?"

Nick took a step closer. He was clearly in her personal space as he whispered into her ear. "Do you feel that?" He paused for a split second. "It's the uncontrollable urge to touch...feel...kiss." He then looked into her eyes with their lips not a breath away. "It's a gift from God that not many people experience in their lifetime. It's called passion. I'm afraid if I don't let you in, we will never have the chance to experience it. That would be a fatal mistake."

His closeness sucked her control away. It was as if his nearness made her forget why she was on the planet, much less her reasons for being there with him. Distance...she needed distance from him.

As if reading her mind, Nick reached behind her without breaking eye contact, and opened the door. "Shall we have lunch?"

For a second, Ericka thought he was going to kiss her. When he didn't she realized she was a bit disappointed. She took a step back. This was not going the way she had planned at all. He had a knack for taking control of things. He'd done the same thing on Saturday. Warnings in the pit of her stomach were going off. Not this man. Walk away. But she couldn't. To complicate matters, she could not determine if the reason she could not pull away was because of Bobby or herself.

"Lunch would be nice," she finally replied, held his gaze, then stepped out of the office.

Outside, the sky was clear blue. The air was filled with the smells of fresh bread from the bakery in the next block, the sounds of traffic and the feel of something special. At least those were Nick's thoughts.

The sounds of merchants at the fresh market stand around the corner and the overhead train track added to a sense of uneasiness in Ericka .

"It's a beautiful day. Let's have lunch in the park. It's peaceful there and will give us a chance to get to know each other without interruptions.

"The park sounds wonderful." Ericka turned towards the parking lot.

"Let's take a walk." Nick held his hand out.

Something inside of Ericka told her not to take his hand. Doing so would create an intimacy that she didn't want. It would allow him to invade her space again.

"Walk?" She looked down at her feet. "Do you see these heels? They are not made for walking. They were made to entice."

"Mission accomplished." His eyes narrowed. "The question is can you keep it?"

Ericka was beginning to hate the man. He was too direct. Somewhere along the line he'd figured her out. She tilted her head towards him. "I haven't met a man yet whose attention I couldn't get...and keep." She stepped towards him. "The question is can you get and keep mine?"

"Oh, how I would love that challenge."

Ericka stepped around him, then turned to face him as she walked backwards. "Where is this park of yours, Nicolas Brooks?" She gave him her most alluring smile.

He walked towards her, placing his hand on the small of her back and turning her in the direction of the park. "Only a few blocks away." Nick pulled out his cell and made a quick call.

"I'm having lunch in the park. Will you call ahead?" He ended the call as they walked in silence for a moment.

"Are you used to having things at your fingertips?"

"I've worked hard to have it that way."

"You're a trust fund baby, Nicolas Brooks. You don't know what it means to work hard for anything."

Nick smiled as he looked around. "I am well aware of the public's opinion of me and my family. The truth is we all work for a living. None of us use our trust funds for much of anything."

"That's a waste." Ericka huffed. "Why have that kind of money if you are not going to use it?

He turned the corner. "Life is about a lot more than money."

"That of course is coming from a man who has it." Ericka smirked. "From us average Joes who have to work for a living, that statement could be seen as an insult."

"The grass is always greener on the other side. Those with money have the same problems as those without. Ours just come with a bigger price tag. At times it's more like a curse."

Ericka stopped, staring at him as if he had lost his mind. "How can having access to an unlimited amount of funds be a curse?"

Nick stopped and returned the glare. "We become targets for those with less who feel we should be forced to share. Some don't think about the damage they leave behind once they get what they want."

Ericka thought about what he was saying as a little guilt seeped inside her gut. "Sounds as if you are speaking from experience," she said as she started walking again.

"Not personal experience." He fell in step with her as they continued. "I have seen the impact on both of my brothers."

They turned another corner and Ericka could see the park a block away. "I'm certain they have moved on from the experience without a dent."

Nick smirked. "That would be true of someone whose steps were guided based on the pocket and not the heart. In my brothers' cases, one was guided by the heart, the other by honor. Either way, they ended up paying a hefty price."

Guilt punch number two, Ericka thought. "Some people may not have a choice. It's a matter of survival."

"Sounds as if you are speaking from experience."

Ericka stopped at the grass once they reached the park. Had she revealed something she did not intend to. She removed her shoes as she shook the thought off. She had to be careful. This man had a way of cutting through her defenses.

"Yes, Nicolas. I've had to make my own way in this world and I don't regret anything I've ever done to survive. For the record, anyone whose heart guides their steps is asking for hurt and disgrace. That is from experience." She walked ahead.

Nick watched her reaction. That was the most honest thing she had said since they met. He smiled. He was making progress.

"We're over by the tree." He pointed as he walked up behind her.

Ericka looked in the direction of a huge maple tree. The trunk looked as if it could seat two large adults on either side. Beneath it lay a blanket, with a basket a bottle of wine and two glasses. The man standing next to the tree looked as if he was expecting them. He smiled the moment he saw Nick, then rushed towards him.

"Mr. Nick." He extended his hand. "It is wonderful to see you again."

"Thank you Raul."

"I understood you had someone joining you. So I took the liberty to add a little something different."

"I appreciate that. How is Lizbeth?"

"Beautiful, as an expectant mother should be." Raul beamed with pride. "May I seat your lady friend?"

The man approached Ericka as she tried to determine how she was going to get to the ground in the dress in a dignified manner. Something about the man's smile was contagious. She smiled back.

"You are as beautiful as my Lizbeth," he said as he whispered in her ear. "Cross your legs and I will hold your hand as I lower you to the ground."

She gave Nick her purse and followed his instructions, surprised by the ease of the maneuver. "Thank you Raul." She smiled up at him. "Is that homemade bread I'm smelling?"

"It's the only way to serve it, nice and hot with butter." Raul turned to Nick. "Enjoy."

Nick removed his jacket and put it behind her back allowing her to lean back against the tree trunk.

"Chivalry is apparently not dead."

Nick smiled and sat down on the blanket across from her. "Let's see what Raul prepared for us." He opened the basket releasing the aroma of pasta and hot bread. "Do you like Italian?"

"What Italian do you know who doesn't?"

"Ah," Nick said as he placed a napkin across Ericka's lap. "Something new about the lovely Ericka. Part Italian, part African-American." He gave her a container. "How many years ago?"

"Twenty-six." She opened the container with glee. "Baked Ziti." She put the container to her nose and inhaled. "Ah, heaven." She gasped while stuffing a piece of bread into her mouth.

Nick was holding a container with a salad. "I take it the salad doesn't stand a chance."

"After this?" Ericka laughed. "Are there any utensils in there?"

"Here you are." Nick looked up as he opened his container. Ericka had started eating. "Are we going to say grace?"

Ericka froze with her fork half-way to her mouth. "Excuse me?"

"Grace. You know the few words of thanks spoken before every meal."

"Oh, that...okay." Ericka put her fork down.

Nick lowered his head and said grace as Ericka lowered hers and watched. "Don't believe in God." Another bit of information about the lovely Ericka."

"It's not that I don't believe in him. I just think he is in some people's lives more than others."

"I take it you believe you are one of the less fortunate," Nick asked as he took a bite of homemade lasagna.

This was a taboo topic. Talking religion was personal...too personal. Ericka spread her legs out and crossed them at the ankles as she continued to eat. "Tell me about your family."

Change of topic, Nick thought kicking off his shoes. He stretched out on his side and rested his head on his hand, with one knee up. His container, now on the blanket in front of him, he continued to eat. "Family. Two older brothers and a sister. What about you?"

Long legs. Thick thighs. Big feet. All three distracted her. Did he ask a question?

"Me what?"

"Family. What about your family."

"I don't have any." She shrugged, "I mean I have a baby brother. We talk every now and then."

"What about your parents?"

"My mother passed away. My father is still in California...somewhere."

Yet another piece of the puzzle surrounding the lovely Ericka, Nick thought as he continued to gather information. "Is that where you live now?"

"No, I'm working out of Atlanta right now."

"What kind of work do you do?"

Ericka froze.

Nick laughed. "This is either your first attempt at a con or you're not very good."

That's just it. She was extremely good at what she did. Working cons had afforded her a life of comfort most people only dreamed of. But this man was proving to be difficult. That's because the con was wrong. Ericka had always picked her targets. She had never been paid to do a con against someone. She would select her target, set her goal and take steps to accomplish what she wanted. This con was all wrong. It was for someone she did not like, against someone she liked too much.

The struggle on her face was a good sign. Having difficultly with a con indicated there was a good soul inside. He sat up. "Let's make this easy. You tell me what you want. I'll give it to you. There will be no bad feelings. Leaving the opportunity to explore the possibility of us."

"There is no possibility of an us," Ericka quickly replied. "I'm here for a purpose. Not to let you sneak into my heart."

"Who said anything about your heart? It's your panties I'm trying to get into."

The laughter in his eyes let her know he was teasing. "You are a terrible tease, Nicolas Brooks."

"I know. So what is it that you want from me Ms. Kennedy?"

Her eyes caught his and held. A slow smile began to form on her face. She put her container down. "You had me from the beginning didn't you?"

"No. Not the very beginning. I thought one of my clients was your target until the intentional bump."

Ericka smiled. "Not my best moment."

Nick nodded his head as he continued to assess her. There was a touch of honesty about her. Not once had she denied why she had come into his life. Whatever the reason, she was here. "God works in mysterious ways."

Ericka frowned. "Excuse me?"

Nick shook his head and reached for the bottle of wine and two glasses. "Nothing." He poured a glass for each of them. "What do you say we start over? Take a few days to get to know me. Then decide if the con is worth it?"

Ericka hesitated, then reached out for the glass. "You are either a very confident man or a fool."

"Gwendolyn Brooks did not raise any fools. She raised children who believe in the goodness of others."

"Everyone does not have goodness in them Nick. I'm sure you know that."

"Ah, a cynic."

"Realist." She pointed to his plate. "Are you going to eat the rest of that?"

Nick looked down, picked up a fork of lasagna and held it out to her lips.

Why does he do these things? They are far too intimate for someone he just met.

He saw the look on her face. "I promise I don't have the cooties or anything close."

She laughed.

A genuine laugh, that reached her eyes. The simple action transformed the lovely Ericka to exquisite, yet cautious Ericka. He waited. "In the immortal words of Billy Dee, are you going to let my arm fall off?"

It sounded just as sexy coming from him. She bent forward and took the offering.

We're making progress Nick thought as he watched her close her eyes, savoring the flavor. "Man, I have to hire him as my cook."

Ericka opened her eyes. "For goodness sake hire the man. If you don't, I will."

They laughed and talked for the next three hours. One of the artists in the park walked over when they finally stood to leave. He gave them a painting of the two of them on the blanket eating. The painting had captured the spellbinding moment on both of their faces.

Nick tried to pay the guy for the painting, but he refused.

"Moments like this don't come along often. When they do, they should be captured and treasured."

When they arrived back at her car. Nick opened the door. Ericka stood behind the door facing him.

"Thank you for a lovely afternoon, Ms. Kennedy." He gave her the picture.

"The pleasure was all mine." She placed it on the passenger seat and waited, thinking he would kiss her. After a few moments, she realized it wasn't going to happen. She got into the car and he closed the door. He stepped back allowing her to pull out.

Ericka was disappointed, as she backed her vehicle out and pulled off. When she reached the entrance to the parking lot, she glanced at the picture, then looked in her rearview mirror. He was still standing there. She put the car in Park and stepped out.

"I would like that," she called out to him.

"What?"

"Getting to know you better."

Nick smiled. "I would like that too."

Ericka smiled, got back into her car and drove off.

Nick stood there for a minute thinking, before walking into the building. What in the hell was he doing?

Chapter 4

"Cannon this is wrong. Nick Brooks is not the kind of man you pull a scam on."

"Let's hope you won't have to go through with it. For now, we only need Singleton to think we are complying with his commands."

"Are you getting any closer to what this is all about? Why does he want this family destroyed? They seem like decent people."

Cannon sat back in his chair at his desk in Atlanta. "I don't know cuz. Only that he wants it done and he wants it done publicly."

Ericka looked out the window of the condo she was renting in Richmond. "I don't know about this Cannon. It doesn't feel right."

"Are you having a hard time finding an opening to this guy?"

"No." Ericka chuckled, "He's an open book. He holds nothing back. I almost feel like I have to protect him from himself."

"Green?"

"No, not at all. He's just a straight shooter. He reads people too damn well and tells you what he thinks. There is nothing green about the man."

Cannon sat forward. "Stick with him until I get a break on this end or you find a way to compromise his firm. Look, we may be going about this the wrong way, but our reasons are just. Bobby is being cheated out of a lot of money and he doesn't deserve that."

Ericka closed her eyes and exhaled. "I know. Bobby is clearly the victim in all of this. But, Nick isn't the person cheating Bobby. It's Singleton."

"There are just too many unanswered questions," Cannon stated. "For instance, he had me to run a full check on the Brooks family. Why?"

"My question is why hasn't the law firm turned over full control of the company to Singleton? As far as they know he is the only child."

"It has to be something in his father's will."

"That's another thing." Ericka set her cup of tea on the table. "With all the money and property that lady owned, why didn't she have a will, too. All you mentioned so far is the father's will. Where is the mother's will?"

Cannon sat back, "Good question. Where is the mother's will?"

"That's what I just asked you. I can't believe she did not have one."

"I think you have a point."

"I'll stay on Nick Brooks. You search for the mother's will."

"If one exists."

***

Sunday dinner at the Brooks estate in Tyson, Virginia was a must if you were in town. Vernon still lived in the east wing of the estate with his wife, Constance, and their daughter, Taylor, when they weren't on the road. With the oldest son James, now acting as the advisor to the President, he and his family had a home in the area. The only two any distance away were the twins. Nicole lived in New York and ran the real estate division of Brooks Industries and of course, Nick who lived in Richmond, but would normally drive up on Sundays for dinner. This Sunday was a wonderful exception. Everyone was home and Gwendolyn could not have been happier. It was apparent by the big grin plastered on her face as she sat at the end of the table.

The conversations were flowing from real estate to music to politics and they had finally come around to Nick's event.

"I saw this really cute guy there," Taylor said to Nicole. All conversation around them stopped.

"What was his name?" Nicole asked, as the two were oblivious to the silence around them.

"I don't know. But he's tall with these muscle-filled long arms and the nicest eyes I've ever seen. Did I say how fine he looked in a tux and had great muscles?"

Ashley nodded. "When I met your Uncle James, he was dressed in a suit and tie, but I could tell what was underneath and I knew I wanted a piece of that."

"I can understand that now. I mean this guy made me feel naked when he looked at me and I was fully dressed."

"That's enough," Vernon shouted. "Nobody is getting a piece of anything around here."

The women looked at Vernon shocked.

"Vernon, don't get upset because your daughter might be getting something you are not," Gwendolyn teased.

"Sex is not a proper conversation for Sunday dinner. Wouldn't you agree Pop?" Vernon turned to his father expecting his support.

"I don't think there is ever a bad time to discuss sex. It's the root of all evil and the start of most love affairs. A very diverse topic I would say." He smiled at his wife.

"Vernon you are acting like you haven't had any since Taylor was conceived," James laughed.

"No, that would be me," Constance stated dryly causing all eyes to turn her way. She didn't skip a beat as she continued to eat.

"Well, we know that 's not the case for Vernon." Nick laughed.

"One mistake, one damn mistake and this family will never let me live it down. Can we please change the subject?" Vernon glared at Nick. "How is your love life?"

"Non-existent for the moment, but I'm working a promising prospect." Nick grinned at Vernon.

"Someone we know?" Nicole asked curiously.

"I just met her last Saturday, so I doubt it."

"The woman in the green dress?" Nicole asked incredulously.

"What woman?" Gwendolyn asked.

"The goddess?" Vernon sat up. "Coal black hair off to the side?"

Nick pointed his fork at his brother. "That's the one."

"How in the hell did you pull that?" Vernon asked proudly. "I was certain she would end up with one of the ball players."

"You're not serious Nick." Nicole stopped eating.

"Why not?"

"Nick, she's a ... skeezer or something Kiki called her."

"She's not a skeezer," Nick replied. "She's a con artist."

"A con artist?" Avery looked up. "What does she want?"

"I don't know. I'm trying to find out."

"Sweetheart, do you think that's the kind of girl you want around?" Gwendolyn asked in a concerned mother's voice.

"She's exactly the kind of girl I want around," Nick replied. "She's intelligent, funny and beautiful, just like you." He smiled at his mother who smiled back.

"While you are right about your mother, I have to question your judgment on having a woman around you known to be a con artist. How would your clients react if they knew this?"

Nicole saw where this was leading and felt bad. She shouldn't have blurted her thoughts out loud. Nick glanced her way and she mouthed, "I'm sorry," and flinched.

"I'm not marrying her or anything like that, Pop. She's an intriguing woman who I would like to get to know better. Nothing more...nothing less."

"Well I would like a little more of the guy I saw at your event," Taylor stated trying to bring the conversation around to her.

"I'm sure Nick would know him," Nicole added to help squash the mess she started. "Describe him Taylor."

"Tall, chocolate and fine."

"That should narrow it down," Ashley laughed.

"Well he did have a tattoo on his back, Uncle Nick." Taylor looked at him expectantly.

"How would you know he had a tattoo Taylor?" Constance asked in that mother's tone every child recognized. "On his back of all places."

"They played a pickup game in the gym," Taylor explained quickly. "I was watching from the balcony."

"What was it?" Nick asked conscious of what they were doing.

Grateful for the question Taylor replied eagerly, "A dragon. It was a full-length dragon tattooed on his back. The tail went all the way down his back."

"Jason Whitfield," Nick and James replied in unison.

"He's the rookie for the Washington Reptiles basketball team," Nick added.

"Oh...hell no." Vernon threw his napkin on the table.

Everyone at the table burst out laughing at his outrage.

Hours later Nick and Nicole were on their way to the private airport in Manassas that the family used for travel. The twenty-minute ride was their time together to catch up on what was happening in their lives. Since neither of them was seeing anyone seriously, their conversations were always lively. They usually finish each other sentences.

"Hey I'm sorry about that thing at dinner. I didn't mean to start a firestorm back there. I was a little surprised by your comment."

"Which one?"

"About the skeezer."

"She's not a skeezer. She's a con artist."

"And she actually told you this?"

"No, Nikki, she didn't have to. It's my job to protect my clients from women like her."

"And who's protecting you?"

"That's what sisters are for." He glanced over at her and smiled.

"You got that right" — she huffed— "I made sure she understood the walls of hell will collapse around her so she better tread lightly."

"Damn Nikki, when did you do that?"

"Saturday night at the valet station. She told me to find my own gold mine. I told her mines explode and collapse."

"Nikki, look." He checked the side mirror before turning. "I like her. Can you give me a little space on this one?"

"You like her, like her, or is this a Nick lay-around until they get too close?"

He shrugged. "Like her...like her."

"Ah Nick." Nicole huffed. "You already know what she's about."

"I know." He shrugged. "But you like who you like."

"You are not going to find a Gwendolyn Brooks on the 'pay me for my services' rack. You know that...right?"

"I know." He pulled into the entrance of the airport. The plane was waiting on the tarmac. He parked the car. "There's something about her. I can't shake."

"Really?" She looked her brother straight in the eyes, then huffed. "All right, you have your space. But trust your gut you'll know if it's right."

Nick kissed her cheek. "Thanks sis. What about you? Anyone special?"

"If you're referring to something on two legs, no. But hey, who knows, a man of questionable morals could be waiting right around the corner for me. You never know." She waved as she walked up the steps of the plane. "We'll talk later."

Nick leaned against the car until the plane hit the runway and took off. He had a two hour drive ahead of him to help him determine what his next move would be with Ericka. Before taking any steps, he wanted to have a conversation with the only other person this could impact. He pushed a button on the console. The sound of a phone ringing vibrated through the car.

"Pendleton."

"You clear?"

"Give me a minute." Nick heard Kiki in the background, then a door closed. "Clear."

"Any new information?"

"No record. Mother died in a fire a few years ago. One brother who went to high school with you. "

"What's his name?"

"Bobby S. Kennedy. "

Nick thought for a moment. "Not ringing a bell. Send me a picture."

"Will do. One interesting tidbit, her cousin is Cannonball McNally."

"The football player?"

"He now owns a private investigation service. From what I understand he's taking a leave of absence for personal reasons."

"Hmm. Where is he?"

"Atlanta. According to our records, Ms. Kennedy was there before renting the condo she has here."

"Is it possible they are working together on a scam?" Nick questioned.

"Not McNally's makeup," Ty replied. "From what I remember Cannonball was pretty reputable. But we leave no stone unturned. We'll check out why he's in Atlanta. It might lead to something."

"He's not based there?"

"No. He's based out of DC. His firm handles private protection for the movers and shakers of politics."

"That's a lucrative account. Why leave that to go to Atlanta?"

"That's what we are going to find out. What's your next step?"

"I'm going to have dinner with the lovely Ericka."

"Watch your back. We are in control for now. Women like Ms. Kennedy have a way of turning things in their favor."

Chapter 5

This was not what she had in mind for a date. Ericka looked around the gymnasium filled with young boys and their parents listening to Nicolas speak. But she had to concede; he had the boys' undivided attention, along with a few mothers. She wasn't concerned with that aspect for she knew she could sweep the floor with any of them. Her plan tonight was seduction 101 with Nicolas Brooks. He may have been able to resist her last week, but not tonight. At least that's what she thought when she left her condo, dressed in a pink, silk, low cut top and flirty flair skirt that moved with every step she took. The outfit was sure to take his breath away...not.

"I have something special I want to share with you today." He said when she stepped out of her car, his smile beaming as bright as the sun above. Here she sat, in a high school gym.

"I was born Nicolas Gunter Brooks." The crowd of fifty Marshall High School athletes chuckled. "Ha-ha laugh as you may, but it was my great-great-grandfather's name. It came with a load of responsibility and expectations. For it was the first Nicolas Gunter Brooks who had the vision of seeing his four boys go away to college at a time when getting an education for African-Americans was against the law." He paused and looked around the room, then began to pace as he captured the young boys' attention. "Imagine that for a minute. Each of you in this room would have been beaten, arrested or hung for being in this school." The boys looked around curiously. "People died to give you the opportunity to get an education. It is incumbent upon you to take every advantage and to honor those who gave their lives so that you can have a promising future. Athletics is your road. I've seen numerous young men, just like some of you, take the opportunity for granted. I suggest you use your God-given talent to make a difference in your lives and the lives of your families." He stopped and exhaled. "The biggest mistake I see in the sports industry is not having a backup plan. Some depend solely on their athletic ability to earn a living. If your knees, your hands, your legs go out, what will you have to make a living from? The average career in the NFL is three to six years...the NBA is four years...MLB is six years. How do you feed your family, or yourself afterwards?"

"I can live off one hundred-twenty million dollars for a long time," one young man joked as he gave high-fives around.

Nick smiled. "The average salary in the MLB is around three and a half million a year...NFL is maybe two million and the NBA is around five million. After you buy your mom the big house, yourself a bigger house, a few cars to show off and let's not forget the baby's mothers, your few millions are gone. Did I fail to mention the ten to twenty percent you are going to pay your agent off the top?" There was a moan from the audience. "That one hundred-twenty million you mentioned goes to the elites and even some of them end up broke once they stop playing ball. However, the smart ones invest in their future to ensure the income they have become accustomed to remains intact. Some have great investors, endorsements and or a second career planned. What all of them have is intelligence. They took the time at a young age to learn about the industry. They took accounting so they can follow what their investors present. They study contractual law while in college so when the time came they would understand the basic language in a contract. Bottom line...they know more than just the game. If you want to just say you played ball for a year or two, okay, don't follow their lead." He stopped and looked around the room meeting the eyes of each young man. "If you want to be an elite, put in the dedication, not only to the skill on the field or court, but to the knowledge in your mind. For it's that knowledge that will keep you in the game long after you stop playing."

He was telling them right, Ericka nodded as he spoke. One of the reasons she never targeted athletes was because their funds were based on their physical ability to play the game. With corporate men, the funds were based on their minds. Brainwork always outlasts physical labor.

Coach Mathew Lassiter straightened from leaning against the wall. He stared at his team. "There are approximately one million high school football players out there. Only seventeen hundred will make it to the NFL and only ninety-two of those are going to play in the Super Bowl. The information Mr. Brooks provided today will separate the boys...from the men." He glared at his players. "He is one of the top sports agents in the country. Yet he's taken time out of his day to school you." Without looking at Nick he asked, "What is your clients' average salary per year, Nick?"

"Sixteen-point-five million."

"Why is that Nick?"

"I only take the best of the best and then I make them better."

"Do you see any in this room you would take?"

Nick looked around. "I see the hunger in one or two. However, it takes more than being hungry. It takes dedication and integrity to the sport, but most importantly, to yourself."

Matt pointed to Nick. "You want to be on his clientele list, be smart. Carry yourself as a gentleman at all times and you might be lucky enough to be sitting across the desk from Nick Brooks with a woman like that on your arm." He pointed to Ericka. She waved as the boys whistled. Matt laughed. "Show Mr. Brooks how we do it here at Marshall."

One young man stood and yelled, "Who are we?"

"The Marshalls," the others yelled back.

"What do we do?"

"We control the key to our own destiny." They all started cheering.

Matt walked over to Nick and shook his hand. "Good talk. As always, I owe you a beer."

Nick gave Matt a pound with his fist. "Anytime you need me, I'm here."

"Any chance you can bring Bryson around?"

"I'll see how we can work it out. The man is all over the place."

"What about Whitfield?"

"Hmmm...He's not there yet, but he's coming around. Give him another year or two to come into his own and I'll have him out here."

"Who's the lady?" Matt nodded in Ericka's direction.

"Mine?"

"Oh, it's like that. I don't rate an intro?"

"So you can try to hit on her, no."

"Excuse me, Mr. Brooks," Nick looked up at the young man who had to be seven feet tall. At six-two, he had to step back to see his face. "My mom would like to have a word with you."

"What's your name?"

"Oh, they call me Coco."

"What's your real name?"

"Charcoal Luscious Brown."

Nick could only stare at the boy. He cleared his throat, then swallowed to keep the chuckle inside. "Where is your mother, Coco?"

The boy pointed towards the doorway where two young girls were talking to another player. "She's right there at the door."

Nick looked, then glanced at Matt. The nod from the coach indicated the boy was telling the truth. "I will be there in a moment as soon as I finish with your coach."

Matt began to chuckle at the look on Nick's face. "They have them young."

"She looks like one of the students."

"Acts like one too," Matt added. "I can see him making the pros, but that name is going to give him hell."

Nick shook his head. "What a choice...Charcoal Brown, or Coco Brown or Luscious Brown. Either way the boy is going to be the butt of every joke when he hits the pros."

Matt hit Nick on the shoulder. "Thanks for talking to the kids and good luck with the mother." Then he walked off laughing.

Nick made his way to Ericka. "I hope I didn't keep you too long."

"I enjoyed your speech. You do this often?"

"Whenever the coach asks me to come in." He tilted his head. "I have to speak to this one parent. Come with me."

Ericka looked in the direction they were walking. "You need me to block for you?"

"You standing next to me looking beautiful should do it."

Ericka smiled as they approached the two ladies.

"Ms. Brown." Nick extended his hand. "Coco indicated you wanted to speak with me."

"I do." The woman looked Ericka up and down. "I didn't expect an audience."

"It's just us." Ericka smiled. "We can step outside the door to speak if you like."

"What I meant was him"— she pointed to Nick— "and me. I don't want everybody in my business when I'm talking about my son."

"The problem is Ms...?"

"Caramel Brown."

Ericka kept a straight face. "Ms. Brown, if Nick speaks to you alone it will jeopardize your son's chance of going into the NBA. NCAA rules prohibit agents from speaking with potential players or their parents. If it occurs it makes your son ineligible. We wouldn't want that to happen with your son...right?"

"Oh hell no...Coco is my ticket out of here."

"Coco?" Ericka asked.

"Yes, my son. Coco Brown. Don't you think that's a sweet name?"

Ericka nodded trying hard to keep a straight face. "Like hot chocolate."

"Right, that's my daughter's name, Chocolate. I thought I would keep the two with the same initials." The woman grinned showing all thirty-two teeth with pride.

"Did you have a question, Ms. Brown?"

"You can call me Caramel. I just wanted you to know my Coco is a good boy. He stays out of trouble and practices all the time. I told him if he gets any of these fast-tail gals out here pregnant, I'm cutting it off. I just want you to know I like you and what you said up there and all. I'm keeping your information cause when the time comes we'll be calling you."

"Thank you, Ms. Brown. I'll look forward to hearing from you."

Not a word was spoken between Nick and Ericka as they walked to his vehicle. Nick opened the passenger door, then closed it once Ericka was inside. He then walked around and climbed into the driver's seat.

"Don't say anything." Ericka touched his arm. "Give me a minute before you speak."

They both sat there in their own thoughts until neither could hold back any longer. Both burst out in laughter. Ericka had tears coming out of her eyes.

"I hope Coco don't get any from any girl until he is out of his mother's house." Nick laughed.

Ericka laughed harder. "Okay...okay. Her name is Caramel. His name is Coco. The daughter's name is Chocolate. If she said her husband's name was Godiva the Chocolatier, that would have done it for me."

"I can't believe she is that young. I thought she was one of the students."

"It happens more than people like to believe, Nick." Ericka sobered. "Young girls find themselves in compromising positions all the time. Not knowing if they should trust the guy. Some are so desperate to feel love, they take it whatever way they can get it. When the guys disappear they feel like they can get the love from a baby. A child never disappears on you."

The atmosphere in the vehicle turned from laughter to somber just that quick. "Are you talking from experience?" Nick asked as he looked over at her.

A surprised Ericka shook her head. "No. Of course not." She laughed nervously, biting her lip as she turned away.

Nick started the car. Another bit of information about the lovely Ericka. She has a soft spot for troubled young girls. He also could sense this was not a topic she wanted to take further. "I think I owe you a meal. I'm thinking...pizza." He smiled at her. "Homemade from the oven to the table pizza. I know just the place. And if you are good...really good, I'll add in a big cup of hot chocolate." There was a moment of silence, then laugher erupted throughout the vehicle.

Her mistakes were building up. For the next three hours, Ericka forgot about the scam. Forgot about Singleton. Forgot about Bobby. She was doing something she never really ever got to do. She was having fun on a date. They were eating pizza, drinking beers, talking and laughing about nothing, yet everything that should matter in two normal human beings lives. Before either of them knew it, three hours had passed. The only thing that made them notice was the chairs turned up on the tables, and the noise level was non-existent.

"I think we ran everyone out of the place." Nick took the last drink of his beer.

Ericka looked around to see the place was empty with the exception of two people standing at the grill. She glanced at her watch, then back at the grill. "They are cleaning the grill."

"It's past their closing time." Nick reached in his pocket and pulled out some bills and placed them on the table. He held out his hand.

There it was again, Ericka thought as she stared at his hand. The intimacy he was extending. She grabbed her purse and stood without taking his hand. "I guess it's time for us to leave." She smiled up at him and walked towards the door.

Another rebuff of the hand. Why, Nick wondered as he held the car door open for her.

"How did you come across such a wonderful place? I could hang out there forever."

"By accident," Nick replied as he slid into the driver's seat. "I was running through the woods in the back of my house and came out on that side road." He pointed across her. "I saw this row of stores and decided to check it out. It's a little town center within the community."

"You live around here?"

"In the woods, behind the stores."

"May I see your home?"

A surprised Nick glanced over and held her eyes. "You want to see my home?"

"I would," then she hesitated. Suppose someone lived there with him. "It's late. We don't have to, it was just a thought."

"No. I love showing off my house. If you really want to."

"Yes, I would."

"Let's go."

Nick pressed his palm to a panel on the porch of his home and the door opened.

As she walked through the foyer of the large rancher, warmth spread through her body. The house was elegant, but if felt like home. She slightly tilted her head to the side as she took the one step down into the great room, then slowly walked through. With each step, the feeling of being at home consumed her more. Trying to shake the feeling and concentrate on what she needed to do, Ericka ran her fingers through her hair then turned in the center of the floor. She stopped as she spotted a piano in front of the floor to ceiling windows. Of course she had seen pianos in homes before, but this one seemed to be the centerpiece of the room even though it was in the corner. She walked over and stood behind the bench. It was a Steinway & Sons baby grand, black with gold lettering. She looked up to see him staring at her. There was a tightening in her chest she hadn't experienced before. Nick was across the room leaning against the fireplace mantle. She didn't hear him come into the room or light the fireplace. It was as if he magically materialized in that space just to tantalize her. He smiled, showing those pearly white teeth and those damn luscious lips and she knew her plan was in trouble.

She licked her lips, then bit into them as their eyes held.

Nick couldn't help but smile. The telltale signs of nervousness were present. "Do you know you bite your lip when you are nervous?"

She stopped, then sat on the leather bench and crossed her legs. "What reason would I have to be nervous?"

"Could it be you are not able to control what's happening here?"

"I'm always in control Nicolas."

"Really?"

Ericka sat back straight, with her chin held high. "Yes."

Holding her gaze, Nick stepped away from the mantle. He watched as the sparkle in her eyes glazed over into uncertainty with every step he took. "You're sure?"

Her normal response would have been a resounding yes, but he was approaching her as if he was a lion with his long powerful strides, and she was his prey. The intensity grew in his eyes letting her know he would not be denied. The warning was there, in the way her heart skipped a beat, her breath caught in her throat and she couldn't pull her eyes from his. By the time he reached her, she wasn't sure. She wasn't sure at all. He walked behind her, gently dragging his forefinger across her shoulder causing the heat to rise within.

He pointed to the space left on the bench. "May I."

Still not able to trust herself to speak, Ericka nodded.

He lifted the cover revealing the eighty-eight beautiful black and white keys. He played a glissando, then eased into a smooth jazz piece. Ericka watched long graceful fingers touching every key as if it were a delicate flower. She followed the movement up his arms, to his shoulders, as the song reached its crescendo. The power radiating through them began to shatter all her confidence. Her pulse began to race the moment her eyes met his. There was an awareness as his fingers continued to pound and their eyes held. It felt as if each note was capturing a small piece of her heart and his eyes were daring her to deny it. The music built as their lips were drawn to each other's. It softened as his lips hovered over hers.

"May I?"

She knew what he was asking and was certain where it would lead, but her resistance left with the last note he played and held until their lips met. He closed the cover with one hand, and wrapped the other around her waist as her lips parted. Then his tongue began playing notes as delicately inside her mouth as his fingers had on the keyboard. Every stroke sent sensations of pleasure coursing through her veins. Their tongues tangoed to a rhythm of their own making and she was powerless to stop what was about to happen.

Nick lifted her onto his lap. The moment her legs opened he could feel her heat calling out to him. All of his senses sent jolts as if lightening had struck and were surging through every circuit. His hand palmed the back of her head, holding her in place so he could plunge his tongue deeper to get a taste of every inch of her mouth. It was as if there wasn't enough of her to quench the desire that was building. He stood and set her on the piano, then slid kisses down her neck to her shoulder.

"You're going to scratch the piano," she moaned.

Nick ran a hand down her legs and knocked her heels to the floor one after the other. "Steinway, baby. It's built with durability in mind."

Her eyes remained on the movement of his lips. "It's a fifty-thousand dollar piece of equipment. You wouldn't want to scratch it."

"Closer to ninety-thousand, but I'm not worried about scratches. The only thing to touch it will be your naked behind, and that is smooth as a baby's."

"How do you know?"

"It's in my hand." He squeezed her to confirm his statement.

She grinned as she brought his lips closer to hers. "You have some smooth moves Mr. Brooks. They say be aware of the quiet ones."

His finger trailed the outline of her cheek, down her neck to the crease between her breasts. "The world doesn't need to know I'm here...I know."

She knew, from the look in his eyes he was speaking literally. "I know you're here." She motioned against his lips.

"How do you know?"

"I can feel you through every pore of my body."

Their lips met, this time it was sweet, sensual, soul searing.

The air hitting her breasts was the first sign that he had unzipped the top from behind and pushed it down to her waist. Next were his lips taking one nipple between them. His tongue circling one, while his thumb followed suit on the other. Ericka was helpless to do anything but cradle him in her arms and hold him to her breast as if he was a baby. Any last strands of resistance faded away when his lips reached her navel, his strong arms lifted her and dropped the skirt to join the top and heels.

Nick laid her back as his hands glided over her magnificent body. His mind's eye would never be able to banish the sight of her lying in nothing but a string thong on his baby grand. It was a sight to behold. He used both hands to smoothly glide the strip of material down her thighs, then dropped them to join the rest of her outfit on the floor. All of her was naked as a newborn baby. Not a strand of hair. Nick put each foot on the keyboard cover, then spread her legs gently open. He touched his forefinger to his lips, kissed it, ran it over the split between her legs and slid it inside. Moisture covered his finger causing him to nearly burst through his pants. He pulled his finger out, spread the juice down both thighs. He licked up one thigh as he removed his shirt and down the other as he pulled a condom from his pants pocket, then dropped them to the floor. He tore the package open with his teeth then covered his erection with the latex protection. He bent securely between her thighs, licking her clitoris with his tongue, then closed his lips around it. He held her down firmly with one hand on her stomach when her body jerked. He wanted every one of her nerve endings in her erogenous zone screaming for him. Once she reached the peak he wanted, he gave her one long lick, a playful scrape of his teeth and she sat straight up panting. He pulled her lower body to him and entered her with one, slow, penetrating move that left her breathless. Their bodies did not move. He wrapped his arms around her back as she wrapped her arms around his neck. Nick kissed her neck as he began to move gently inside of her, first in a slow circular motion. He could feel her muscles clenching him, but he wasn't ready for things to come to a head...not yet. He pulled out, then brought her bottom to meet him. His hand held her there, as he moved in...then out...then in...and out...in...out until her body took over the motion. Now both his hands were in her hair, pushing it away from her face. As he kissed her eyelids, she continued to move in....and out with more force, he kissed her nose, she pushed harder. He parted her lips with his tongue and dove deep into her mouth. Her body pushed harder, faster as the rhythm of his tongue increased. The deeper his tongue went the harder her body met his. Her intensity was so strong her nails dug into his back. He could feel her wanting to crawl inside of him to get what she needed...desired from him. Nick's hands moved to her hips, stopping her motion, he pulled completely out, then slammed back into her causing everything around them to explode. She screamed out his name as he continued to pump vigorously into her until his explosion matched hers. He sat back on the leather bench with her arms wrapped around his neck and his arms around her waist. He held her tight as he kissed her neck, her shoulders, any part of her skin he could reach until his heartbeat began to slow down.

Once his strength returned he picked her up, carried her down the hallway through the double doors of his bedroom. They lay on the bed still entwined as he whispered. "Round two."

Ericka's laugh was as giddy as a schoolgirl's with her very first love. While the first session was intense, this one was exploratory. For hours they explored each other's bodies, not leaving an area untouched, by lips. She thought his hands, those wonderful long fingers of his were magical, for everywhere they touched she felt sensations unlike anything she had experienced before.

That hand that she had avoided for a week was now her focus, as they lay on the ruffled bed embraced in the warmth of each other's arms.

As she played with his fingers, Nick teased. "You like that hand now?"

"I do." She brought one of his fingers to her lips and kissed it.

"You want to tell me why you were afraid of taking my hand, before?" Ericka knew what he was asking. He could tell by the way her body tensed.

"We are having way too much fun to relive the past." She turned her body to face him. "Nick..." she hesitated.

"Don't hold back Ericka. What's on your mind?"

He looked down at her with such sincerity. The guilt of her reasons for being there seeped in for a moment. She wanted to tell him that what they just shared was an exception and not a rule. For whatever reason she did not want him to think she slept with every target she conned. She did not want him to think being with him this way was about money.

Nick watched as the play of emotions showed on her face. He wanted her to open up and tell him why she was there. But for whatever reason, he did not like seeing the turmoil he was causing her.

Ericka's hands caressed his chest. "You took dance lessons, didn't you?"

"I did." Nick kissed her neck, and sighed. She wasn't ready. He would give her the time she needed to come clean. For now he wanted to enjoy whatever time they would have together. "When I was in high school my coach said a dance class would help my foot movement on the court. So I took a class and liked it. Every Tuesday and Thursday after basketball practice I would go. The guys laughed, at first, but then they saw the ease of my movements on the court and a few of them began coming to class."

"Are you as good at dancing as you are on the piano?"

"I've got moves," He pulled her body over his.

She straddled him. "I've got a few moves myself," she grinned as her body moved against his.

"Do you?" Nick adjusted his position under her. "Show me and don't hold back."

"I don't hold back. When I give, I give all I got."

"That's what I want Ericka. All you have."

Ericka slid on to him, pulled her hair off her shoulder and held it on top of her head. She closed her eyes, then began to move slowly up and down as he held her firmly.

For the first time in her life Ericka knew she was in good hands.

Chapter 6

"I can't do this, Cannon." Ericka took a drink from the glass of lemonade as they sat outside of a restaurant in the Buckhead area of Atlanta. She and Nick had spent two days together making love, laughing, making love, talking, and making love some more. Ericka shook the memory away.

"This is a good man. I don't know why Singleton wants him disgraced and I'm not sure I care why."

"Let me tell you what I've found out." He pulled out a piece of paper and gave it to her. "This is a copy of Singleton's father's will."

Ericka glanced through it and shrugged her shoulders. "It leaves everything to his wife and son."

Cannon nodded, then gave her another piece of paper. "Now read this."

Ericka read the second document and looked up at him somewhat confused. "Isaac has a child?" She put the paper on the table. "What does that have to do with Nick?"

"This is where things get a little interesting." Cannon sat up. "According to this document, the mother of Isaac's child was a Gwendolyn Spivey. Gwendolyn Spivey married an Avery Brooks." He raised an eyebrow.

"Avery and Gwendolyn Brooks are Nick's parents." She frowned. "You think Nick is Isaac's son?" She asked shaking her head. "No." She pushed the paper back to Cannon. "No way."

"Not Nick. He's too young and he's a twin. I'm thinking one of the older brothers may be Isaac's son."

"So go after one of them and leave Nick alone."

"It doesn't work like that for a man like Isaac." Cannon shook his head. "I think his plan is to destroy the whole family. But there's more. I followed up on your question about Isaac's mother's will. According to her housekeeper, she said she knows Mrs. Singleton did have a will. In fact, she was the one who drove Mrs. Singleton to your mother's house the day she gave her a copy. She doesn't know what was in the will but she knows it exists. That's why she was surprised when Isaac got everything. But when he gave her one hundred thousand dollars for her service to his mother, she never said anything."

"That's the will my mother showed to you?"

Cannon nodded. "If we can find that will, Bobby is due to inherit half of what Isaac has claimed."

Ericka sighed. "Cannon," she looked away then turned back to him. "I want to help Bobby get what is rightfully his, but I can't do this to Nick."

"If you don't, Isaac will find someone else to do it. You better believe that. Hell, he has instructed me to go after the sister now. You don't need to know that, but the play is in motion."

"What in the hell is his problem with this family?"

"It's all about the Benjamins."

"But there is plenty to go around."

"Singleton is not the sharing type. That's part of the reason he didn't make it in the NBA. He's not a team player. He's selfish. After that murder charge, no team in the league wanted to deal with that and his problem is he's also selfish on the court. They didn't care how talented he was."

"Somebody has to put a stop to this."

"I think we can, but you have to play it out Ericka. Singleton is expecting a status in two weeks."

"Hello, it's Ericka, right?"

Ericka and Cannon looked up to see Nicole Brooks and another woman standing not ten feet away from them. What in the hell was she doing in Atlanta?

"Yes, it is." Ericka turned to Cannon. "Would you give us a moment?"

Cannon had just received a complete dossier on the woman, so he knew exactly who they were and the consequences of them seeing him and Ericka together. He stood and put on his most charming smile. "Good afternoon, ladies. If you would excuse me."

Nicole nodded her head but never took her eyes from Ericka. "Funny seeing you here in Atlanta with another man. Is he your next target?"

Ericka smiled. "Nicole, right? You have your brother's eyes."

"We share a lot more than that." Nicole removed her glasses. "You weren't able to get what you wanted from Nick so you've moved on, I hope."

"I love it when women try to analyze my life." She chuckled. "No, I haven't moved on from Nick nor do I plan to."

Nicole looked off then turned back with a sigh. "Look why don't you go find a ball player to marry and leave my brother out of your plans?"

Ericka stared at Nicole for a long minute. "If a ball player was who I wanted I would have one. However"—she looked around shrugged her shoulder, then focused back on Nicole— "I choose not to live my life waiting for a man to dish out his shit and then stand back and ask may I have more of your shit please. Ericka stood, picked up her purse and put her shades on. I choose to be the one dishing. You should try life my way. Loosen those curls. You might like it." Ericka turned, but Nicole caught her by the arm.

Ericka jerked away. "That's crossing the line, Nicole. But out of respect for your brother I will not knock you on your ass."

Nicole stepped in her face. "Respect? If you had any respect you would get a job and stop depending on decent people to support you.

Alicia, Nicole's assistant stepped between the two women. "We're causing a scene. Let's walk away."

"Yes, Nicole...walk away."

"You may want to consider doing the same thing Ericka." Nicole said as Alicia pulled her away. "Gold mines blow and collapse. Remember that."

Ericka kept her eyes on the two women as they walked away. Any thoughts she had of a possible relationship with Nick just vanished. She turned and walked purposely over to Cannon, "Two weeks, Cannon, two weeks. You find what you need to get what is due to Bobby before I have to take this step with Nick. "

"Are you getting in too deep with this Brooks character?"

"Just find another way to do this, please."

Seeing how upset she was getting, Cannon agreed. "Okay, let me ask you this. Your mother had a copy of a document she showed me. Would she have showed it to anyone else? A friend, or a neighbor...anyone?"

Ericka thought for a minute. "The only person I can think of is old Mrs. Crabtree. The woman would tell mom every time I climbed out the window. The old bat."

"Every neighborhood has one. Somebody who doesn't have anything else to do but mind somebody else's business." Cannon nodded. "Where does she live?"

"Her house was behind us on Maggie Walker Avenue. Her bedroom was on the back and so was mine."

"I'll start there."

"Find what you need quick. I need to get out of this situation before I end up being the one hurt." She turned and walked out.

Neither Cannon nor Ericka noticed the men following them.

"I have the woman," Tower I aka Jake, spoke into his cell phone. "You take Cannon. I'll report back to the boss."

"Watch your back," Tower II aka Peace, replied.

***

There were two people, other than his brothers, that Ty Pendleton trusted with his life; Tower number one, Jake Turner, and Tower number two, Peace Newman. Both had been middle linebackers on his college football team and were drafted into the NFL on different teams. Jake Turner busted a knee in his third year and Peach Newman sustained a concussion in his fourth. The injuries ended their careers. Thanks to the deals Ty helped them sign, both were financially set. However, neither was ready to be sportscasters for any network and decided for a more lucrative, action-filled position as bodyguards for the Pendleton Agency. Their duties consisted of a variety of responsibilities, but were not limited to anything needed by their friend and the man they simply referred to as Boss.

Both were in Atlanta gathering information on Ericka Kennedy and an old friend to Peace Newman, Tower II. "Cannon is not the type of person to set up scams, Boss. I'm telling you what I know."

"If you believe you can approach him without compromising your mission reach out to the brother." Ty sat up. "If Mr. McNally is into something that will cause problems for Brooks-Pendleton, are you prepared to end your friendship?"

"My loyalty is to you, Boss," Peace stated. "You want Cannon handled...it will be done. Bank it." Peace disconnected the call as he watched Cannon drive into the parking deck of B7Beats Recording Studios. The file showed Lawrence Cannonball McNally was representing Singleton Enterprises in the acquiring of the studios. The deal was in the delicate stages of negotiation, but it looked as if the takeover was inevitable. Peace looked at the paperwork again. Why would Cannon be involved in something of this nature? It wasn't his thing. He was into security like him and Jake. Peace decided to sit back and observe...for now.

Chapter 7

"I was beginning to think you stood me up." Nick stood with open arms to Ericka as she entered the restaurant. He noticed her hesitation, but then she walked into his embrace. He kissed her neck. "Bad trip?"

She leaned into his gentle touch and longed for something she knew could not be. "Not great." She slowly pulled away.

Nick pulled the chair out for her as she unbuttoned the double-breasted white trench coat to reveal a canary yellow dress underneath. He gave the coat to the waiter to check in as she sat. "Will a large glass of Chardonnay help?"

"Yes." She nodded without hesitation.

Nick held up his hand as the waiter approached. "A bottle of Chardonnay, thank you." The waiter nodded then walked away. "Is it something you can talk about?"

Ericka closed her eyes as she sighed. "Why are you always so nice, so considerate?"

He took her hand and held it so she could not pull it away. "You make it easy."

"Nick." She tried to pull away, but he held on. She looked up at him. "I wish you wouldn't. You're making things difficult." She looked around before completing her statement.

"That was the plan, Ericka. I thought I made myself clear from the beginning. Once you knew me better you would do one of two things. Tell me what you want from me so I can give it to you. Or, have you so head over heels in love with me that you can't do whatever it is you planned to do." He shrugged as the waiter returned with the wine. "Leave it, I'll pour. Thank you," Nick said to the waiter.

He picked up the bottle and began to pour. "This is where you say, Oh Nick I can't hurt you for it would be as if I hurt myself. Then you fall to your knees and beg my forgiveness for even thinking of pulling a scam on me." He handed her the glass with the most ridiculously innocent smile she had ever seen.

Ericka gave him an incredulous look, then slowly began to smile as laughter begin to build inside of her and spill out. "You play dirty, Nicolas Brooks."

"Ah, that's what I want to see...laughter in your eyes. They sparkle when you are sincere with your laughter. Like black onyx that's been polished to a spit shine. During the throes of passion, they turn a midnight blue. When you are about to indulge in a bit of fiction they turn jet black. My favorite is when they are ebony. It's when you are just...you. No pretense, no scheming, just Ericka being Ericka." He sat forward and held his glass across the table to touch hers. "That's when the heat between us starts as a slow burn. As we talk the intensity of the burn builds. The only thing fueling it is the essence of you and me. No outside forces pushing us to do or saying anything. It's just...us." He tapped his glass to hers, took a drink then ran his tongue across his bottom lip.

She was losing the battle. Whenever she was alone, Ericka could come to terms with what needed to be done. When Nick was within fifty feet of her, the desire to be with him increased and the drive to help Bobby vanished. It was clear she was losing her damn mind.

"You're conflicted because you are fighting a losing battle."

"How do you know what's going on in my mind?"

"I see it all over your face." He tilted his head and stared at her. "It hurts that I'm the cause of your turmoil. Then again, it's a sign that what you feel you have to do, isn't going to be easy. That's a good thing." Nick put his glass down. "Just tell me what you need. I'll give it to you."

"It's not..." She looked away, shaking her head. "It's not that simple." She looked up and held his gaze. "If this was for me, I would have let it go the other night. What we shared was...amazing, just freakin amazing. I don't experience that with men, Nick. That was new for me." She drank the glass down, then set it on the table. "As wonderful as it was, it scared the living hell out of me." Nick refilled her glass. She picked it up. "I don't know if I should be running for the hills or what?" She gulped it down and sat the glass back on the table.

Nick put his hand over the top. "Do you trust me Ericka?"

The question caught her off guard. What was more surprising is she had to think about it. The normal response would be a resounding no. But sitting there, looking into his eyes, she knew her perspective on things had changed. She did trust him.

"Trust isn't easy for me Nick."

"It's not for me, either, but I trust you to do what is right when the time comes."

"Why? You know I'm here for a purpose. This didn't just happen for Nick. Why would you trust me?"

"You never denied why you came into my life." He sat back.

"That doesn't change the reason I came into your life, nor does it make what we are doing right."

Another piece to the puzzle ran through Nick's mind. There is a 'we' involved. But was fitting all the pieces together important anymore? Did he care why she was there? Ericka was placed in his life at this time for a reason. Neither may be privy to the reasons at this time. Hell, at this point he wasn't sure if she was there to help him through something or vice versa. What he did know was simple. They did share something special. The night they made love was meant to be. No one would ever be able to tell him anything different.

"When you are ready, tell me. For now, let's enjoy being with each other for however long it lasts." Nick held his out hand. "Do we have a deal?"

Two weeks went through Ericka's mind. That's how long she would have with him before a decision had to be made. She took his hand. "Deal."

The next five days were heaven to Ericka. She had never laughed so much or felt so treasured in her life. The days were filled with teasing phone calls or text messages and at night they held each other, savoring every moment. The walks in the wooded area behind his home became their favorite pastime. This was where they shared their dreams for the future. This was where Nick really found the essence of Ericka Kay Kennedy.

"If you could do anything in the world and not worry about money, what would it be," Nick asked as they walked hand in hand home from the pizza place.

Ericka looked up at the bright stars with the blue sky as their backdrop and huffed. "I would spend my time teaching young girls how to deal with their emotions and hormones. You have to catch them early, say around ten or eleven. You know, before they start smelling themselves as my mother used to say."

"What would you tell them?"

"Nothing," she replied as she looked up at them. "I would just listen and when they ask questions, I would be there to answer. Or have others around to help them deal with the changes in their bodies, the mental games boys play when those changes occur. How to defend themselves from the boys and men that will come in and out of their lives."

"You realize, boys need that too."   Nick tilted his head as he looked at her. "They need someone to talk with them. Explain the changes that will be taking place in their bodies. The impact of quick decisions based on those changes. The right way to talk to girls, how to respect them...treasure them...love them."

They both stopped and stared up at each other, for a long moment. Ericka, looked away. "I guess we all need someone to listen at a young age, before mistakes are made."

"Mistakes can be corrected."

"Not all, Nick. There are fatal mistakes that can't be altered no matter how much you pray." Ericka continued walking and Nick followed.

Upon their return to the house, Nick poured two glasses of wine and they sat in front of the fireplace on the floor. "Tell me something," Nick said as he pulled her into his arms and they leaned back against the sofa. "Do you trust me?"

"You asked me that before."

"I did."   Nick sipped his wine. "You never answered."

Ericka nodded her head, then looked up at him. "I do. I do trust you."

Nick smiled as he kissed the tip of her nose. "How much do you trust me?"

She pulled back a little. Stared in his eyes. "What are you up to?"

Nick grinned. "I'm going to put your level of trust to a test." He stood and held his hand out. She took it without hesitation. "Come with me." He put her in front of him as they walked the hallway to his bedroom. He unzipped the back of her dress, then pushed it down her shoulders. "You're not going to need that."

She glanced over her shoulder. "Oh, really." She pulled the clamp from her hair. "I guess I won't need that either," she said as she sauntered into the room in nothing but the black lace boy shorts she wore.

"You are scandalous," Nick said as he licked his forefinger and ran it down the center of her back.

"Words will never hurt me, Nicolas Brooks," she said as she lay back across the bed and spread eagle.

Nick opened a box he had brought home earlier in the day. He pulled out a black satin blindfold. Turning, the sight of her on his bed, her long wavy black hair fanned behind her like a silk blanket, her dark nipples perky and ready and those thighs that caught his attention the first night they met summoned him to forget the trust test and take her as is. The trust factor was too important for them. He straddled her. "Will you let me put this on?"

Ericka hesitated, then smiled. "Only if you promise to do nice things to me."

Nick bent over and kissed her lips. "Oh...I promise." He slid the mask over her head, then over her eyes. "No peeking."

"Okay," she laughed.

He reached into the box again, then came above her on the other side of the bed. "Hold your hands out." She did. He placed the object in her hand. "May I put this on you?"

Ericka took the item in her hand. She felt the two connecting pieces and lowered her hands.

Nick waited as the emotions played across her face.

She held it up to him. "Yes."

Nick kissed her, took the handcuffs from her. He put one around her wrist, ran the other around one of the poles on his sleigh-style headboard, then completed the process around her other wrist. He walked out of the room and returned moments later.

Ericka did not fidget, or move in anyway. She was paralyzed with fear. Not that Nick would do anything to hurt her, but with the thought of surrendering herself to him so completely. Would the past replay again? The last time she gave herself completely it cost her her mother's love. What would this cost her?

"I would never hurt you, Ericka."

The words were spoken with such sincerity. "I know you." She felt him sit on the bed next to her.

"Part your lips for me."

She did. Something warm and sweet touched her lips. The tip of her tongue touched it. She opened wider and bit. She began laughing as she chewed.

"I thought you would enjoy strawberries with dripping hot chocolate." The laughter from her was so real, so genuine. Nick enjoyed every sound. He understood her turmoil, yet she trusted him enough to go through with his test. "You know, the thing about chocolate, is it tastes good on just about everything." He dripped it over one nipple, drawing a line from her breast to her navel. He did the same on the other nipple joining the line right where her belly button dipped. He then spread the warm chocolate from the belly button to each thigh forming two connecting V's.

It was his tongue that circled her nipple. She could feel the warmth of the chocolate spreading over her breast, before his mouth covered it, completely devouring the chocolate and her self-control. His lips went from one to the other as if he was playing a song that only he knew the melody to. As his tongue traveled to her navel, following the trail of chocolate, she could feel his thighs above her head. He had reached between her thighs when she felt his heat on her cheek. He was balancing himself above her on his hands and toes as if doing pushups. He went down each thigh licking the hot chocolate, pushed up, then lowered his head between her legs. She brought her legs up, pushed her body up to meet his lips. Then squealed at his touch. Her head went from side to side from the desire that was building from the intimate touch of his tongue each time she pushed her body up, the motion building in frequency each time. The handcuffs were pulling as she moved to get closer to his tongue. Desperate to keep him where the fire was now burning out of control, she locked her legs around him. His tongue dove deeper inside, his lips captured her nub, and sucked until her body bucked feverishly, her scream echoing around the room as he took everything she released and kept sucking, licking and kissing until her legs had no power left in them.

Ericka kissed the only thing she could reach and found the taste hot and sweet. He had covered himself in chocolate. She almost laughed out loud, but was too engrossed with the sweet, salty mixture of him and chocolate. She licked and sucked what she could reach, but he still held the tip of him out of reach. She lifted her head trying to meet his, but he was in full control. He kissed her thigh and lowered the tip of him to her lips. She kissed it. Parted her lips and waited. He did not move.

"Nick."

He could feel her breath on him as he lowered the tip of him to her parted lips. When they closed around him, he wanted to lower all of him into the wet, hot silky feel of her mouth. But this was a test of trust. He had to show her, she could trust him, even when he wanted nothing more than to let his control go. He pulled up, as he closed his eyes, he lowered himself a little further and moaned as she closed her mouth around more of him. He pulled up again, giving her a moment to adjust. Her head came up and grabbed him. The heat, the sucking pressure from her mouth was draining his strength, but he meant he was not going to lose control. He was not going too deep.

"Take what you want Ericka. It's all yours, baby."

He pulled up, but not out, he followed her mouth, pulled up and back in as her mouth moved around him. It was at the point where he had to pull out. When he tried, she closed her mouth, locking her jaws as she frantically swirled her tongue around him, sucking, and sucking until he bucked and fell to her side.

He quickly slid on a condom, shifted positions and entered her as if his life depended on having her right that minute.

She wrapped her legs around him, pulling him as deep into her as she could. He was her lifeline at that moment and she was swimming up to him with all the passion and love she had.

His lips covered her mouth, his tongue diving as deep as he was inside of her. His hand caressed her behind, as he drove deeper and deeper. He had to touch her in a place where no other ever dared... her heart.

Their bodies exploded causing ripples of pure ecstasy to race through their veins. Legs tightened around his waist, his hands squeezed her behind as his lips fell to her neck, she screamed out. "Nick!'

Nick reached up, grabbed the key, and released one cuff.

Ericka pulled her hands free and circled his neck.

They kissed and held each other until the natural high began to slowly release them.

Nick removed the blindfold, wrapped his arms protectively around her, said a silent prayer, and they both...slept.

Ericka missed the warmth of Nick's body next to hers. She reached out. The bed was warm, but empty. One eye opened, then another as she looked around. There was a sheet over her and the room was dark. She sat up, wrapped the sheet around her and went in search of Nick.

She walked down the hallway to the great room. He wasn't at the piano, the fireplace or in the kitchen. She walked to the other side of the house and found him in his office.

She walked over, straddled his lap and kissed his neck. "What are you doing?"

Nick looked up to see her hair tossed all around her shoulders, her lips still swollen from his kisses and the sheet that was enhancing the silhouette of her body. "Working on a contract." He smiled as he looked over her shoulder at the monitor.

"Can't that wait until in the morning?"

"You have something more enticing for me to do at three in the morning?"

"I do." She smiled and reached around to turn off the computer.

"Wait, let me save this." Ericka watched as he saved the information then put the black book in the drawer. He locked it, picked her up and took her back to bed.

She stared at the desk as he carried her down the hallway. She was certain that was the book he kept his passwords in for his home computer. She tightened her hold around his neck wishing she had never seen it.

Chapter 8

Nicole pulled up to Nick's house, grateful to have the escape and looking forward to a weekend of doing nothing but listening to music, having a few bottles of wine and enjoying a little laughter. The real estate world was not very kind these days. Sales and rentals were great, but dealing with the good old boys, who believed a woman's place is barefoot and in a kitchen, tended to get to her from time to time. When it did, she would go home for a visit or come here to Nick's place and just hang with him. She put her palm on the panel outside the door and walked in. Music was playing, the fireplace was burning, but she didn't see Nick's car out front. She struggled, thinking it may be in the garage.

"Nick," she called out as she took off her coat and hung it in the closet. "Nick," she called out again as she walked through the great room over to the bar. She pulled a bottle of her favorite wine from the wine cooler, and was pouring a glass when she heard a movement behind her. She turned to see the woman, Ericka, walking towards her in one of Nick's shirts.

"Hello, Nicole, right." Ericka smiled.

"What are you doing here?"

"Waiting for Nick to come back."

"Come back from where?"

"He went to handle something for one of his clients." Ericka walked over, leaned across the island and began eating a bunch of grapes.

Recognizing the motion as a mark of territory, Nicole set the bottle she was pouring from, down at the other end of the island. She didn't like the woman, and liked her being at Nick's place even less.

Nicole leaned across the island and stared the woman down. "So...you're here visiting with Nick."

"I am. And you?

"I live here from time to time. So, why were you in the west wing since Nick's rooms are in the east wing?"

"Taking a tour."

"I'm surprised Nick would leave you here...alone."

"Why?"

"Oh I don't know. You're a stranger could be a good reason. He doesn't like strangers roaming around his house."

"I'm not a stranger to Nick. He knows me well."

Nicole smirked. "I doubt that. He met you the same night I did. That was barely two weeks ago."

"Apparently, you are wrong, for here I am...alone...at his home."

Nicole drank down her glass of wine, trying hard not to smack the smart heifer. Instead, she picked up the bottle and poured another. She then walked in the direction from which Ericka had come. "I'll take this to my room before this becomes a pissing match you have no chance in hell of winning."

"Have I offended you in some way?" Ericka asked as Nicole walked by.

"The fact that you asked that question and don't give a damn if you did or did not, is offensive enough. I'll wait until Nick gets back, then I'll be out of your way so you can do whatever it is you plan to do."

"What make you think I'm here to do anything, but spend some time with your brother?"

Nicole slowly turned back to face her. She walked towards her and stopped a foot away. With the glass in her hand she pointed to Ericka. "Women like you come after my brothers all the time. Some of you luck up and get a payday; others leave with no more than what they came with. Two, who are much better than you, ended up married to my older brothers. Don't think for one moment I will allow a con artist like you to come at Nick without a fight." She took a step back. "You've been warned." Nicole finished the glass, turned and walked away.

Ericka stepped in front of her. "You don't know me, Nicole. I'm not the bitch you make me out to be."

"Does Nick know about the guy you were with in Atlanta?"

"That was my cousin."

"Heard that one before." Nicole went to step around her.

Ericka stepped in front of her again. "Look, Nicole, I'm trying to avoid any problems with you. The man you saw me with is my cousin, Cannon."

At this point Nicole could care less. "Don't make me ask you again. Get the hell out of my way."

"You know, I'm trying here. My norm is to tell you to kiss my ass and move on. But for the sake of your brother, I'm extending the courtesy of an explanation of what you saw in Atlanta."

Nicole put the bottle and glass on the bar.

Ericka smirked. "Oh, you plan on doing something with your hands?" She shook her head as she walked by Nicole. "Dumb-ass, little rich girl, don't know when to let go."

Before she knew what was happening, Nicole had grabbed her by her hair and pulled her back. Erica didn't think twice, she swung as she fell back, catching Nicole on her jaw. That's when all hell broke loose.

Nicole swung her against the bar, jumped on top of her and started swinging.

Ericka had just wrestled Nicole to the floor when she felt a strong arm pull her away.

"What in the hell is going on in here?" Nick yelled as Nicole jumped up from the floor grabbing at Ericka. "Stop...damn it!" Nikki stopped. Nick held Ericka at his waist in one arm, as he kept Nicole at a distance with the other. "Nikki go to your room...now!"

"What in the hell do you mean go to my room?"

"Now!" Nick pointed as he sat Ericka on her feet.

Nicole grabbed her bottle from the bar. "Poor little rich that..." she said and walked off to the rooms in the east wing.

Nick brushed Ericka's hair away from her face. "Are you all right?" He kissed her temple.

She pulled away. "I'm fine." She stomped off towards his bedroom.

Nick stood in the middle of the floor for a moment replaying the scene he walked in on. A few seconds passed and he bent over in very quiet laughter. A moment later, he wiped his hand down his face, exhaled, then went to check on Ericka.

He found her in the bathroom at the mirror with a cloth wiping away the blood from her lip. He reached in the medicine cabinet and pulled out cotton balls and Band-Aids. He closed the cabinet, and reached for the cloth.

Ericka jerked it away from him. He took it back, picked her up and set her on the vanity. He ran the cloth under the water, then wrung it out. He pushed her wild hair out of the way, then applied pressure to the cut on her forehead.

"You want to tell me what happened?"

Ericka did not say anything for a moment, she was too damn mad. Then she huffed. "I guess I pissed her off."

"No, you think?" Nick frowned, then smiled as he put the cloth down, then put the cotton ball on the cut, and a bandage on top. He braced his arms on either side of her. "My sister went through high school fighting the popular girls. She didn't take anything off of them and she's not going to take it off of you."

"You don't even know what happened."

"Somewhere in your remarks did you use the word dumb?"

Ericka thought for a moment. "I'm.... not exactly certain what words were used, but that could have been one."

"That's why you got your ass whipped."

"She just got the jump on me. If you hadn't come in, I would have gotten mine."

"Wouldn't have made a difference." He grinned as he picked up the damp cloth rinsed it, then began to clean her bloody lip.

"You find two women fighting over you funny?"

"There's nothing to fight over, Nikki is blood. She will always be a part of my life."

She stilled his hand. "So that makes me what...expendable?"

"No. That makes you Ericka. The woman whose trust I'm trying desperately to gain so she will open up to me." He kissed her bottom lip. "I'm going to check on Nikki now."

Ericka sat there for a long moment watching the empty doorway Nick walked through. Did that just happen? She sat there with a wet cloth in her hand just staring off into space. She slowly slid down off the vanity turned and looked at herself in the mirror. Her face was messed up. Her hair tangled all over her head. She brushed it back with her hand and just stared at herself. She reached in her pocket and pulled out the flash drive where she'd saved the information from Nick's computer on Jason Whitfield's account. The transaction was set up. All she had to do was push send. But she couldn't do it. The decision was literally in her hands. Should she do what Isaac Singleton requested or should she trust this thing she had with Nick? Thing...exactly what did they have? She thought back to the lunch in the park, the pizza dinner, the walks in the woods, making love on the piano, making pushup love, as they called it. She smiled at that. Then his words of a moment ago came back to her. Nikki is blood. She will always be a part of my life." The smile disappeared.

Nick stood in the doorway of the bedroom Nicole used whenever she stayed over. She was lying across the bed with a glass of wine, reading from her tablet without a scratch on her. "So Laila remains undefeated."

Nicole turned to see her brother in the doorway. "Not funny, Nick." She turned back to her tablet.

"No Nikki, it's not funny to walk into my house and find my sister fighting with an invited guest."

Nicole dropped her tablet on the bed, put her glass on the nightstand and stood with her arms across her chest. "Let's talk about that, Nick. Why is she here?"

"Are you serious right now?"

"Yes Nick I am. You said yourself she was a con artist. She was after something from you. So help me understand, why would you invite someone like that into your home? If you want to hit that, take her to a hotel, five-star if you must, but you don't bring women like her into your home."

Nick stepped inside the room and closed the door. "She's here because I like her, Nikki. I want her here."

Nicole threw up her hands. "You want someone in your house that is after your money?"

"She's not after money Nikki. I would give that to her, no questions asked and she knows it."

"You think she's here because she likes you?"

"Is that so hard to imagine?"

"No, Nick of course not." Nicole exhaled. "Look. You and I experienced James' disastrous marriage to Katherine. We are still living through the hell of Vernon and Constance. We vowed we would look out for each other. Whenever one of us saw the other going in that direction, we would speak out. Well Nick you are going head first into one with this woman. And I'm not talking about your mind."

"Ericka is different from Katherine and Constance. You should take the time to get to know her."

"I don't want to get to know her. She is trouble. What makes you think she is any different?"

"The mere fact that she never claimed otherwise. She never denied why she came into my life."

"I'm lost then. You know this, yet you let her in your private space."

"I like her Nik."

That was the second time he said that. Nicole stepped back and looked at her brother. Really looked into his eyes. She shook her head. "Don't tell me that Nick." She looked up at him. "You are falling in love with her. Someone you know is out to take you for a ride."

"I asked you to give me some space on this."

"I gave you space and you allowed this woman to get closer...too close. She is a no-good skeezer and you expect me to just let her hurt you?"

"I expect you to respect my decision on who I choose to have in my life. Let me say that part again. My life, Nikki. If it's a mistake, it's my mistake to make. Does this conversation sound familiar?" He raised his voice. "Think back to when I had this very same conversation with Pop about my career choice. Do you remember?"

"Nick, this is different. I'm not trying to control you in any way. I'm trying to protect you from someone who you know is out to hurt you."

"I'm a grown man, Nicole. I can protect myself. Step away from this."

"Nick," a stunned Nicole huffed.

"Step back, Nicole. I'm not going to ask again." Nick held her glare for a moment then turned and walked out the door.

Nicole couldn't believe what had just happened. They never had harsh words with each other...never. They always had each other's backs even against their parents. She picked up her tablet, purse, grabbed her coat out the closet and left Nick's house.

Nick walked into his bedroom to find Ericka gone and a note on the pillow where she'd slept.

You spoke of fatal mistakes, well, I
made one.
Please remember things are not always
What they seem.
Ericka

He heard the front door close and was pretty sure that was Nicole leaving. As he read the note, he did not miss the undertone of the last sentence. Whatever she came to do was going to happen. All he could do now was pray he had taken the right precautions. His cell phone chimed and he knew before answering it was going to be about Ericka.

Chapter 9

"It's done," Ericka said as she took Interstate 95 South towards Atlanta. "I'm on my way back to Atlanta now."

"It's two o'clock in the morning, Ericka. Are you driving?"

"Yes. I need the time to clear my mind."

"I was going to call you in the morning. I have some information you will not believe. I also have a copy of Estelle Singleton's will. It's not signed and by itself it's not enough, but it is going to put a damper on Singleton's parade."

"Will it help Bobby's case?"

"Yes."

"Then what I did was for nothing," Ericka said as tears rolled down her cheeks.

"Anything that was done can be reversed. I'll put the disc with the information in my safe until you get here."

Ericka hung up the telephone and shook her head. What she did could not be reversed. She broke a trust and hurt someone she cared for. Some one who made her feel what she had always wanted.... loved.

***

"Mr. Brooks, I called the moment the alert posted. All evidence indicates it came from your home computer. Once we ran through the verification process, we approved the transaction and disregarded the alert."

"Take the exact amount from this account." Nick pulled a card from his wallet and gave it to the accountant. "Put it back in Whitfield's account."

"I can do that, but it will not erase the transaction trail."

"I'll sit down with Whitfield and explain what happened." Nick turned to Ty. "We know what. Now we need to determine the why." Nick shook his head in confusion. "If she wanted money she could have taken it from me. Why Whitfield?"

"You have a hundred million sitting in a bank account?"

"Several," Nick replied. "There's something else in play. What can be gained from taking funds from a client's account?"

Naverone walked into the office. "Kennedy just arrived at Cannon McNally's home in Atlanta. She apparently drove through the night."

"What do you know about McNally?" Ty asked.

Naverone sat on the edge of Nick's desk. "He's not dirty. Have no idea what he's working on, but I can vouch for him."

"His cousin just embezzled one hundred million dollars from us."

"That's his cousin," Naverone reiterated. "Not Cannon. Speaking of the beautiful Ericka, do you want me to pick her up?"

"No," Nick replied.

"Why not?" Naverone stood as she glared at Nick.

Ty put the note Nick had shared with him on the desk and stood. "Because things are not what they seem to be." He glanced at Nick. "Don't carry this weight on your shoulders. You did all you could to deter this from happening. I agree, there is something else in play."

"What happens if the media gets wind of mismanagement of funds by the agency?"

"How would the media find out?" Naverone asked. "We have a full lid in place."

"Just follow me for a minute," Nick stated. "It's not about the money. She could have taken that from me several times over. It would be a lover's crime...me against her. By taking it from a client she's taking on an entire agency. She knows the agency will come after her, not just me." Nick stood and walked around to the front of the desk to stand between Ty and Naverone. "What if this isn't about me at all? I was just a means to discredit the agency in some way?"

"Word gets out that significant funds are missing from a client's account, other clients will get jittery. Start looking at other agencies." Ty added.

"Could cause a mad exodus of clients," Naverone concluded.

"We put a full lid on those we control," Nick added. "What about those who know, but we don't control?"

"Such as Ericka and Cannon, if he's involved," Ty finished the statement and pulled out his cell phone. He dialed a number. "I need Rosa in the next five minutes." He hung up. "I'm going home. Nick you should give Ericka a call. Get a reaction from her."

"I've tried. She's not taking my calls."

"Keep calling. It may take a year, but she will eventually answer."

"You're sure about that?"

"Yes."

Naverone watched as the door closed. She stood there looking from Nick to the space Ty left vacant. "I am apparently going about getting a man all wrong. I thought treating them with respect and honor was the way. Kiki turned him down for a year. Ericka is trying to ruin your career. Yet, both of you chased after them. I'm changing my tactics," Naverone announced, then walked out of the room.

Nick turned away from his desk, held his head back and wondered. What would Ericka gain by ruining his reputation? He pulled out his cell phone and dialed her number. He knew she wouldn't pick up, but he had a message for her. "Trust is like faith. You believe in something unseen. I put my trust in your love for me. Trust me enough to come back."

***

Armed with the information he needed, Ty, with Tower I and Tower II behind him, entered the private dining room where Isaac Singleton sat with his date. He was momentarily stunned by the discovery of the identity of the woman sitting at the table set for a romantic dinner for two. The woman had the decency to jump away once she recognized him. Singleton did not move.

"This is a private room," Isaac snarled.

"Nothing in this town is private to the right person, Mr. Singleton."

Isaac's eyes narrowed. "You know my name. It's evident you do not know me. If you did you would know better than to interrupt me while I am entertaining."

"I am certain Mrs. Brooks will not mind giving us a few moments." Ty's eyes locked on Constance and held.

She quickly stood. "I'll step outside." She said to Isaac as she eyed Ty suspiciously.

Ty nodded to the Towers. They both turned and walked out, closing the door behind them. Ty put an envelope on the table, then took a seat. "I'm a man of few words and less time. Inside the envelope are the shares to your company, which I now have access to. You have until Tuesday morning at nine a.m. to reverse the actions taken against Nicolas Brooks on your behalf."

Isaac sat up and snatched the document from the table. He quickly glanced at the names promising the sale of their shares if needed to Tyrone Pendleton. "What the hell is this?"

Ty stood. "Have your accountant explain it to you. Tuesday, nine a.m." He walked to the door then stopped. "Come near my company or anyone connected with any of my companies again and I will not be so polite." Ty walked out of the door.

Constance quickly approached him. "Isaac just purchased the recording studio my daughter is signed with. We were discussing the renewal of her contract."

"You are exploiting your daughter for a questionable lay and a few zeros in your bank account. If I were your husband that...would be my primary concern."

"How dare you speak to me in that tone."

Ty turned back to her. "I spoke to you out of respect for Nick. Other than that I would not have bothered."

***

Nick pulled up and parked next to the black sedan in front of his home. The only one in their family that did not bother to drive himself around was Vernon. Nick could count on one hand the number of times Vernon had visited him. His guess was Nicole spoke with him regarding her concerns about Ericka at Sunday's dinner. He got out of his car, waved at the driver, then stepped through his front door.

He was not prepared for the scene that met him in the living room.

"Nick," his mother rushed over and hugged him. "Let me look at you." She took a step back and smiled. "You are still the most adorable baby. You just can't help it."

The smile covered his face as he pulled his mother into his arms again. "He kissed her cheek. "You always know the right thing to say."

"Nicolas."

Nick's eyebrow rose. "Your husband, on the other hand."

"Oh, stop it," his mother smiled, took his hand and walked in the direction of his father and brother, both of whom were sitting on the sofa in front of the fireplace with a drink in their hand. "Hello Pop, Vernon." Nick hugged both of them, then sat in the chair across from them.

"A hundred million. Are you in trouble son?"

"No Pop, I'm good."

"Tell me what's going on." Vernon sat forward, concerned for his brother.

"Nothing is not a good response at this point," Avery said.

"One hundred million was embezzled from one of my client's accounts. I simply replaced the funds."

"Have you been able to track the transactions." Vernon asked.

"Yes."

"Then the person is in custody." Avery nodded.

"No." Nick stood, walked over to the fireplace and leaned against it to face his family.

"Why the hell not." Vernon shot up. "If you need help finding them, it can be arranged. We will find them."

"I know where they are."

Vernon frowned as he and Avery glanced at each other.

"It's the woman?" Gwendolyn stated as she watched her son. "And you are in love with her."

Nick exhaled as the eyes of his father and brother bore into him. "Yes."

Vernon's hands flew up in the air in disgust. "Nick." He turned away and sighed.

Avery stared at his youngest son. He was the sensitive son, who had a heart of gold. The thought of a woman using that for ill-gain angered him. However, this was not a time to scowl. This was a time to support. "Have you spoken to the client who was affected?"

"Yes," a surprised Nick answered his father.

"Good, keeping the trust in that relationship is important. Have you kept your partner in the loop on things?"

"From the very beginning."

"Where the hell is she?" Vernon paced angrily. "I'll have her put under the jail for this."

"That's not the way to handle this, Vernon."

"How in the hell do you handle criminals? I put them in jail." They all turned in mock surprise. Vernon freed more criminals as their attorney than Avery ever freed on legal terms. "You know what I mean."

Avery and Gwendolyn passed a glance between them. "How do you want to handle this son." Avery turned to Nick.

"I want to give her a chance to make it right. Hear me out, Vernon," he added before his brother could voice another objection. "I believe something else is in play. Ericka could have taken the money and much more, directly from me. She had access to everything here. But she took it from a high profile client with limited funds. The action was sure to cause an investigation."

"She took if from the first account she found," Vernon commented.

"No, she is much smarter than that. I'm telling you, there is something else happening that has nothing to do with money."

"So you want us to do nothing?" Vernon asked, sarcastically.

"I'm asking you to trust my judgment. You know I would not jeopardize my clients or put them in danger in any way. It's my job to protect them."

"Yet, this woman got close enough to do this," Avery stated. "Could this be a test run to detect vulnerabilities in your system?"

"It could be," Nick acknowledged. "I don't believe it is."

"Nick," Vernon cautioned. "If this gets out, it could cause irreversible damage to your agency and your career."

"I know," Nick sighed and looked away.

***

The sounds of the city were too loud. It's funny. Those sounds comforted her at one time. Now she needed the sounds of the silent night. The crickets that could be heard through Nick's window, the trees rustling during the night, the sound of his soft snore and the warmth of his arms as he held her. She missed the simple things about being with him. The walks in the woods, the songs at the piano, the laughter of just being together was killing her, she missed them so much. Somewhere along the line Nick Brooks stole her heart away. She never thought she would need a person so much. It had been three days since she left his house. *Nikki is blood* kept going through her mind for days. Tonight the words from his message were taunting her. *I'm going to trust in your love for me.* He had to know what she had done by now, yet, he was still trusting her. "Who in the hell does that," she cried out? The hurt she caused him so far had prevented her from taking the next step ordered by Singleton. She was to contact the media with a tip on the missing funds. Money was one thing. It could be replaced. A man's reputation was something different and she could not bring herself to ruin Nick. She just could not do it.

Her cell phone rang. She looked down at the table to see the call was from Cannon. For a moment she was disappointed. "Hello."

"There's been a change in plans."

"What does the ass want now?"

"He wants the funds returned."

Ericka sat up in bed. "What?"

"He want the funds returned tonight. He will of course compensate you for your time."

"The bastard couldn't pay me enough for what he's done." She got out of bed to send a message to Nick. "Do you have what we need to help Bobby?"

"We need more. But I'll keep looking. You take this opportunity to get things worked out with Brooks."

I wish it was that simple. "I'm going to let him know he has access to the funds. Then I'm cutting my losses and going home."

"You're going back to California? Why? From what you told me, this man cares for you and I can see you care for him. Ericka, that doesn't come around that often. Don't throw it away. Make things right."

"I can't make things right. As much as Nick will try, he will never trust me again. And I can't blame him."

"I think it's a case of you being afraid to face him. You think he may reject you."

"Why shouldn't he?" Ericka asked angry at the turn of events. "I stole from him."

"You did," Cannon agreed. "Funny, I didn't see any cops at your door. A man with the means of Nick Brooks could easily find you. Why do you think he didn't hunt you down? Just something to think about." Cannon paused. "Your assignment is officially over. He wants confirmation the funds are returned ASAP."

Ericka hung up the telephone. From her computer she sent the account number to the bank account in the Cayman Islands to Nick's private number.

***

It was two in the morning. Nick was at his piano. The house was quiet. Not the normal quiet, that sound he was used to. This was emptiness. The house felt empty. For the first time, no music flowed through him. He felt nothing. His mind was filled with thoughts of Ericka. He set his drink on top of the piano and softly played the melody to *I Can't Make You Love Me*, Tank's version. His father's support both pleased and surprised him. They stood out on the balcony and talked for a while. His father explained his mission to gain his wife's trust after another man had betrayed her. It took years for her to trust. It was his patience that led her to loving him. "There were many days I had doubts that she would ever love me the way she loved the other man. I held on," he said. "I had no other choice because I loved your mother just that much. If you love this Ericka and you believe in her, stick to your plan to gain her trust. If she is anything like your mother, she will make you thankful every day for the rest of your life."

Nick stopped playing and took a drink. He set the glass back down. He heard his cell phone buzz. This time of the morning meant one of his clients had an issue. He closed the top down, thinking he couldn't sleep anyway. He might as well work. When he checked the message it was a group of numbers. With his name and Jason Whitfield next to it. It took him a moment, then it hit him. At least, he hoped he knew what it was. He dialed Ty's number. "Meet me at the office and call the Rosa woman. I think I have the number to the account in the Caymans."

Chapter 10
Three Months Later

It had been a long day. Meeting with clients, team owners and the deposition for his father's attorney had taken its toll. Who would believe at the age of sixty his father would be facing a paternity suit? The family knew it was all connected to the dealings of a mad man, Isaac Singleton. It was inconceivable a person would take the steps Singleton had, over the last three months, out of jealousy, but it was the only reason anyone could come up with.

His cell phone rang as he drove towards home. Nick pushed the voice button on his steering wheel. "Brooks here,"

"How did it go today, Nick?"

The relationship between him and Nicole had been strained until she met Xavier Davenport. A pretty decent man she'd paid fifty thousand dollars for at an auction. Nick still laughed at the way they met, but he believed

Xavier was perfect for his sister. Once this mess with Singleton was over, he would dance at Xavier and Nicole's wedding. When Singleton plans for Nick imploded, and the embezzled funds he hired Ericka to embezzle were returned, he then set his sights on Nicole. He ruined an international real estate deal and had paid someone to file a frivolous lawsuit against her. When that did not work, he hired an ex-employee to file a paternity suit against his father.

"Do you have any idea why this man is after us?"

"Not the slightest idea. Xavier mentioned the man Cannon was the one to approach him about me."

"Cannon is Ericka's cousin."

"If you reach out to her do you think she would give you information on him or the Singleton guy?"

"I've reached out several times and there has been no response on her part."

"Keep trying, Nick. If you still care for her after all this time and all that has happened, it's not just a fling. She touched something deep in you. I have to believe you did the same for her."

"Change of tune from a few months ago," Nick smiled.

"Like you told me, you can't help who you like. The last thing I would want is to stand between you finding the happiness I've found with Xavier. Whatever you do, don't give up on her."

"We'll see how things go. When do you meet with Pop's attorney?"

"Tomorrow. He's requested to speak with Xavier as well."

"Xavier? Why?"

"He thinks Xavier can open the door to the whole Singleton conspiracy theory."

"Since he pulled back on me, I can't help on that front."

"That's what I don't get. Why did he suddenly pull back on you?"

"Have you met my partner Ty Pendleton?" He laughed. "He is not a man you want to go up against."

"I'm finding out, my fiancé is the same way."

"Good, with Xavier in your life, you are protected and kept busy so you can stay out of my business."

"Ha ha. Love you little brother. We'll talk later."

To say Nick was ready for a hot shower, a drink of Hennessy and long night of sleep was an understatement. The thought of Nicole's happiness brought a smile to his face, but it also brought Ericka to his mind.

It had been ninety days. The only contact was the account number to the funds she had taken. They were all surprised to find the entire amount untouched and the account in Jason Whitfield and Nicolas Brooks names. In essence she had not taken the money, only put it in another place. They were all still puzzled by that revelation. However, Vernon didn't care. The impropriety of the transaction could have caused irrevocable damage to his name as an agent if it had gotten out. He wanted her to pay.

Wiping the thoughts from his mind, Nick punched the button on his console to open the double wrought iron gate to his estate. Looking through the windshield as he drove towards the house, it was hard not to notice how bright the stars were in the sky. It was something he had been avoiding for the last three months. Noticing brought on other images he preferred to forget.

There was an early board meeting at his agency, Brooks-Pendleton, so he decided to park in front of the house rather than driving to the garage in the back. He placed the palm of his hand on the door pad. The deadbolt unlocked. Nick stepped inside, turned to close the door behind him and his world turned black.

The sensation burning the hairs on the inside of his nostril was enough to make him bolt up. When he did, Nick was immediately pulled backwards. His eyes flew open and narrowed on the object restraining him. He yanked on them.

"What in the hell?"

"They are called handcuffs. We've used them before. I have to be honest, I'm surprised you still have them."

It had been months, but he would've known that scent anywhere. Nick looked towards the foot of his bed. He knew the legs that sat in his chair crossed at the knees. He could still feel the thighs that were exposed under the dress around his waist. And yes, he remembered the handcuffs and all that took place the weekend she disappeared.

His eyes narrowed. "I keep them close as a reminder."

The impact of his smooth voice did not escape Ericka's senses. The calmness and confidence still radiated through her as if it was the first time ever hearing it. How she wished she could change her actions, but it was too late for that. All she could do now was make it right and pray it would be enough.

Ericka uncrossed her legs, stood then walked around to the side of the bed. She put a finger with her long, red-painted nail to her lips, then shook her head. "I should have undressed you before putting you on the bed." She smiled down at him." That would have made the night interesting. Don't you think so?"

Nick eyes shifted around the room as a thought occurred to him. There is no way she could have carried him from the living room to his bedroom. He yanked at the cuffs.

"Who's here with you?"

"Do you remember the night we used these? You asked me to trust you. I did." She closed her eyes. "It was the single memory that kept me sane for the last eighty-seven days." She inhaled and opened her eyes. "Now I'm going to ask you to do the same. Trust me Nicolas," she looked down at him with pleading eyes. The tension in the room was so thick it was as if there was another person in the room. This was all her fault. It would be up to her to get them back to their comfort zone.

Nicolas relaxed. His mind was no longer racing with possible outcomes of his situation.

Gazing into her eyes he could see she wanted...no...needed his trust.

"Trust goes two ways Ericka. If you ask for my trust you have to be willing to reciprocate. Can you do that? Can you trust me enough to tell me everything?"

"Yes." Ericka did not have a choice at this point. For her own sanity, she had to give this man a chance. Living without him was no longer an option. Her life had changed and it was because of him. Never before did she want a lifetime. Now she did and she wanted it with Nick.

"Take the cuffs off. Let's talk."

Ericka reached over his head to unlock the cuffs. Once he was free she stepped back. "I have someone you need to meet."

"Cannon McNally."

"Yes. As I'm sure you know, he's my cousin."

"Let's go meet him," Nick said as he held the bedroom door open.

Ericka hesitated, then walked out of the room. When they reached the kitchen, Cannon was sitting at the table. He stood as Nick approached. To his surprise Nick extended his hand.

"Nicolas Brooks."

"Cannon McNally."

They shook hands, then Nick walked over to the bar pulled out a bottle of Hennessey and three glasses. He put the items on the table then took a seat. "Tell me why Isaac Singleton has declared war on my family," he said as he poured a glass for each of them.

"The root of all evil, money," Cannon replied as he took a drink.

"I'm listening."

Ericka took the seat at the head of the table. Nick sat at the right, Cannon to her left. "I have a little brother. His name is Bobby Kennedy."

"Funny a Bobby Kennedy played football at my high school when I was there."

"He's one and the same." Ericka nodded her head. "Most people call him Bobby Singleton."

Nick remembered Ty mentioning the name, but had not put the two together. "Bobby Singleton Kennedy?"

"Yes," Ericka acknowledged. "It was my mother's way of giving him a part of his father."

"My aunt died a in fire a few years ago. Before she died, she showed me a will leaving one third of the Singleton's Estate to her son," Cannon explained. "She asked me to check into the family to see what kind of people they were before she told Bobby about his father and the estate. Before I could get the investigation going good, she died. Not long after my aunt's death, Estelle Singleton died. At the time I thought the will would be read and Bobby would get his inheritance. That did not happen. A few weeks after her death, the newspaper reported Isaac Singleton was the sole beneficiary to his father's fortune and would be taking over the reins at Singleton Enterprises. When that happened, I called Ericka to tell her about the document her mother showed me."

"Why Ericka? Why not Bobby?"

Cannon smirked. "Bobby is a very nonchalant kind of person. He's the type that would say I'm doing okay. Let him have it and be done with it."

Nick shrugged his shoulder. "Then why not let that be his choice?"

"I promised my aunt I would ensure Bobby was not shafted and would receive what is rightfully his. Once that's done, then Bobby can do whatever he wants with his inheritance."

"And you two are not expecting to receive some portion of Bobby's inheritance?"

Ericka took offense. "I have my own. I don't need Bobby's inheritance or anyone else's."

Cannon sat up. "It's a fair question," he interrupted Ericka. "After what we took, you have the right to question our motives. The answer is no. Neither of us wants anything from Bobby."

"I can't stand by and let this man take what is due to Bobby," Ericka explained a little calmer now. "My mother and I did not see eye to eye on a number of things. But we both loved Bobby."

"Bobby's a grown man." Nick poured another glass of Hennessey. "Let him handle his business."

"Singleton has taken that choice from him," Ericka stated. "We have to give Bobby the opportunity to handle his business as he sees fit. The only way to do that is to bring Estelle Singleton's will to light."

"Okay, take her will and contest what Singleton is doing?"

"That's where things get complicated." Cannon shook his head.

Nick refilled his glass. Ericka pushed her glass towards him. "You've had enough."

"Excuse me?"

"You've had enough." Nick nodded to Cannon to continue. Ericka reached for the bottle. Nick caught her hand and just held it.

Cannon saw that Ericka was no longer protesting, so he continued. "There are two wills. One, Estelle's cannot be found. The other, William's will, has an amendment. Earlier I told you Estelle's will split the estate three ways. One third was to go to Isaac, their oldest son. One third was to go to Bobby, William's son by another woman. The other third was to go to Isaac's child." Cannon took a drink. "See according to William, he felt remorse for forcing Isaac to abandon the young girl he impregnated while in high school. He was sent off to college and the girl was left to fend on her own. In his amendment, William gave one-half of his estate to the child. The law firm has been charged with finding the child. Then there's a second qualifying factor. The child must be of good moral character. William and Estelle were a bit disappointed in Isaac and wanted to ensure someone with some remnants of decency would have a part of Singleton Enterprises. That's where your family comes in."

"My brother is Singleton's son," Nick stated. "Or so he thinks?"

"That's what he knows."

"Let me get this right." Nick took a drink, then sat forward. He looked from Ericka to Cannon and chuckled. "Singleton came after me, Nicole and my father to ruin our public reputation to discredit his own son?"

"You are making it too simple," Cannon offered. "In Singleton's mind, he has to destroy the entire Brooks family. Not just which ever one is his son."

It was then that Nick realized they did not know who was Isaac's son. "Vernon. My brother Vernon is Singleton's son. Why not just go after Vernon?"

Ericka felt the loss of his warmth the moment he took his hand away. It took her a moment to focus on his question. "The Brooks are so powerful, once you rally around it's hard to discredit any one. You would have to destroy the foundation. That would be your father. Coming after you and Nicole was to solidify his claim once his father's attorney locates your brother."

"Okay." Nick was shaking his head, trying to filter through the craziness. "Stop the madness. Present both wills to the court and call it a day."

"That was the plan." Ericka smiled as she shook her head.

"Was?" Nick looked from her to Cannon.

"Yeah, was. Until Xavier Davenport."

Nick frowned. "What does Xavier have to do with this?"

"He and a friend broke into my house and stole the documents from my safe."

Nick laughed. "What?"

"He had taken it upon himself to become Nicole's savior. I attempted to eliminate his impact, he, in turn, came after me. They stole the documents and used them as collateral to get me to back off of Nicole. William and Estelle's wills were in the safe."

"That's why we need your help, Nick." Ericka took his hand. "We need you to get the documents back from Xavier."

"They who?"

"I don't know the other man," Cannon stated, "I can tell you, he was dangerous."

Nick sat there staring from one to the other not knowing what to think or believe. "You know the best way to get to the truth?" he asked as he pulled out his cell phone. "Xavier, I know it's late. I need you to come over." He pushed the button to end that call, then dialed another number. "I need you at my house." He disconnected that call then stood. "Have you two eaten?" He walked over to the refrigerator.

"No," Ericka replied as she stood and joined him. "What do you have?"

They started pulling items from the refrigerator as Cannon looked on. He liked the man. Nick Brooks was good for Ericka. It was the first time he had ever seen this side of her. From time to time when they would meet up, he would see the diva, going from one man to the next. But watching her in the kitchen with Nick, there was a calmness about her. All the edginess of the last few months had disappeared as if by magic. Maybe that's what love did for a person.

"You want me to refresh that drink for you Cannon?" Nick asked as he looked over his shoulder.

"No, I'm good. I have a feeling I'm going to need to keep my mind clear."

"Oh, you will."

Twenty minutes later Xavier and Nicole walked into the house. Nick walked over and shook Xavier's hand. "Thank you for coming. I think...everyone knows each other, correct?" Nick asked as he scanned the faces around the room, which was now suddenly filled with tension.

"Ericka." Nicole nodded

"Nicole," Ericka replied.

Cannon stood. "Davenport." He extended his hand.

Xavier hesitated.

"You two know each other?" Nicole asked looking from the man she remembered seeing with Ericka in Atlanta, to Xavier.

"Do you remember when I asked you if the name Cannon McNally meant anything to you?"

"You're Cannon McNally?" Nicole asked.

"I am."

"What's going on Nick?"

"I'm preparing some dinner. We are going to eat, drink and talk. Nikki would you get a few bottles of wine from the cellar. We are going to do this one time with all parties at the table."

Xavier and Nicole looked at each other. "Okay." Nicole put her purse on the table and left the room.

"I take it you are the reason I'm here." Xavier glared at Cannon.

"I am. You have something I need back."

Xavier grinned. "Do I?"

Sensing the temperature in the room rising, Nick hit Xavier on the shoulder. "Have a seat man. I'm about to awaken your taste buds." When Xavier did not move, Nick nudged him. "Come on man, have a seat."

Xavier slowly pulled a chair from under the kitchen table and sat across from Cannon, as he did the same.

"See, we are all going to get along as we solve this mystery." Nick walked over to where Ericka stood watching the scene unfold.

"I'm not sure this was a good idea," she whispered to Nick. "There are a lot of hurt feelings in the room."

"Including mine." Nick glared at her. "With everyone at the table we can stop the madness and work out a solution.

"Nick," Ericka started to speak.

"Not now. We are going to handle this first. Then we will work on us." He turned to the oven to check on the steaks.

At least he used the word us, Ericka thought as she finished with the salad. Nicole came back into the room with four bottles of wine. She turned as the front door opened to see Vernon and Naverone walk in.

"Hey." she kissed Vernon on the check and smiled at Naverone.

Vernon froze at the sight of Ericka in the kitchen. "Have you called the police?" he asked while glaring at Ericka.

"No Vernon." Nick stepped in front of her. "The police aren't needed." He took the bowl with the salad from her hands and placed it in the middle of the table. "We are all going to sit, eat, drink and talk." He pulled out a chair. "Have a seat Vernon."

Vernon looked around assessing everyone. He stopped at Cannon. "McNally."

Cannon smiled and extended his hand. "Brooks," They both began to laugh.

"It had to happen one day." Vernon shook his hand. He exhaled, then pulled out a chair for Naverone.

Before she took the seat, she walked over to Cannon. "Good to see you, big boy."

"You're killing me Naverone...killing me." They hugged each other.

Vernon raised an eyebrow. "You two know each other?"

Naverone smiled, then took the seat Vernon held out. "Something like that." She looked around the table at the food. "Looks good Nick."

Nick looked over at Nicole who was now sitting between Xavier and Naverone. They both shrugged their shoulders with a quick glance at Vernon. "Anyone freaked out at this point, hold it until we get this entire story out in the open." Nick held the chair next to Cannon out for Ericka and he sat next to her.

Everyone bowed their head in prayer, except Ericka. She just waited.

"Cannon has a story he wants to tell," Nick said as he opened a bottle of wine and begin filling glasses around the table.

Cannon nodded, then retold the story to everyone at the table.

Everyone around the table was silent for a minute. Nick and Nicole glanced at each other then at Vernon.

"To summarize" —Vernon leaned back with a glass of wine in his hand,— "Isaac is looking to destroy my reputation."

"He wouldn't have far to go." Cannon grinned.

Vernon nodded with a smirk. "Did you know it was me he was looking to destroy?" He looked up at Cannon.

"Not until tonight." Cannon sat back. "What would you have done had you known?"

"Oh the stories I could tell." A second passed and the two fell out laughing.

The others around the table glanced at each other. "Either of you care to share," Nick asked.

"Oh, hell no." Vernon laughed, then sat up. He put the wine glass down and picked up the Hennessey, The bottle was almost empty as were most of the plates on the table. "You have any more of this?"

Nick nodded. "Of course." Ericka walked over to the bar and pulled out two bottles. She removed the wine and replaced it with the Hennessey. Nicole gathered several shot glasses from the bar and spread them around. Ericka began moving the plates over to the counter top. Nicole chipped in. They both reached for Nick's plate at the same time. Nick looked up at his sister on the left to Ericka on the right. Neither was letting go. He sat back to allow them to work it out. Nicole let go, raising her hand in surrender.

"Nicely played," Vernon whispered to Nick. The men at the table laughed.

"Do any of you think it's a coincidence that Estelle Singleton and Felicia Kennedy died within days of each other, or is it just me?" Vernon was leaning back in his chair, then took a drink after asking the question.

"You think there was foul play?" Cannon sat forward.

"Based on what you have told me, if I'm Singleton, I would get rid of the second will and anyone who knows of its existence." Vernon glanced around the table. "I would eliminate Estelle, the person who the will was given to and the person who had it drawn up. Two out of the three are gone. Who did Estelle Singleton use as her attorney?" Everyone looked around. "Anyone want to bet the man is dead?"

"Anyone want to put a bet on the date?" Cannon added.

Vernon grinned. "So we have an unsigned copy of Estelle's will. Does anyone know if a signed copy exists?"

"The copy Aunt Felicia showed me was signed," Cannon stated.

"That went up in the fire," Ericka stated. "Where is Estelle's signed copy? The attorney would have given her one."

"That would have been the first one I destroyed," Vernon stated. "Would your mother make a copy? It's an important document. Is it possible?"

Ericka said, "If she did I have no idea who she would have given it to."

"What about Bobby?" Nick asked.

"No," Cannon replied. "When Aunt Felicia died I spoke with him in-depth and went through all of the documents we could find. He knew nothing about the will. The only items in her safe deposit box were, her will and the deed to the house."

"Maybe it's time Bobby knew what was going on," Nick stated. "If what we are saying is true, this man has killed three people that we are aware off."

"What reason would he have not to eliminate the remaining threat?" Vernon raised an eyebrow.

Naverone pulled out her cell. "I'll put someone on Bobby. I'll need his address," she said to Ericka.

"You really think Bobby is in danger?" Ericka asked. "And if that's true, aren't you in danger too?" She looked at Vernon.

Naverone held the phone away from her mouth as she spoke, "I have him covered."

Vernon grinned. "I'm covered."

"How do you think Constance is going to react to that?" Nicole smiled.

"Constance is rather busy these days trying to hold on to Singleton," Cannon stated. He looked up at Vernon, "No disrespect."

"None taken," Vernon replied. "As long as he keeps his distance from my daughter."

Cannon sat up, but hesitated before he spoke. "You realize your wife is more of a threat to Taylor than Isaac...don't you?" Cannon held Vernon's gaze. "That contract with Snake was her doing, not Isaac's."

"Oh, I don't think we have to be concerned with Snake." Nick shook his head.

Vernon nodded in agreement. "No, I think Snake is very clear on Taylor. Wouldn't you agree Xavier?"

Xavier took a drink. "We could always remind him."

Nick and Vernon looked at each other and laughed. "No...I think he's good."

Cannon looked from the two to Xavier. "What did you do?"

"I'm telling you, it's the quiet ones you have to be afraid of...be very afraid," Vernon teased.

"I have no idea what you two are talking about," Nicole chimed in, "But we need to decide what we are going to do about this man. Poppa is due to go to court next week over some crap he made up with Stacy. How can we put a stop to that?"

"Dad could always ask for a continuance," Nick suggested.

"That would play right into Singleton's hands. To the public that would only mean Pop is trying to find a way out."

"I agree with Vernon on that," Cannon stated. "Isaac has looked at his plan from every conceivable outcome. He has reporters on his payroll to do nothing but spread gossip on your family."

"How did you get involved with Singleton," Vernon asked curiously.

"I took a leave from the firm to follow up on Aunt Felicia's request to help Bobby. I went to Atlanta and set up an accidental meet with him. He asked what I was doing these days and I told him." He glanced at Vernon, "I handle sensitive issues for special clients."

Vernon grinned. "He took it from there." Cannon nodded. "That brings us back to Nikki's questions. Now that we have more facts, what is our next step with Singleton?"

"We need that disc back." Cannon glanced at Xavier.

Xavier did not respond for a long moment. "If we return the items, how do I know you will not come after Nicole again?"

"This isn't about Nicole, it never was," Cannon replied.

Nick could feel the tension between the two men. He had no idea what happened with them, but there certainly was no love lost between them. "I'm asking you to give the items to me, Xavier," Nick chimed in. "You know I will not allow anyone to harm Nikki."

Xavier looked away from Cannon. "He pissed me off."

Vernon chuckled. "It's a Davenport thing."

"Damn right." Xavier nodded. He pulled out his cell phone and placed a call. "I need the items we took from the safe in Atlanta."

"Removed...removed. Not taken." Adam Lassiter's voice came through the speaker.

Xavier grinned. "All right. The items removed from the safe."

"They're in Atlanta? You shouldn't bring items removed across state lines."

"Where in Atlanta?" Xavier struggled to keep from laughing.

"Safe deposit box in the name of Lawrence McNally, the bank at Monarch Centre."

"Where's the key?"

"On McNally's keychain."

Cannon pulled out his keys frowning. He went through them and found one he did not recognize.

"Appreciate it. I need one more favor. Find the attorney used by an Estelle Singleton about two to three years ago. I need to know his or her name and if he is dead."

There was a hesitation on the other end. "Okay...you know for a quiet man you sure have a lot of cloak and dagger stuff going on. Tell me something. What are you doing with the items?"

"Giving them back."

"Giving them back? What's the point in removing them if you are only going to give them back? I'm going to have to find somebody else to hang with if you keep doing dumb things like that. I'll hit you up tomorrow with the info."

"Situation calls for it," Xavier replied then disconnected the call.

"Who was that?" Naverone asked.

"If I tell you, I'll have to kill you."

Cannon stood shaking his head. "I guess I'm on my way back to Atlanta.

Nick stood. "It's been a long day. The bank doesn't open until nine. Bunk down here and leave in the morning."

"Take the jet," Vernon said as he stood. "Bring the items to my office tomorrow. Between the two of us we can find a way to shut down Singleton."

Chapter 11

Ericka was in the kitchen keeping busy as Nick showed Cannon to the guest room. He didn't say a word when he entered, but she knew he was there. She turned and met his seductive brown eyes.

"I can't make you love me if you don't, but I will never give up trying. Call it a fool's errand or being blinded by love. Either way, you got under my skin, Ericka Kennedy. Nothing you do will ever change that. Stay, or leave in the morning with Cannon, that choice is yours. I will not chase, you have to want to stay. It's been a sleepless three months without you and no decisions have to be made tonight." He held his hand out. "Let's go to bed, get some sleep. If you are still here when I wake up, I will have my answer and so will you."

The man was too damn sweet for his own good. How could she do anything but beg for his forgiveness and love him. She put the cloth she was holding down, walked over and took his hand. The warmth of his hand flooded her with contentment. She was home. It wasn't going to be an easy adjustment for her, but she vowed in that moment she would never do anything again to lose his trust.

Nick closed the door behind them as they entered the bedroom. He stripped her down to her undies, then he did the same. He pulled the comforter back as she slid under the sheets. He slid in next to her, gathered her in his arms, used his hand to close her eyes, he closed his and they fell asleep.

***

Naverone drove as Vernon watched the night scenery along the ninety-minute drive. She glanced at him knowing his mind was working on payback for Isaac Singleton. "I want you to know I don't visit people in jail. Whatever is going on in your mind is not worth you losing your freedom. You are a highly intelligent man. I am certain you can come up with a way to make him pay that is legal."

"Do you have any idea how intoxicating the fragrance you're wearing is?" He turned back to the window.

"Sweet talk is not going to change the topic."

"I think it will. You can barely resist me as it is."

Naverone smiled. "This situation...with Singleton isn't just about him stealing an inheritance from Bobby Kennedy. If he has his way, he will be stealing from you as well."

"I wouldn't take it. I would give it to the Kennedy kid. Old man Singleton doesn't owe me a dime. If anything, I owe him." He thought for a moment before sharing his feelings. It wasn't something that came easy for Vernon. "I always knew I was different growing up. Not because of anything my parents did. They loved me unconditionally. Believe me, I gave them reason after reason to get rid of me. No matter what I did they were always there to correct me in a loving way. My brother, James, he caught it from me. Anything I could think to do to him, I did it, but he never turned his back on me until I slept with his wife. That was the lowest I've ever stooped." He paused. "He literally tried to kill me that day. I was living dangerously back then. In some way, I think I wanted to just end it all. Not many understand misery to the point of giving up on ever having a happy life. To the point of thinking why wake up every day to deal with the same unhappiness. It wasn't until James held me over that balcony about to drop me , that I realized how deeply I had hurt my brother. It took me a while, but I vowed I would make it up to him by being a better person. The man he always thought I could be. For me, James was my nemesis. He was the one I had to always outdo. He was my father's son...his real son. I was my mother's child. Pop never treated me that way, but it was inside of me all my life. It was a demon I had to beat. I thought I had. I thought I had passed the dangerous mark where I could cross that line. When James pulled me up, I thought okay, I have a chance here to be a good person. Singleton has pulled be back to the brink."

Naverone knew this was a time to listen. Many questions entered her mind, but she felt she would learn more if she let him talk. Now, she had to speak and prayed she had the words to keep him on this side of the line.

"Why did you sleep with James' wife?"

"Because she was his wife." Vernon smirked. "She was something that belonged to him and I had to have whatever he had."

"Why do you think she slept with you?"

"At the time, I had no idea. It's not like she didn't know the kind of person I was. She lived in the same house with me. Later I concluded she wanted out of the marriage. She couldn't just leave. James had to leave her. Alimony is a strong motivator in our family."

"Do you think your brother has truly forgiven you?"

For the first time since they'd entered the car he turned and genuinely smiled at her. "Yes I do. Not only him, but my family, for putting them all through hell all those years without him in our lives."

"Have you forgiven yourself?"

He hesitated. "I have, but I will never forget the look in his eyes."

"What about Constance?"

The interior of the vehicle was silent for a full five minutes before Vernon answered. "Other than my mother and my daughter, I've loved only one other woman. That was Genesis Morgan." He did not look at her when he mentioned her best friend. "The night I told Constance I was in love with Genesis, she told me she was three months pregnant. She wanted the Brooks name and I wanted to be a part of my child's life. That ended my chance at happy ever after. I never tried to love again." He hesitated. "Now there is you. I told Genesis I have never met a woman that made me feel more alive than you. I've seen enough crap in my life to have the good sense to grab onto you and not let go."

"You can't do that if you cross the line." The darkness did not hide his jaw tightening. "I know there are many facets to you Vernon. I choose to focus on the good, the man who turns my head every time you walk into a room. But I know there's a dark side. It doesn't frighten me, but I do fear for others. I don't know what it would take to keep you from crossing that line."

"You," Vernon replied.

There was silence again before Naverone spoke.

"Your life is too complicated to add me to the mix. You have this thing with Singleton to work out and then there's a thing called a marriage you are in with another person. I'm too good to be the other woman even for the great Vernon Brooks."

"You are correct. Doesn't make me want you any less." He turned to face her. She was a beautiful woman. Part Cherokee, part African-American, Rene Naverone had made his knees buckle the first time he met her in Nick's office. "I would walk through the fires of hell to have your legs wrapped around me for one hour. Climb Mount Everest without a rope to have one taste of the juice that flows between those thighs. Give my life over to Christ to have you in my life for eternity. You say all I have to do is get rid of my wife. I would do that and so much more to have you look at me as if I'm the only man in the world. For you I would give my life."

The vehicle suddenly veered to the right. Naverone pulled over and put it in Park. She reached over, grabbed his tie and pulled his lips to hers. Not a word was said as she ravished his mouth, tasting every crevice with her tongue. Branding his tongue as hers and hers alone.

Within a minute, her body was pulled across the center console and stretched on top of him in the seat he had reclined at some point. The dress that reached her mid-thigh had been pulled up. His hands cupped her behind and squeezed as he took total control of the kiss. His hand moved between her thighs until his finger reached the moistness he sought. The other hand wrapped around her waist holding her captive in his embrace. Her moan caught in his throat the moment his fingers entered her. Pushing down, her body began to move with the movement of his fingers as they probed deeper inside. Her hair fell cascading around his face like a silk scarf. Their lips parted, her body shifted. He thought she was trying to break away, but she sat partially up to allow him to go deeper. The hand securing her waist moved up her back, as his lips captured the bottom of her earlobe. "Rene," he moaned at how deep his fingers traveled. He wished that was him in side of her, but that had to wait. He moved, bringing her body to the side of his then proceeded to use his thumb to add to the beautiful assault he was launching. With her thighs now closed around his hand, his fingers weren't going anywhere until he brought her to the brink of no return. She parted her lips to say something, but Vernon entered and his tongue ravished her mouth as his fingers played melodies inside.

"Ah...Ah...Ah..." Naverone moaned as the juices stored inside her burst and spread over his hand.

Vernon didn't stop, his fingers played in the juice flowing from her as he continued to brand her lips, her tongue, every inch of her mouth, his.

Naverone's hands roamed down beneath his belt, into his pants. She took him in her hand and moved with the same motion he was using on her. The gasp of air that escaped him encouraged her to take his thick...long...hot...member to meet where he had taken her. He felt like the handle of her 357 Magnum. And Lord knows Naverone loved her guns. She caressed, pulled, and massaged him in her hand until the heat was almost unbearable, both inside where his fingers were still waging war and in her hands where she didn't want to let go. Their breathing was heavy to the point where they had to break the kiss. Vernon's lips rested on her neck, as hers were perched on his throat when they both lost all sense of being as stars shot from their eye sockets and juice flowed from their bodies.

He held her, there in his arms and knew he would never do anything to lose her. Vernon kissed her temple. He caressed her a little more, then withdrew his fingers. He pushed the button on the side to raise the seat back up.

She placed her booted feet on the other side
of the middle console as he lifted her body and
placed her back in the driver's seat. They
locked eyes as Vernon pulled out his
handkerchief from his suit jacket pocket and
handed it to her. He took his fingers and
sucked them clean, one by one, as she looked
on.

"You know I'm like a dog with a bone. Once
I get a taste, I don't stop until I've had it all."

Naverone was about to go for round two
when blue lights flashed behind them. They
both began to laugh as the officer approached
the door.

"Is everything okay?" The officer looked
around the inside of the vehicle.

"Just a little war we thought was better
fought on the side of the road," Naverone
explained with a flick of her hair across her
shoulder.

The officer glanced around once more.
"Let's move it along."

"Of course. Officer." Naverone started the
vehicle and pulled off without looking in
Vernon's direction.

***

The birds were singing, fresh air was
coming through the window and coffee was
brewing as Nick opened his eyes. He looked
around. Ericka was not there. He pushed the
sheet aside and walked over to the door when
he heard a sound behind him. He turned
towards the closet and took a step back. There
she was, hair wet and her body wrapped in a
towel. In the closet, going through the shelves
with his sweat pants. He watched with a smile

as she pulled a pair out, unfolded them then held them to her. She placed them on the dresser and began rolling the legs up. He watched her put them on. Next she checked the drawer where he kept his t-shirts. She pulled one out, dropped the towel and pulled it over her head. The glimpse of her brown nipple stirred him, making his briefs a bit uncomfortable. He watched as she stepped back to look at the outfit in the mirror. She ruffled her hair and shook her head. She didn't like what reflected back, she pulled the top off. That was Nick's undoing.

In three long strides, he was behind her. His hands capturing her breasts as he kissed the back of her neck.

"Nick," she whispered as she reached back putting her arm around his neck. "I missed you so much."

He turned her to him and kissed her with the urgency of a man reaching for a lifeline. Then he pulled away. He braced his hands on the dresser at her sides and in a low seductive voice he spoke, "You made a conscious decision to deceive me. My mistake was believing you would come to your senses before doing what you did."

"I put the money in yours and Jason's name."

"It's not about the money Ericka. The money was replaced within hours of you taking it. It's about trust...you trusting me enough to tell me why you had to do this. You said you loved me. You can't love without trust."

"I never told you I loved you Nick. That's a fatal mistake in my line of business."

Nick nodded. "Then you made a mistake. For you told me with your body. By the way you touch me, the way you look at me, the way you wrap your legs around me, the way you take me inside of you. The way you release your love to me. You hold nothing back. The way you are holding on to me right now. If you didn't love me, this whole situation would be something different. I would let Vernon have his way, lock you up and leave. Without a minute's regret. But that's not the case. Is it?" Nick picked up his shirt and placed it in her hand. "You can continue to lie to yourself, Ericka, but you can't lie to me. It's morning and you are still here." He stood willing his body to step away. "I want forever Ericka. No doubts, no wondering are you going to be home when I get here. I want the same trust that I give to you." He stepped back. "Can you give me forever?" He held her gaze, then walked out of the closet.

Ericka heard the shower. She sat on the floor in the closet contemplating his words. He was asking her to commit. To put her heart in his hands. As much as her body ached for him, could she let go of the past? Could she once again do something she hadn't done since she was sixteen? Give her trust completely. Still holding his shirt in her hand, she wrapped her arms around her drawn knees and rocked. She didn't know how long she'd been there, but she knew the moment he walked back in.

His feet were wet standing there above her. She followed his long powerful legs up to where the towel wrapped around his waist. His chest glistened from the dampness. She looked into his eyes as tears streamed down her face. "I want forever." She leaned forward and kissed his feet, then ran her hands up his calves. She kissed his knees, then reached up and pulled the towel from around his waist. Her hands roamed up his thighs as she came to her knees. She gazed up into his eyes. "Please forgive me. I made a mistake, one that I will spend the rest of my life making up to you."

Nick bent down to her and wiped the tears from her eyes. "I forgive you." He kissed her nose as he pushed her backwards. "I forgive you." He kissed the corner of her mouth. "I forgive you." He kissed the opposite side of her mouth. He held her face between his hands. "What's more important is...I love you. I love you. I love..." She pulled his lips to hers before he could finish. They fell onto the carpet in the closet and made sweet love.

An hour later, they were still there, tangled in each other's arms. He was twirling his fingers between hers.

"Do you remember asking me why I hesitated so long to hold your hand?"

He sat up on his elbow and looked down into her eyes. "I do."

She smiled, then inhaled. "When I was sixteen I called myself being in love. Stephen was the love of my life. I ate and slept Stephen. For months, he would walk me to school and just talk about any and everything. Then he started holding my hand. That was just the sweetest thing for me. Every morning he would hold my hand all the way to my first period class. He would say, that's his way of joining our souls forever." She smirked. "That went on for six months and I was on top of the world.

All the girls envied me because that's all my boyfriend wanted was to hold my hand. That changed to kissing in the seventh month and my first sexual experience in month eight. In month nine I saw our lovemaking on my friend's phone. Needless to say I was devastated and began hyperventilating. That caught the cafeteria monitor's attention. The phone was confiscated, our parents called and the rest was history. My mother flipped her lid when she saw that video." She closed her eyes. "She never once asked for my side of what happened. She called me every name in the book. A week later I was shipped to my aunt's in California. Mind you, she was my father's sister who I only knew by name. Two months later I found out I was pregnant. My aunt was very clear on the fact that she was not going to raise any babies. I gave birth at seventeen and the baby was put up for adoption."

He took her hand and kissed it. "I like holding your hand because it warms my heart. I'm not a surgeon or anything close to it, however, I've been told that the fourth finger on your left hand has a vein that runs directly to your heart."

"Is that a fact?" She smiled.

"It is." He laid back down and pulled her to him. "I believe any hand you hold has veins that run to your heart. Want to know why?"

"Why?"

"Because each time you take my hand, my heart begins to race and a contentment comes over me. Unlike what happens when your body touches mine."

"What happens then?"

"Nothing is content. Everything becomes a wild beast that needs to be tamed."

Ericka straddled him. "Let's tame that beast."

Chapter 12

Geraldine Morgan had worked with Vernon for a number of years and knew his moods better than most. She recognized the '*don't mess with me* signs' the moment he stepped off the elevator.

"Good morning, Mr. Brooks." She stood and walked behind him into his office.

"Mrs. Morgan. I need everything off my table today and possibly the entire week. Have Franklin take the lead on the Costen case. Get me everything you can on Isaac Singleton, concentrate on the murder trial of Matt Peterson." He paused for a moment. "Get me the prosecuting attorney for that case on the line." He took off his coat. "Call my father to see if he is free for lunch or earlier."

Geraldine was writing as he spoke. "Got it. Cannon called stating he is in transit. He'll be here before noon. Nicole called stating you better not leave her out of the loop." She knew how to get him to climb down a notch. "Nicolas called stating he has meetings until three. He will check in then. Now, you want to tell me what's going on?"

Vernon took a seat, sat back in his chair and stared at her. "Isaac Singleton has waged war against my family because of me. I plan to stop him."

Geraldine nodded. She did not need the details. All she needed was direction. "What do you want to start with?"

"The paternity suit against my father." He sat up. "Rene Naverone will be coming by with her team. Send them right in when they arrive."

"She's already here. They are in the conference room." Vernon smiled. Hmmm, another way to bring him back from the brink of destruction. Over the years it had been her job to keep Vernon from blocking his own blessings. It had been a while since she had seen the signs. But she recognized the mood and knew she had to be on alert. She turned to walk out of the door. "I like her. She doesn't take any crap off of you."

"Who?"

"The owl in the damn tree. You know who?" Geraldine smiled and walked out of the room.

Vernon took a deep breath. She was right Naverone did not cut him any slack. Well, he smiled, thinking she did cut him a little taste last night. And what a taste it was. Geraldine returned with a file in her hand.

"I thought this would get you started. This is the file on Stacy Crane. It may be helpful."

Vernon sat up taking the file. He opened it and began reading. "See if we can get any medical information on her. Since this is a paternity issue, we may be able to subpoena it if need be." He looked up suddenly. "Get me a copy of the opposition's discovery report. I want a list of all witnesses they plan to use. I want to know the color of the underwear she was wearing each time she claims she was with my father."

"Details?"

Vernon looked up at her raised eyebrow. "The importance of knowledge is not just having it but knowing how to apply it."

"Another Vernon the master quote?" Geraldine asked, as she looked over her shoulder while walking towards the door.

"No, that one came from Confucius." He grinned.

Geraldine had just reached her desk when the phone rang. "Brooks and Associates," she answered as she motioned Naverone to go in. "I warmed him up a little for you," she mouthed.

Naverone smiled as she entered the office. "Good morning sunshine. I understand you are brightening up everyone's morning with your testy attitude."

Vernon walked around the desk, pulled her into his arms and proceeded to kiss her senseless.

Naverone basked in the embrace for a moment, then pulled back. "Kiss me like that again and I'm going to break your knees." She pulled him by his lapel and returned the kiss." When finished, she pushed him away. "We're supposed to be professionals. Not making out in a car like horny school kids."

"You started it." Vernon smiled as he watched her walk over to the chair in front of his desk. She crossed her legs and he swore he was just kicked in the gut. He groaned, wiped his hand down his face then took a seat behind his desk. "What do you have for me?"

"A plan to collect a DNA sample from Peter Crane."

"The results of the paternity test will be disclosed in court." Vernon sat back as she listened.

"Why wait until then. Aren't you tired of playing this game according to Singleton's rules? I say let's get in front of him. Start making our own rules. Let him play catch up for a change."

Vernon sat up. "Okay. What do you have in mind?"

Naverone smirked. "What is the one thing a high school boy can't resist?"

"Girls," Vernon replied without hesitation. "We older boys aren't much better." He grinned at her.

"Concentrate."

"It's difficult to concentrate when your thighs are exposed and calling out to me. Vernon come taste these smooth sexy thighs. Remember how sweet we were last night?"

Naverone pointed to her face. "Up here Brooks."

"Like that's better. Now I'm looking at your lips which are swollen from our good morning." He tilted his head to the side as he teased. "Imagine what our good nights will be like."

"Peter Crane, the eighteen year old son of Stacy Crane is the topic on the table."

"Right." He sat up straight. "You have a way to get his DNA? If you succeed we could use it as collateral to have the case dropped before going to court. There's one problem with that. The public will think my father bought them off."

"Not if it comes with an apology and the real father steps forward."

A message came to Vernon's phone. "My father will be here at ten." He looked at his watch. "That gives us less than an hour to put this plan together."

"Already done." Naverone sent a text message from her phone. She looked up. "I have two of my girls who will approach the kid after school. She pulled up a picture of Peter on her cell. "He's a good looking kid." She showed the picture to Vernon. "Athletic, smart, straight, all-American kid. Attends private school on Park Avenue. Tuition is around thirty thousand dollars a year. Well within her means when she worked at Brooks International. Have no idea how it's being paid now. The kid has a steady string of girls chasing him. They are usually at a spot called Dango's after school." There was a knock on the door. "That would be for me," Naverone said as she stood and walked over to the door.

Two girls walked into the office. "Vernon Brooks, brother to Nick." She pointed as the girls walked towards him.

Vernon stood extending his hand. "Good morning."

As he moved another chair to the desk, Naverone introduced them. "Vernon, meet Karess Parker. She has an Army background with a stint in Afghanistan. Her specialty is knives, spear, bow and arrow or any sharp item."

A petite woman, with her hair in a ponytail, black tunic top over jeans, with boots shook his hand. "It's a pleasure to meet you."

"Raven Junee." She looked like an innocent sixteen-year-old dressed in a thigh-high skirt that showed her muscular thighs, a midriff top, and three-inch high heel boots that accentuated her legs. "She came to us via the Marine Corp, then Secret Service. Her specialty is the martial arts. She can kill with her bare hands, or her thighs, your choice."

"Hello." She shook his hand and they all took a seat.

Vernon began to laugh as he sat behind his desk. "Beautiful and dangerous. The kid doesn't stand a chance."

"That's the idea." Naverone smiled. "Raven has an appointment to meet with the admissions director at the school who has arranged for Peter Crane to give a tour of the campus. Karess is going to go along as a friend who may be interested in attending the school as well."

He looked at Karess. "Cherokee?"

"My family roots are here in Virginia near Stafford County."

"How old are you?"

"A girl never tells." Karess smiled.

Vernon turned to Raven. "You're not telling either?"

"If I tell you..."

"You have to kill me." Vernon waved them off as they smiled at each other. "Tell me your plan."

"We are going for the simple cheek swap if we can get it. If not we going to get a sample of his blood."

"Do I want to know how?"

"No," Raven replied.

"How soon can this be done?"

"Two days tops," Karess replied as she stood. "The samples will be stored and turned over to Dr. Mason."

"Harry Mason at Quantico?"

"Yes. No chain of custody issues."

"Our plane leaves in two hours." Raven stood to join her. "We'll send info once we make contact."

"If all goes well, we will be back in Virginia by Wednesday. Have the results by Friday, if not sooner." Raven shook Vernon's hand when he stood.

"We are scheduled for court next Tuesday," Vernon stated. "I would like for this to be resolved before then."

"I'm going with the girls. I will be meeting Taylor at Nicole's place."

"Taylor?"

"Yes, your daughter."

Vernon grinned. "I know she's my daughter, thank you. Why are you two meeting up?"

"I promised to introduce her to Jason Whitfield. So we'll be stopping in DC before coming home." The look on Vernon's face was priceless. Naverone laughed out loud. "You need to get a grip." She laughed and started to follow the girls out the door, but Vernon stopped her.

"Rene, where is Genesis?"

"Why?"

Vernon caught the nip in the air. "Because I asked."

Naverone hesitated for a split second. "She's covering Bobby Kennedy."

"Okay." Vernon held her gaze. He walked over to her. "Genesis was in the past. I told you how I felt about her because I do not want any secrets between us. Are you okay with that?"

Naverone did know how she felt about it. "Did you two ever..."

"No. We never made it to that point. She was with butthole and I was with Constance."

Naverone smiled at the nickname Genesis always called her ex. She held her head down. "I was jealous for a minute."

"Just a minute?" Vernon kissed her nose.

"Maybe two when Genesis told me about you two."

"The last thing I want to do is come between your friendship. Is this something you can handle?"

"There's no alternative. We're in too deep." She held his gaze. "But if you screw with me one time, I'll kill you in your sleep."

"If you're beside me it will be a sweet death." He kissed her as she pulled away and walked out of the door.

Not long after their departure, Avery knocked on Vernon's door. "You too busy for your Pop?"

Vernon stood and smiled as he walked over and hugged the man who'd raised him. "I'm glad you could make it."

"Sounds important," Avery said as he started to sit in front of the desk, but Vernon stopped him.

"Let's sit on the sofa. You want a beer?" Vernon looked over his shoulder as he walked towards the bar area of his office.

"It's ten in the morning, son."

Vernon nodded. "I'll bring two for each of us."

Avery frowned as he reached for the bottle his son was offering. "What's going on, son?"

"Someone is going to be joining us soon, but I want to talk with you one-on-one before that."

Avery opened the bottle and took a drink. "Okay. You have my undivided attention."

Vernon smiled. Pop had been saying that exact thing to him since he was a child. When he said, 'Pop can we talk', his father would stop, put down whatever he had and look him straight in the eye and say those words. "Simple question first." He took a drink then looked at his father. "Is there any chance Peter Crane is your son?"

"No chance in hell," Avery replied, then held his son's glare. "Next question."

Vernon laughed. "All right Pop. Tell me all you know about Isaac Singleton."

Avery snorted, shook his head and sat back on the sofa with the beer bottle in his hand. He tilted the bottle. "Tell Geraldine we are going to need more of these."

Vernon smiled. "We have plenty."

Avery sat up, drank the contents of the bottle, put the empty one on the table, then took another. "I hated that boy from the moment I met him. Couldn't stand the ground he walked on."

"Is it because he walked those grounds with Mom?"

"You're damn right," Avery growled at his son.

Vernon tapped his beer bottle against Avery's. "You got the girl Pop." He chuckled. "You can let that anger go, for now."

"Singleton is not the type you let anything go with. You have to stay on your p's and q's around that ass." Avery shook his head again. "Vernon, the one thing I never did was talk bad about your father. I always figured one day when you grew up you would run across him and find out on your own the kind of man he was."

"I never had reason to, Pop. I had you."

Avery's expression softened with that statement. "That's right." He held his chin high. "You did." He smiled, then exhaled. "I met your mother at a civil rights conference at a library near Fredericksburg. There weren't many Blacks living in the area, so naturally we gravitated towards each other at the conference. My goodness." He smiled. "Your mother with her cornrows and that coke-bottle shape had every head in the room turning."

"My mother in cornrows?"

"She did them herself. I watched her." Avery laughed. "God." He sat back glancing out the window as if looking back on that time. "I swear I fell in love with her the moment I saw her. She had on a Dashiki top, bell-bottom jeans and this dumb bag she called a purse with strings of beads hanging from it. Oh...she was a sight. She had just turned sixteen at the time. I was in my first year of college at Morehouse. Your grandfather knew I was trouble." Avery laughed. "He came over, patted me on the shoulder and said. 'She will never know you are interested if you stand back here gawking.' I straightened my tie, walked on over and started talking to her. She told me she had a boyfriend, but hell, I didn't care. He wasn't there. So we started talking. I lived in Atlanta, she lived here in Virginia so there wasn't much we could do. I would call and talk to her just about every day. We became good friends fast. Every Saturday we would look at Soul Train together. Your grandmother used to fuss about the telephone bill back then. But, I told her to take it out of my allowance. There was no way I was going to stop talking to her." He laughed. "From time to time, she would mention Isaac, the great basketball star. I would act like I cared, but I didn't." He looked at Vernon. "I knew he was wrong for your mother from the very beginning. The summer after I met Gwen I went to Howard for a six-week program. We hung out on the weekends, when we could. She asked me to go with her to one of Isaac's basketball camps so I could see how good a player he was. So one weekend I went. He was the asshole of a peacock I thought he would be." Avery laughed. "Around all his boys acting like he was all of that. He was...but he didn't have to act like it. You know." Vernon nodded as he took a drink of his beer and continued to listen. "He didn't like me being with his girl. He tried calling me out. Challenging me on the court. I declined. I told him, that's your lane. I'm more effective in the courtroom than on the basketball court. He came over and shoved me. Saying 'you trying to call me dumb in front of my girl?' I said no. I'm just saying you're the basketball player. We have two different courts. That's your court. 'Damn right. In fact get the hell off my court'. Gwendolyn was hot. She pushed him and told him, 'stop acting like a jerk. He's my friend that I wanted you to meet.' Isaac was pissed then. 'He's just trying to get in your drawers. Coming around here in a tie and shit. It's a basketball court. Take your country-ass back to Atlanta'. I knew how to walk away when someone was acting like an ass. I threw up my hands and said. 'Cool man.' I turned and walked out. Gwen came running out behind me. She said 'I'm sorry Avery for the way he acted. I'll take you back. I told her no. I'll take the subway back. She should stay, clear things up with him. But I told her he was right. I don't mean about trying to get into your panties. But I do like you. I like you a lot. He can see that. It's the reason he's acting like he is. I would do the same thing. I'll call you later, I said, then caught the subway back to Howard. We didn't talk for a few days. But when we did, it was as if there was no break. Things changed for them then. He would guilt her into doing things. 'If you love me you wouldn't say no to me.' I would say maybe he has a point. But she would counter with 'no I do,' There was always some hesitation. Like she knew something wasn't right, but he was her boyfriend so..." He exhaled and looked down. "I will never forget that phone call from her. She was so scared. So scared. She found out she was pregnant and Isaac the boyfriend had been shipped off to college and his parents wouldn't even open the door to talk to her mother or take her phone calls. I told my father as much as she had told me and begged him to take me to her before she did something foolish. Back then, they had abortion clinics, but I didn't want her to do that. We drove from Atlanta to Fredericksburg that night. He talked to me all the way asking if I was sure this was what I wanted to do. I told him if Gwendolyn would have me I was going to marry her and her child would be our child. It took some convincing her mother and Gwen, too, for that matter. But, we got married that Saturday. We brought Gwen back to live with us. We stayed with my parents so she wouldn't be alone in a strange city. Once she had you, we stayed for about six months, then we got our own place. Your grandfather tried to keep us in the house." Avery laughed. "I think he just wanted to keep you there. I finished law school. Worked with your grandfather's firm for a while then moved back to be close to her mother, before she passed away. We never heard anything from Singleton. We sent pictures and information on you from time to time. Then one day I came home and Gwen was cursing up a storm. She had received a letter from some attorney stating to stop attempting to contact Isaac Singleton or they would charge her with harassment." Avery laughed. "She called the man some of everything in the book. But after that day his name was never mentioned in our home again until that day at the house after Nicole's trial."

Vernon sat there for a long moment after his Pop had stopped talking. "You loved her and me that much?"

Avery turned to his son, who was sitting next to him and stared into his eyes. "Still do."

Vernon reached over and hugged his father. They held on to each other, acknowledging the love that was flowing between them. They broke away. "We are going to take the bastard down." He stood, walked over to his desk and pushed a button for Geraldine. She had sent him a text letting him know Cannon was there twenty minutes ago, but there was no way he was going to stop his father from talking. "It's time you know what all this crap is about."

Cannon walked through the door. "You ready for me?"

Vernon nodded, as he walked towards the conference table on the other side of the office. "Join us over here Pop. Cannon my father, Avery Brooks. Pop, this is..."

"Cannonball McNally. Man I used to watch you play and flinch every time you hit a man. You were a beast. You used to shoot out of that pocket like a rocket. I loved watching you play."

Cannon smiled. "Thank you, Sir."

"Pop, Cannon is going to share some information with us about Isaac Singleton. When he finishes we are going to determine the legal way to bring this man down."

Avery cleared his throat. "You know Constance is still talking to this man." He looked up at Vernon.

"It's okay Pop. Constance is free to do what she pleases. I've secured a condo for her with all the amnesties she can stand. All I need from her is to file for divorce so I can move on with my life." He sat at the table. "What we are about to embark on takes priority in my life. Before this night is over I am going to have a plan in motion to take over Singleton Enterprises and give it to its rightful heir. With any luck, Singleton will be up under a jail where he should have been years ago. He is going to curse the day he ever met Gwendolyn Spivey."

Avery looked at Cannon, then back to Vernon. "Damn, son."

Chapter 13

By that night, the ladies had made contact with Peter Crane. Naverone believed the plan was progressing according to plan. Now, she had to keep her promise to Jason Whitfield and Taylor Brooks. She pulled out her cell as she stood outside Nicole's Place where Taylor was staying. "Jason, this is Naverone. Do you have things in place?"

"Yes, yes. I swear I do."

"Don't mess up. Don't have any girls around, none of your boys and make sure your place is clean."

"I got it all covered, Ms. Naverone. I promise I will not mess this up."

Naverone smiled. She was beginning to really like this kid. "We'll be flying out in an hour. We should land around seven, your time. We'll meet you at the game."

"I'm gonna show her my skills." Jason bragged as he gave a high-five to one of his boys.

"What was that?" Naverone's attitude changed in a flash.

"That's just my boy Clint. He's gonna be gone by time you get here. He's out Ms. Naverone...He's out."

"Look, there are rules with this girl Jason. Don't make me break my foot off in your ass."

"No, no, Ms. Naverone. It's not like that. I swear I will show her nothing but mad respect. I was talking about my skills on the court...the basketball court. Nothing else."

Naverone exhaled. "Did I tell you who her father is? If that's not enough remember her uncle knows people who can make your ass disappear and so do I."

"I know, Ms. Naverone." Jason hesitated. "I promise I won't mess with her like that. I really just want to meet her. I think she's cool. Like someone I could really hang with, you know."

"I know Jason," her voice softened. "Just know she's precious cargo."

Naverone disconnected the call and prayed she was doing the right thing. With kids, anything could go wrong. If it did, she would not only have to answer to Constance, but Nick and Vernon, too. She exhaled as she walked through the door. What could she do, she was a sucker for love.

***

Raven and Peter hit it off quite well. Two of his friends and Karess were walking behind them as they headed to Peter's house.

"I have to be back at the hotel by nine or my parents will have a fit," Raven said as they reached the doorman.

"We'll have you on the subway by eight. The subway goes right under your hotel." Peter said as the door was opened for them. Raven hesitated as she looked back at Karess. "I don't know. Maybe we should go back to the hotel now." She said more to Karess than to Peter.

Karess walked past them. "Oh come on. I want to see a little bit of New York while we're here. Don't be such a baby."

"I'm not being a baby," Raven replied with a pout.

"It's going to be all right. I live on the third floor. We'll stay for a little while then leave...okay." He gave her a boyish grin.

"Okay," she replied and followed them to the elevator. A look passed between her and Karess as the boys high -fived each other behind their backs.

The elevator stopped. "This is me," Peter said as they stepped off the elevator.

Raven looked around. "Is your mom home?"

"If she is, it's no problem. She stays in her room most of the time."

"Yeah, that's why we hang out here," his friend said, cheesing from ear to ear, as Peter opened the door.

The apartment was tastefully furnished, tans and brown. A living room, dining room, and kitchen could be seen from the entrance. There was a hallway that led to a small bathroom, an office and Peter's bedroom across from that. A set of double doors was at the end of the hallway. Raven took that to be his mother's room.

"Nice place." Karess dropped her tote bag on the floor as she scanned the place. They were just high school kids, but who knows what kind of things they might have up their sleeves. It's always good to get your bearings.

Raven sat in the chair close to the edge with her bag still hanging on her back, while Karess flopped down on the sofa.

"Hey, you guys want something to drink?" Peter asked from the kitchen where he and his friends had disappeared.

Raven and Karess glanced at each other.

"What do you have?" Karess asked as she heard the loud whispers floating back and forth. She shook her head as she stood and started looking around at pictures on the entertainment stand in the living room. She took out her cell phone and snapped a few quick pictures. She stopped and pulled an old black and white from the shelf and motioned for Raven to come over.

Raven took the picture from Karess and held it, as she took a close up on her phone. The boys walked back in the room.

"Hey, these are some cool pictures," Karess stated. "Some of them are old. Who are they?"

"Relatives and folks," Peter replied as he gave them each a glass. The alcohol could be smelled a mile away.

Raven and Karess looked at them. "Aren't you guys having anything?"

"No, we're good," all three replied.

"So," —Raven put her glass on the table— "You said you had the curriculum book here?"

"Yeah," Peter looked at the glass, then at her. "It's in my bedroom. Come on, we'll go get it. You guys hang out here."

"We got you covered." The boys sat in the living room with Karess.

Peter and Raven went into the bedroom. "This is really nice of you to let me use your book."

The tall, lanky kid, looked at her in a bashful way. He looked back and closed the door. "Don't drink the glass I gave you. It's has alcohol in it," he whispered.

Raven frowned. "Alcohol? Why?" Inside she was smiling. She wasn't going to have to kick the boy's ass after all.

"Well, the guys thought it would be fun to get you and Karess drunk. I don't think it's a good thing to do."

Raven kissed him on the cheek. "Thank you for telling me."

The kid blushed. "I'll get the book for you." He started going through the books on the shelves as Raven looked around. There were pictures on the stand next to a few trophies. You play basketball?"

He looked over his shoulder at her and smiled. "Yeah, but I'm not that good at it. The coach figured since I was half-Black I could play so they put me on the team."

Raven smiled. "Yeah, I get that sometimes too." She picked up a picture from the desk. "Who is this?"

He turned with a book in his hand. He gave her the book and took the picture putting in back on the desk. "That's my dad."

"Oh, he's at work?"

"No, he doesn't live here. My mom said he wasn't comfortable living in the New York area so he went back down south."

"Oh. So you visit with him during the summer. That's what my cousin does. She lives here, well not here, she's in Jersey, but she comes to Georgia to visit with us during the summer."

"No, I've never met my dad. Maybe one day."

"Maybe," Raven replied. "Hey, we should share something."

"What do you mean?"

"Well if I decide not to go to your school I might never see you again. I would like to have something to remember you by." She pushed her hair across her shoulder.

Peter eyes widened. "Okay, like what?"

"I don't know." She looked around, then she pulled her bag off her shoulder, reached inside and pulled out a stick of gum. She unwrapped it and put one end in her mouth. She bent over and kissed him pushing the gum into his mouth. When she came up for air, she had a small round container in her hand. She put the gum in there. Then looked up at Peter. "You're a good kisser."

"We can do it again." He reached for her, but she pulled away.

"I have to go. We've been in here a long time. Karess is out there by herself."

"Can I call you sometime?" Peter asked. "You know to try to convince you to come to our school."

"We'll see. Walk me to the subway."

"Okay." He eagerly ran out the door behind her grinning.

His two friends were on the sofa, laughing like someone had told a funny joke. "What's so funny?" Peter asked as he stared at his friends.

They looked at him, then at Raven and fell out laughing again. Raven turned to Karess.

Karess picked up her bag, and shrugged her shoulder. "I told them your secret, then they drank whatever was in those glasses and just started laughing."

Raven rolled her eyes. "What secret did you tell them, Karess?"

She looked over her shoulder as she walked towards the door. "That you are really a boy named Randall."

The look on Peter's face was priceless. His hands flew to his mouth as he started wiping his tongue off with his hand. "Oh man," he yelled as he turned and ran to the bathroom. His two friends fell to the floor, rolling with laughter.

Raven and Karess shook their heads and walked out the door.

They were in a taxi heading to the airport when Raven put the small container inside a baggie. "That wasn't too difficult."

Karess placed a call to Naverone. "Mission accomplished. If the plane is still here, we can get this to Quantico tonight."

"Meet us at the airport in an hour," Naverone replied as she turned to Taylor. "We're going to have some company on the plane."

"Good, maybe they can help get my nerves under control."

Naverone smiled. "Ahh...the nervousness of meeting someone new."

"It's really funny. I mean, I don't know this guy, never met him. But there was something about his eyes." Taylor sighed. "Maybe my mom is right. I shouldn't be meeting this guy. I mean he is a ball player and all the TV shows blast on their lives in the fast lane. I really don't want to be a basketball girlfriend."

"You know better than anyone how untrue things can be on TV and in the press. Just look at what your Aunt Nikki just went through," Naverone said as the car traveled towards the airport. "At the end of the day, he is a person just like you. When he saw you, there was an attraction just like when you saw him. Both of you are going to be a little nervous and that's okay. You're supposed to be."

"Were you nervous when you first met Daddy?" Naverone gave her a sideway glare. "Oh please." Taylor smirked. "You feel the fireworks going off when you walk in the room. I expect to see clothes being stripped off and legs up in the air."

Naverone burst out laughing. They weren't far from that the other night. She looked out the window. "Nothing is going to happen with me and your dad until he is divorced from your mother." She turned back to Taylor. "How do you feel about that?"

"Them divorcing?" Taylor turned to her. "They should have done it years ago. If Daddy knew half the things I do, I'm not sure Mom would still be alive."

"You know, your dad has done some things, too."

"But you know what, I never saw it. If he did, he never let me see what was going on." She turned away. "Do you have any idea what it feels like to know your own mother would pimp you out to the highest bidder? That's what she did to me. I told her I did not want to work with Snake. I didn't like him before and I like him even less now." She turned back to Naverone. "She saw the dollar signs on that contract and didn't care what I had to go through. What kind of mother does that?"

Naverone didn't say anything for a while. "You're out of that contract now, Taylor."

"Yes, thanks to my dad. But now I can't sing or perform with anyone else for five years. And I don't deserve that."

The car pulled onto the tarmac next to the plane waiting for them. Naverone stopped Taylor before she got out of the car. "You are a very talented special young woman. Fate has a way of recognizing people like you." She kissed her cheek. "Let's go meet that man of yours."

Taylor smiled as she stepped out of the car. And just like that, the perky, indestructible twenty-year-old was back. "He better step right or he's history before the war even begins." She snapped her finger in the air as she rounded the vehicle.

Naverone smiled. She was really beginning to love this girl.

***

"The Washington Raiders stadium was packed almost to capacity. What a contrast that was to last season." The announcer spoke to the capacity crowd. "The kid by the name of Jason Whitfield has brought this building new life."

"I wish they would stop saying that." Jason said as he turned the television monitor off.

Taylor and Naverone turned to see Jason standing in the back of the room they had been escorted to.

He was just as she remembered. Tall, dark and oh so fine, with eyes that could light up the sky.

Jason smiled at the woman who had captured his imagination and had not let go. He prayed he didn't say anything stupid. He walked over in his grey suit, white shirt and contrasting pink tie and took her hand. He did not kiss it because he did not want to be presumptuous. He simply shook it, then let it go. "Hi, I'm Jason. I'm glad you could come to the game."

"Taylor," she tiptoed up and kissed his cheek. "Thank you for inviting me." They simply stared at each other, not saying a word.

"Why does that bother you?"

He knew she was referring to the announcer's statements. "It makes it seem as if I alone brought this building to life. It's the team. I'm just one member of twelve who make the games worth seeing."

"Good answer," Nick said as he walked through the door and stood right in between the two.

Naverone almost laughed out loud it was so clear what he was doing. She looked to see Ericka standing in the doorway shaking her head. "Get your boy." She laughed.

Ericka walked over, grabbed Nick by the back of his suit jacket and pulled him from between Jason and Taylor. "Get over here." She turned to Jason. "We're going to give you a few minutes to talk."

"Umm, then you need to get dressed for the game," Nick stated. "Five minutes." He nodded as Ericka pulled him out of the door.

She peeked back in at Naverone. "You, too. Give those kids five minutes."

Naverone looked at Jason with narrowed eyes. She pointed two fingers from her eyes to his.

The door closed behind them and all Jason could do was stare. "You are prettier in person."

Taylor smiled. "You're not too bad yourself."

He grinned. "Look, I'm not too good at this first meeting thing, but I really would like a chance to spend some time with you. If you're not busy after the game would you like to have some dinner or go dancing or something?"

"I'll take both, please." Taylor smiled.

Jason broke out in a grin. "Okay, okay, we can do that."

"My dad and my uncles are very protective of me. I think it's because I've never really been on dates or anything."

"You've never been on a date?"

"No, I've been working since I was thirteen. So it was studios and stages for me."

"Wow, I guess I better get this right then, hum?"

"I don't have anything to compare it to, so you should be good."

"May I kiss you?"

Taylor was surprised by the question. She had kissed before in videos but never for just because. "Okay."

Jason surprised himself. He bent down, gently kissed her lips, then pulled away. He smiled at her as she opened her eyes and looked at him. "You taste like home."

She wanted to ask him what he meant, but Nick knocked on the door and came in. "Times up. You need to dress for the game and you need to come on out."

"Uncle Nick, out," Taylor commanded.

"You, too. Now." Taylor rolled her eyes. "No you didn't just roll your eyes at me."

Jason laughed. "I'll see you after the game." He turned to walk out the back door that led to the team room, as Taylor pulled Nick out the door leading to the court.

The passes they had put them in floor seats right behind the team. When the game started it was Ericka, Nick, Taylor and Naverone. By the end of the game, it was Nick, Ericka, Naverone, then Taylor. When they went to meet Jason at his car, Ericka refused to let Nick anywhere near Taylor.

"Look Nick, I got them tonight," Naverone said pushing him into the sedan waiting for him and Ericka.

"Are you sure Naverone?" Nick grinned. "I can back you."

Naverone couldn't help it, she laughed at Nick who was playing his role as overprotective uncle to the hilt. "No, I'm good."

He whispered in Naverone's ear. "Make sure she has a good time."

Naverone nodded and closed the door to the car.

"Thank you," Taylor said as she walked over to Jason's SUV. "He's going to be okay. He said to tell you to have a good time."

"I have my bodyman with me, " Jason said. "We'll be okay."

"Oh, I know you will. Because her body girl is going to be with her." She pointed inside the car. "Let's go."

Once inside, he decided against going to the club where the team hung out after the game. He really wanted to spend some time with Taylor, talking. They opted for a private restaurant near the Capitol building. Unfortunately, Jason was still recognized. A few patrons tried to get their picture, but Naverone and Jason's bodyman blocked them. After a while, people got the message. Every now and then Naverone would look behind her to see the two talking and grinning at each other. She had to smile.

"He must really like her," the bodyman said. "None of his boys are around. Didn't even come to the game."

"Is that a good thing?"

"Oh, yes. They are a pain in my ass. But he's a good kid. Just have a few leeches who make him think he owes them something."

"Your job is to protect him from that." She raised an eyebrow at him.

"I do what I can, but you have to let them come to terms with valid friendships and baggage."

Naverone nodded.

"She good people?"

Naverone smiled. "Yeah. First crush."

"You know he got this home-girl that keeps hounding him. Her name is Keisha. Don't let her mess with your girl's mind."

"Keisha have a last name?"

"Jackson." He nodded.

"I appreciate the information." Naverone pulled out her card. "I have a feeling these two are going to be seeing a lot of each other. Here's my information."

"I know who you are. Rene Naverone, Secret Service." He tilted his head towards Jason and Taylor. "I know who her other uncle is, too. Advisor to the President. I check out who is coming around my people." He took the card and gave her his. "We'll keep them right as long as they need us."

She glanced at the card. "You're with McNally." She put the card in her pocket. "Keisha Jackson, hmm?"

He frowned and shook his head. "Trouble with a capital T."

Naverone looked around and caught the tail end of what she thought was their first kiss. She almost melted then and there.

Chapter 14

Cannon walked into the offices of B7Beats Tuesday morning to be in place to gather the information needed to make the takeover of B7Beats, successful and swift. He keyed into his computer, then pulled out the burner phone Vernon had given him. He dialed Xavier's cell phone number.

"I'm in." He disconnected the call.

Xavier turned to Adam, who was sitting in the vehicle next to him. "He's in."

"I don't understand. One minute the man is our enemy, the next minute we are working with him." Adam talked as he hacked into Cannon's system. He pulled up a list of the current stockholders, public and private. "Got it." He looked at Xavier. "Are we going to give this back too," he asked incredulously.

Xavier looked at him and grinned. "No, we're going to own B7 by the opening bell tomorrow.

"You know you go to jail for insider trading...right?"

"That's why we are not going to trade anything. We are just taking. Well borrowing...not really borrowing." He hesitated as he looked around then turned back to Adam who was still looking at him waiting for an answer. "We are taking something to give to the rightful owner."

"Mmm, hmm" Adam said then turned back to his computer. "I have the entire list. What do you want to do with it?"

"Now, we are going to get all the information we can on everyone on that list"

Adam pushed a few buttons. "Done. Now what?"

Xavier frowned at him. "What do you mean done?"

Adam looked over at him, then switched screens on his computer. He clicked a few buttons. "Webster's says: having finished or completion..".

"I know what it says in the dictionary," Xavier laughed. "Let's get the hell out of here." He started the vehicle. "We're supposed to meet up with someone named Rosa Sanchez at Brooks-Pendleton."

Twenty minutes later Xavier and Adam were inside the building being escorted to Rosa Sanchez' office. "She's expecting you." The woman pointed to the office. "Mr. Pendleton will join you shortly."

"Thank you," Xavier said because Adam's head was still down in the computer. He knocked on the closed door.

"Come in."

Xavier opened the door to find an exotic beauty looking up at him from a room filled with computers. "Rosa Sanchez?"

"Yes. Xavier Davenport." She extended her hand. "It's a pleasure to meet you. I understand we have an interesting project for the day." She smiled as she looked past him.

Adam's head shot up. "What is that fragrance you are wearing?"

Rosa tilted her head and laughed. "What an odd question?"

Xavier thought so too, as he raised an eyebrow at Adam.

"It borders on heavenly." Adam smiled at the woman, then extended his hand as he pushed Xavier out of the way. "Adam Lassiter and you are?"

"Rosa Sanchez," she replied.

"And the fragrance?"

"Chanel, Allure-Sensuelle. A common fragrance."

"It's a mixture of the chemicals and your biological scent that makes the fragrance unique."

"Will you stop with the chemicals and biological and hit this list?" Xavier looked exasperated.

Rosa laughed as she walked over to the computer. "I understand you have a list I need to analyze."

"I do." Adam sat in the empty seat next to her at the desk. He looked up at Xavier. "This is going to take a while."

"We don't have a while. We have to move quickly."

Adam walked over to him and whispered. "Look, I already have the list analyzed. Just give me an hour as I work it out her way...."

"Done."

They both looked at her. "Done? What do you mean done?" Adam asked.

"Done, as in finished or complete." Xavier smiled.

Adam went and stood over Rosa.

"I have an algorithm I used for reasoning. See." Rosa pointed to her screen. "I took the names and figures from your list, placed them in and let the computer determine which stockholders should be approached first." She turned to him, looking over her shoulder. "But you already know that, don't you Dr. Lassiter?"

Adam smiled. "So you know my work?"

"I do."

Xavier rolled his eyes upward as Ty walked through the door.

"Do you have anything for me, Rosa?"

"Yes sir, we do," Rosa said. "I think we should compare the two lists produced to ensure accuracy, then we can set things in motion."

"I don't think you are going to have a lot of push back," Adam stated. "My preliminary investigation shows some executives were about to make a move. Rumor has it many are not happy with the direction he's trying to take them. You may be able to takeover and keep most of your executive staff in place. I suggest you use what is referred to as the Dawn Raid. Get brokers to buy a substantial holding in B7 as soon as the stock market opens in the morning. It will mask that you are the one purchasing the shares until you are ready to divulge it." Adam stopped talking and smiled.

"Who are you?" Ty asked.

"Oh, I can't tell you. If I do..."

Ty held up his hand. "I know." He turned to Rosa, "Do what he just said. Discreetly contact the executives at B7. Offer double for anyone willing to sell. Keep Pendleton out of it."

"Got you Boss," Rosa replied.

Ty turned to Xavier, "Let's leave this to them."

"My pleasure," Xavier replied. The two left the room.

Adams smiled at Rosa. "Shall we have some fun?"

***

Wednesday morning by nine-fifteen, brokers had purchased fifty-two percent of the stock in B7Beats. By nine-thirty, Ty Pendleton was in the conference room of B7Beats where all employees were told to gather.

"Good morning. As of nine-fifteen this morning I became the controlling owner of B7. To some this may be seem like a hostile takeover. I'm here to assure you it is not. I have no interest in running B7. I do have an interest in keeping it from being destroyed."

"What in the hell is going on here?" Isaac stood in the doorway with Cannon behind him.

"Good of you to join us Mr. Singleton." Ty nodded. "Have a seat. As I was saying..."

Isaac walked to the front of the room where Ty stood. The Towers stepped in front of Ty blocking Isaac's approach.

"Get the hell out of my way," Isaac demanded. The men did not move.

"Step aside," Ty said and they both moved to stand behind him, as Cannon did with Isaac. "Mr. Singleton, this is an information-only meeting. Your views or questions will be addressed in private. You can have a seat with the other employees or you can wait in my office until we are finished."

"You are finished. What do you mean your office? What in the hell are you doing here, Pendleton?"

Ty glanced at the employees and smiled. "It seems I am doomed to repeat myself." He glared at Isaac. "As of nine-fifteen this morning I became the controlling owner of B7."

"I have forty-eight percent of the stock in this company..."

"I have fifty-two," Ty cut him off. He saw the shocked look of understanding slowly show on Isaac's face.

Isaac turned and glared at the executives, who had to have sold all of their shares to Pendleton. He huffed and nodded his head as he locked eyes with each.

"You should have better communications with your executives, Isaac. If you had you would have known they were unhappy."

"I don't need business advice from you, Pendleton." Isaac sneered as he walked towards the door.

"On the contrary, I believe you do." Ty turned his attention back to the employees. "As I was about to say. There will be no layoffs, no changing of positions." This beautiful young lady in the corner is Rosa Sanchez. I would like for each of the executives to give her a plan for B7. Whoever presents an innovative future for

B7 will head up the team to accomplish that
task. All contracts will be honored. Any talent
who wishes to leave us, don't give them any
trouble. I want the people at B7 to be happy
here with us."

Isaac stood outside the door fuming. "How
in the hell did this happen? Why were you not
aware of this?"

"You pulled me out to work on the Brooks."
Cannon replied coolly.

"I should take all of those bastards out.
Every last one of them."

"I think it would be more prudent to check
your other business ventures," Cannon
narrowed his eyes on Isaac. "If they took B7 so
easily, what else could they be doing to
retaliate?" For the first time in their
partnership, Isaac seemed rattled.

"How did they know the stockholders?"

"Public record."

"Not all," Isaac shook his head as he
thought. "We have private investors. Pendleton
had to get their shares to have controlling
interest. Someone inside B7 had to feed them
that information." He turned to Cannon. "Find
out how this happened."

Cannon's cell phone buzzed. He looked at
the caller, then at Singleton. "It's Crane."

Isaac frowned. "Take it?"

"Cannon." He listened, then took a step
away from Isaac. "Was there any indication
what it's about?" He listened more. "I'll be
there." He hung up the telephone.

"Crane and her attorneys have been called
to the judge's chambers at three this
afternoon."

Isaac raised an eyebrow expecting more.

Cannon shook his head. "No indication why?"

Isaac's mind was racing. He had covered all the bases with Stacy Crane. They had enough information to damage Avery Brooks' reputation. "Contact the attorney handling the case. See if he has some insight." The meeting was breaking up. Employees were coming out of the conference room, most with smiles. "Ingrates." Isaac sneered as he eyed each of them.

He approached two of the executives as they exited the room and was immediately blocked by one of the Towers. "I still own a good portion of this company."

"Tell it to the Boss," Jake replied.

"Unpleasant things happen to people when they cross me, Pendleton," Isaac's anger was now getting the best of him.

"You are not the only one," Ty stepped to the man. "While things happen from your end, people disappear from mine." The dead stare Ty gave him left no question as to his meaning. Ty stepped back and shrugged. "I'm the least of your worries. You...pissed off Vernon Brooks. I believe he warned you." Ty smiled. "Hell has no fury like what you are about to behold. You take care now." He turned to the towers. "Escort Mr. Singleton from the building." The two men took a step towards Isaac, but Cannon interceded.

"I have him," he stated. The two men hesitated until Ty nodded, then they stepped back.

Cannon turned to Isaac. "Mr. Singleton." He walked to the elevator and pushed the button.

Isaac glared at Ty. This wasn't his fight. It was Brooks'. He remembered what Vernon said the last time he saw him. "Brooks never issue threats. We advise you of our intentions. You've been warned.

If Isaac thought his morning had a bad start, his afternoon was turning out to be disastrous. As soon as they stepped outside the B7 offices, his cell phone sounded. He looked at the caller ID and paused.

"Isaac Singleton," he answered recognizing the law firm.

"Mr. Singleton, Thomas Letcher from Letcher, Barnes and Wentworth. The partners require your presence at a meeting this afternoon at two p.m."

"I have a full schedule, Mr. Letcher." Isaac's eyes narrowed. "Would you give me some indication what this is about?"

"The estate of William and Estelle Singleton. We'll see you at two p.m." The called was disconnected.

Isaac stared at the phone for a long time.

"Is everything all right, Mr. Singleton?" Cannon asked, knowing the answer."

Isaac was too angry to answer. He slid into the backseat of the sedan and told his driver to go.

Cannon smirked. "That damn Vernon." He shook his head and dialed a number. "He's on his way."

Vernon sat back in his office chair "Good job Cannon. When will you be back?"

"As soon as I pack up here. Ericka and I are going to meet with Bobby tomorrow."

Vernon nodded. "It's time."

"Give him hell." Cannon disconnected the call, then dialed Ericka's number. "Have you let that man up for air yet?" he teased when she answered.

Ericka giggled like a schoolgirl. "Nick is fine. Good of you to question his well-being."

Cannon smiled. If nothing else good came from this situation with Singleton, he knew Ericka had come out on top. Nick was the perfect man for her and Cannon could not be happier. "I don't have to ask how you are doing."

"I'm good Cannon." Ericka beamed. "Now that you've settled on Virginia and Nick, what are you going to do?"

"You know Nick and I were talking about that. I think I want to start a mentoring program for girls. I don't have all the details yet, I'm just working through the plans now. But, I'm pretty set financially. I think this would be a great way to give back, you know."

"Sounds like a plan. I'm happy for you cuz." He huffed. "Before you start, we have to get Bobby straight."

"I know." Ericka sighed. "We will sit him down tomorrow and tell him everything we know including all we know about his father and brother."

"I hate interfering. Bobby has a good life. But he needs to know."

"That's my only hesitation." Ericka sighed. "Bobby is a simple man. He doesn't need or ever wanted a lot. He may not want this. But he deserves to know and make that decision for himself."

"Aunt Felicia would be proud of you right now." Cannon smiled. "You are getting your life together and doing this thing for Bobby. It's what she would have wanted."

Ericka was silent for a moment in her own thoughts. "It's the only way I can make amends Cannon." The sadness from not mending fences with her mom was about to take over when a beep came through the phone. "Hey that's Nick. I have to go." And that quick, she disconnected the call with Cannon and was speaking to Nick.

"How's it going?" she asked knowing this was a big day for the Brooks.

"I'm wrapping up a meeting and heading to the attorney's office, then the courthouse. I need to be there for my family."

"It's time for the good guys to start fighting back. I hope your brother gives him hell."

"You hope? We are talking about Vernon. That's a definite. Singleton is not going to know what hit him, a tank or semi-trailer, by the time Vernon is done. I'll be home as soon as this is over."

Nick looked up to see his family gathered. He disconnected the call and joined them. He stopped when he reached them and smiled. "Man, we are a good-looking bunch." The family laughed as Gwendolyn kissed him on the cheek. "Butchie," Nick shook his hand. "The president keeping you busy?"

"Not busy enough to miss this." James looked at Vernon. "I get to see you in action."

Vernon smiled. "You're in for a treat." He turned to his father. "Are you ready?"

Avery took Gwendolyn's hand. "Let's do this."

***

Isaac reached the building that housed his father's law firm. On the flight to Virginia, he wondered what the call was about. The timeframe on locating his child wasn't up. His contact in the firm had no further information on the activity to locate the child. It's possible they could have gotten wind of the B7 takeover. But that was a company he acquired after he became CEO. Whatever the reason, he wanted it over with. The meeting at the courthouse was in an hour. He wanted to know what that was all about. First things first, Isaac thought as he stepped out of the sedan.

"I should only be fifteen to twenty minutes. Wait here," he said to the driver.

Mr. Wentworth greeted him at the door. "Mr. Singleton, happy you could join us. We are in the main conference room."

"We?"

"Yes," Wentworth replied as he adjusted his bowtie. "We are happy to report there's been a development."

Wentworth opened the door to the conference room as Isaac glanced over his shoulder and narrowed his eyes at the woman he had compensated to keep him informed. A feather could have touched his forehead and knocked him over from the shock he took when he walked through that door.

Sitting on one side of the long conference table was the entire Brooks family. All the children, Avery and the woman he hadn't seen since she was a sixteen-year-old girl, were at the table.

"Mr. Singleton," Mr. Letcher stood. "We are pleased to inform you we believe we have located your child."

Vernon stood and smiled. "Hello Isaac."

It took every ounce of willpower for Isaac to step into that room. When Wentworth closed the door behind him, the simple click caused him to jump. Then he regained his decorum. He looked from Vernon to Gwen to Avery. "What proof do you have?"

Gwen stood. Avery caught her hand. She gently pulled away.

"Stop her," Nicole whispered to Nick.

"I'm not stopping her." He chuckled.

James stood and followed his mother as she walked past him. She stopped in front of Isaac with her petite body, folded her arms across her chest and glared at him. "Are you calling me a liar?"

Isaac did not skip a beat. "And you are?"

Gwen raised her hand to slap him, but James held her back.

"Why don't we all take a seat," Letcher stated. "Mr. Singleton, please." He pointed to a chair on the opposite side of the table.

Isaac hesitated, then sat. James escorted Gwen back to her seat, but remained standing behind his mother as he glared at Isaac.

The agent who traveled with James stood in the doorway. "Is there an issue, Mr. Brooks?"

"No," James replied, his arms folded across his chest as he glared at Isaac.

The agent looked around, then closed the door.

"Well," Letcher cleared his throat. "Mr. Brooks would you like to have a seat?" he asked nervously.

"No," James replied.

Letcher cleared his throat again. "Very well." He turned to Isaac. "Mr. Singleton, we have spent the last two hours taking depositions from Mrs. Gwendolyn Spivey Brooks, Mr. Avery Brooks and of course Mr. Vernon Brooks. "We believe we have fulfilled the obligation stated in the amendment of William Singleton's will. We are satisfied that Vernon Brooks is of good moral character, as required. We believe he is your son. Do you disagree?"

Isaac had prepared for this moment. He did not expect it to come this soon, however, here it is. "It's been a number of years, forty to be exact. I was not certain back then that this woman was carrying my child. The reason is the very man sitting next to her, Avery Brooks." Avery held Gwen's hand to keep her still. "I believe she was screwing both of us at the same time. Both of us were sons of wealthy parents"— He shrugged his shoulder,—"who knows what other boys she was so free with. So my question again is do you have proof?"

Every Brooks male in the room was on his feet when Isaac made his statement. It was James who reached him first. He had Isaac pinned up against the wall before the agent could burst through the door.

Vernon wedged himself between James and Isaac as Letcher, Barnes and Wentworth ran to the corner of the room.

"James," Vernon cautioned. "This is what he wants." He pulled at James' hands, then looked over at the agent. "You want to give me a hand here."

"Butchie, put him down this moment," Avery yelled out.

James eased up as the agent began to pull him away. Vernon, adjusted his suit, turned to face Isaac and whispered. "You were warned." He followed James back to his seat.

Isaac was cheering inside. "You call this a family of good moral standards?" he seethed. "You have a daughter whose sexuality is questionable, a son over here who has embezzled funds from his clients. And this one, the one you claim to be mine, fathered a child with his own brother's wife." He looked at the partners who were just retaking their seats at that moment. "You call this a family of good moral character? I think not."

Vernon pulled out a document. "I believe we have given all the time we plan to spend on this situation. This is a petition to freeze all assets connected to Singleton Enterprises until such time that it can be determined who the rightful heirs should be. In addition, there is a request for an accounting of all funds, property and holdings of William, Estelle and Isaac Singleton."

"You have no rights to request such an act," Isaac yelled across the table furious.

"I have every right." Vernon smirked, then looked at his family. "I've written all the contingencies I will allow Mr. Singleton in this document. I trust that Letcher, Barnes and Wentworth will see to it that it is followed to the letter." He checked his watch. "I believe we are due in court. Let's go Pop." Vernon smiled as his family walked out of the room.

Gwen stopped at the door. "Thank you Isaac. If you hadn't been the ass that you were, my son would not have had the father that he needed." She smiled at Avery. "You get a special treat tonight."

"Oh mother." Nikki frowned. "In public? People are around."

Everyone laughed not noticing that James had not left the room. He stared at Isaac. "If my son's name ever comes out of your mouth again, they will be the last words you ever speak." The look James gave Isaac spoke volumes. It let him know this was not a man he wanted to deal with. James turned and walked out of the room.

Isaac turned to the partners. "What are you going to do about this?"

Letcher picked up the document Vernon left. "Follow this to the letter until the matter is resolved."

***

The courthouse was not as busy as one would expect in the afternoon. Mornings were packed with cases, but in the afternoon things tended to dwindle down a bit. The hallway leading to the courtroom had a few people in it, but not enough to block the view of who was arriving or sitting outside the court waiting. The Brooks clan was standing, with the exception of Gwen and Nicole who sat on the bench. When Stacy Crane and her attorney turned into the hallway, all the Brooks stood and watched as the woman they knew was lying walked towards them.

"Avery, I'm sorry it had to come to this, but it's time for the truth to be told." Stacy smiled and turned to Gwendolyn. "You're looking well, Gwen."

"Thank you, I can't help it." She smiled back letting the woman know she was not getting to her. Stacy huffed and walked off as she glared at Nicole. "First Isaac and now Stacy." She looked at Avery. "Let's please squash these bugs and get on with our life."

"Where's Naverone?" Nick asked Vernon.

"She's with Taylor in New York. She's going to see the boy play again." Vernon frowned.

"He's a nice kid, Vernon." Nick grinned. "I give him a hard time just to keep him in line. Taylor could do much worse."

"I prefer she not do at all."

James laughed. "Overprotective, are we?" He looked at Vernon.

"This from a man who almost choked the life out of someone for mentioning his son." He looked up at Nick. "What was that, fifteen minutes ago?" They laughed.

"The judge is ready," the clerk called from the door. "Only the two parties and their attorney," she said as she looked at all the people in the hallway.

Gwen kissed her husband. "Squash them," she said as they walked through the door.

They walked through the courtroom to the back door leading to the judge's chambers. Vernon held the door for everyone to enter.

Judge Tyree looked up as they entered. "Ahh, the cherry on top of my already ecstatic day." He sat behind his desk. "Mr. Tillman some information has been brought to the court's attention. If I find you were a party in this deception, wasting the court's time, possibly tarnishing a man's reputation, I will have your license."

"Your Honor, I have no idea what you are referring to," Stacy's attorney feigned being insulted.

The judge put a file on the desk. "Take a look. The results were received yesterday straight from Quantico." The attorney picked up the file and looked at the papers inside. "That's right, Avery Brooks is not the father of one Peter Crane. In fact, we know your client has been aware of the real father from the beginning." Vernon handed the folder he was holding to the judge. He pulled the picture out. "This is the father. His results are on the back page. Ms. Crane," the judge looked between Vernon and Tillman. "Why have you perpetrated this fraud on the court?"

Stacy stood slowly, on wobbly knees. "Your Honor, I worked for Avery Brooks for over twenty years until his daughter fired me. Now I have no way to support my son. The Brooks family owes me."

"No. Ms. Crane. Harvey Brooks owes you. I suggest you contact him since he has been proved to be Peter's father."

"Your Honor." Avery stood. "I have no issues helping Ms. Crane financially. She was once a loyal employee of our firm, however, there are extenuating circumstances."

"Ms. Crane I believe Mr. Brooks has just saved you. I was about to throw you in jail along with your attorney."

"I was not aware of any of this until this moment, Your Honor."

The judge looked at him skeptically. "Very well. What do you need Mr. Brooks?"

"We request her testimony against Isaac Singleton." Vernon gave the judge another document. "We believe Ms. Crane and Mr. Singleton conspired to ruin my father's reputation."

"I don't believe in people being compensated for doing a dirty deed, however, if all parties agree, I'll allow it. Now get out of my court so I can spend the day with my grandchild."

Vernon grinned. "Thank you, Your Honor."

They walked back into the hallway. "How much Avery?" Stacy asked indignantly

"Not a dime," Gwen stood. "I have no idea what you are referring to, but if it has anything to do with that woman receiving a dime of Brooks money the answer is no."

Everyone was on full alert. There were only a few times when Gwen Brooks raised her voice. When she did everybody stopped and listened. All eyes were on Avery. He took his wife's hand, whispered something in her ear and turned to Vernon and nodded.

"Let's go home everyone," Avery stated. "This leg of our journey is over."

They began to file out. "Well what does that mean?" Stacy called out.

"It means you don't get a dime." Nicole laughed. "Nada.... Nothing. Go tell that to the bloggers." She walked away laughing.

Nick reached into his pocket and pulled out an envelope. He handed it to Vernon then followed his family out the door.

Vernon turned to Stacy. "Let's make a deal."

Chapter 15

The beast had been unleashed, again. Isaac knew it the moment he walked out of the offices of Letcher, Barnes and Wentworth. They were going to pay for what they did to him. They were his parents, his alone. No one had any rights to what was his. He owned the estate. He tried to show them how far he would go to keep what was his, but they didn't take heed. Just like Terrell Bell. He told the bench-warmer not to show him up on the court. What did he do? Made four back to back three pointers when Isaac was having an off night. The coach pulled Isaac and had him on the bench in the fourth quarter...the fourth quarter. Isaac Singleton don't sit the bench for nobody. He knew, when he told the kid to come to the club, he was going to take him out. When he stepped on his feet, well that gave him the reason. He didn't mean to kill him, just shoot his knees out. But hey, the fool ducked and the bullet went through his brain. Should have taken heed, Isaac thought. Now, it was Brooks' turn. He didn't care that the man was his son. Vernon was after what belonged to him. His thoughts turned to another loose end, the other kid. Damn, he thought. He was going to have to take him out.

The driver dropped him off at his childhood home. It was the one place Vernon Brooks did not attach anything to. The house and the original headquarters of Singleton Enterprises in Fredericksburg were available to him to work and live. Every other office was on lock until an accounting could be made.

The more he thought about it, the madder he became. By the time he was done, no one would have any claims on what was his. The entire Brooks clan would come to feel his wrath. He pulled out his cell. "Cannon, get me everything you can on Jason Whitfield."

Cannon hesitated. "I thought you was pulling away from anything connected to Pendleton."

"It's not about Pendleton. Get me the information."

"Yes sir." Cannon hesitated. "Mr. Singleton, the Crane case was thrown out of court this afternoon."

"What happened?" he snapped.

"Paternity test came back."

Isaac huffed. "We knew we would lose. Get me the information." He disconnected the call.

"You may have won the morning. But the battle is still raging." He unpacked his bag and changed his clothes. Driving the dark SUV he kept at the house, he put in the address to BSK

Lawn Care Services. He parked across the street near the park he knew the kid walked through to get to his apartment and waited. You have to know your enemies as well as you know yourself. He knew the kid's routine. Had followed him a time or two to see what he was about. Bobby Kennedy was a health freak. He ate healthy, ran miles a day for no reason, rode bikes and played a little ball here and there. Hell, he had the nerve to join him on the court for a pickup game once. The kid had skills, but nothing compared to him.

Isaac checked his watch. It was a little past five. Traffic had picked up a little, but nothing compared to the interstate or the traffic in Atlanta. But his nerves were on edge. The idea of him having to fight for what was his at the age of sixty wasn't right, it just wasn't right.

"But they will pay," he said out loud with a grin. He pulled out his cell and dialed a number. "Constance, baby. How you doing?" he said with the sincerity of the Grinch.

"Isaac, I've been calling you. Where are you?"

"Not far away. Are you expecting Taylor to come by tonight?"

"No, she's in New York with that Jason boy."

"Jason Whitfield?" He shook his head. "That kid is no good for her. As her mother, you should put an end to that."

"That new woman in Vernon's life has more say about that than I do."

"Vernon," Isaac sat up, "has someone else in his life?"

"Yes. Some woman name Naverone, Navaronni or something like that."

"You know, Constance, I want us to be together without Vernon between us, but he is my son and I feel so guilty about loving you. I just can't see how him having a new life and being happy is fair to you. It just doesn't' seem right, baby. He's replacing you with a new woman in his life and your daughter's, too. I don't know babe, it seems like there should be something you can do about that."

"What can I do Isaac? Vernon has all the cards in his court."

"Not all," Isaac stated as he thought. I'm leading her to the fountain. Now drink the damn water.

"What do you mean?"

Isaac sighed. "I mean, he can't do anything unless you sign those divorce papers. As for Taylor, you are her mother. Not this other woman. Call her home. Demand it if you have too." He paused. "Constance... No. I'm not going there."

"What?"

Isaac grinned. "Well, baby isn't Taylor still a virgin?"

"Yes."

"Well, I hate to say this, but I know the life, babe. I lived it. If this woman keeps taking Taylor around this ball player, well...her status is going to change. You should talk to Vernon about that. You are her mother. You should have some say in her life."

"You are right. I'm calling Taylor right now."

"Good. Let me know how it goes." Bobby came out of the door just as she made the statement. "Baby, I'll come by tonight, we'll talk more about it. I have to go into a meeting now."

She was saying something, but he had disconnected the call. He started the vehicle and looked around. The little traffic that was coming through had slowed to a crawl. There were a few people with dogs in the park, a woman sitting on the bench reading a book and another walking towards Bobby. Not too many people. He pulled out and slowly started driving towards the kid. He glanced through the rear view mirror, scanned the corner, then checked the people in the park. He waited until Bobby was about five feet from the curb when he slammed on the gas pedal and the vehicle bounced forward. He saw a movement to his right as the woman sitting on the bench jumped in front of the vehicle, knocking Bobby backwards into the middle of the street right at the moment of impact. Isaac didn't stop or look back. He knew he had missed the kid. He cursed and punched the steering wheel, kept his foot on the gas and swung around the corner and out of sight.

"Get off my man." A woman stood above the couple in the middle of the street hitting the woman from the bench with her purse. Cars had swerved around them stomping on brakes trying not to hit them. People in the park were running over to see what happened.

The woman looked down at Bobby. "Are you alright, Mr. Kennedy?"

Before he could answer, the woman swinging the purse was giving it her all. "Get off of him. Get off him.

Suddenly she was on the ground and the other woman had a gun drawn pointing at her. "Hit me with that damn purse one more time and I swear I will shoot you."

The woman turned back to Bobby. "Mr. Kennedy. I'm Special Agent Morgan with Secret Service. You are in danger I need you to come with me." The woman on the ground moved. Genesis turned with the gun still on her. "Don't move."

"What's going on?" Bobby asked as he stood, wiped himself off, then walked over to the woman on the ground.

"You know that woman?" Genesis asked.

"Yes, it's my girlfriend, Patrice."

Genesis took a step back, exhaled and put her weapon away. By this time a police car had pulled up. Genesis pulled out her credentials and told them to stand back. "Mr. Kennedy, you don't know me. But we have reasons to believe your life is in danger. That vehicle just tried to run you over. That solidifies it for me. I'm going to ask you to come with me."

"He's not going anywhere with you," Patrice yelled. "You're a mad woman."

"No," Bobby said to Patrice, trying to calm her down. "This woman just saved my life. I saw the vehicle coming. Hell, I damn near felt the impact." He turned to Genesis. "What is this all about?"

"Let's go somewhere safe so we can talk. I'll have your sister Ericka and cousin Cannon meet us there." She looked at the woman. "She can come to, but I'm telling you, lift that purse and I'm going to shoot you."

***

Genesis entered Vernon's office with Bobby and Patrice in tow. The police officers stayed outside and waited to get a statement from her.

"I thought this would be the safest place for them until Ericka and Cannon arrive." She held the door as Bobby entered.

Vernon was a bit surprised. From all the talk and keeping things away from Bobby, he had the impression that the man was some type of weakling. He was wrong. Bobby Singleton Kennedy was a good six-two, probably two hundred and twenty solid pounds and as handsome as his sister was beautiful. He had to laugh when he walked through the door.

He extended his hand. "Vernon Brooks. So you're the one causing all the confusion."

Bobby shook his hand. "Sir. Don't know about the trouble, but I am Bobby Kennedy."

Vernon nodded his understanding. "We're trying to clear things up for you."

"Vernon," Patrice screeched. "What is going on here?"

"Patrice." He glanced at Genesis.

"The girlfriend." She gave him a sideways glance.

"Ahh..."

"Yes, I am and I want to know what's happening here," she replied with a huff and hands on hips.

"I always thought you would end up with Nick."

The wind was knocked out of her sails a little with that statement. "Nick was too slow."

She put her arm in Bobby's. "I'm with Bobby now."

"Good." Vernon nodded his head. "I'm certain Nick will be relieved...to know you're happy," he added. He looked up at Bobby. "Please, come in make yourself comfortable. This is going to take a while."

"We have plans, Vernon," Patrice explained.

"Your plans are changing. Please have a seat."

"I'm going to give my statement to the officers," Genesis said as she headed towards the door. "I'm certain they will want to speak with you, Mr. Kennedy."

"Not a problem," Bobby replied and he and Patrice sat on the sofa in Vernon's office.

"Ask Geraldine to order some dinner." He looked at the couple. "Any preferences?"

"Whatever you have is good," Bobby stated. "Well, I don't do red meat, or too many carbs, so no French fries or anything of that nature," Patrice stated. "Oh and I'll need purified water, thank you."

"Are you under the impression that I'm a waitress?" Genesis frowned at the woman. "You'll have whatever comes in." Genesis glanced at Vernon, shaking her head as she walked out the door.

"Mr. Brooks, the agent mentioned my sister. Ericka is here...in Virginia?"

"Yes," Vernon replied as he took a seat across from them. "In fact, she's staying with Nick. I contacted them when Genesis called about the incident. They will be here shortly."

Bobby nodded. "What is this all about Mr. Brooks?"

"Oh just call him Vernon," Patrice said. "His father is Mr. Brooks."

Vernon raised an eyebrow at the woman. "She's right," he said. "Vernon is fine." He sat forward. "Bobby, this is a private situation. The less people know, the safer they are." He glanced at Patrice.

"Bobby and I don't keep secrets from each other. You may speak freely in front of me." Patrice was nodding the entire time she was speaking.

"It's fine Mr. Brooks. Patrice is good."

"Okay." Vernon crossed his legs, sat back and began. "Bobby, your father is a man named William Singleton. He passed away a few years ago leaving a pretty sizable estate."

"William Singleton of Singleton Enterprises?" Patrice questioned.

"Yes." Vernon nodded. "This will go a lot faster if you hold your questions to the end."

"Okay," Patrice replied and sat back on the sofa.

Vernon smiled, then continued. "Singleton has one son in his marriage, Isaac Singleton."

"The ball player who went to jail for killing a man?" Patrice asked.

Vernon shifted his eyes towards her. "That's right."

Bobby put a hand over Patrice. "Honey, you know, on second thought would you help the agent with the food order. I don't want to risk an upset stomach or anything."

"Of course." Patrice stood, nodding her head. "I'll take care of that for you, sweetheart." She kissed his cheek and ran out of the room as if on a mission.

"That will keep her busy," Bobby said to Vernon. "I pray the agent won't kill her."

Vernon smiled. He liked Bobby Kennedy. "She'll be fine." He sat forward with his arms braced on his knees. "Isaac Singleton, your half-brother is a dangerous man. He believes his father's estate should all go to him. The problem is two-fold. William's will has an amendment that gives half of the estate to a long, lost grandchild. That grandchild is me." There was no reaction from Bobby so he continued. "Williams' wife Estelle was made trustee over his estate. I believe she had issues with the way her son was living his life. I was not her confidant, so please know all of this is conjecture. In an effort to leave her husband's legacy in reputable hands, she sought out your mother. In her will, Estelle divided the entire estate, hers and her husbands into thirds. One to their son Isaac, a third to the unknown grandchild, me, and the last third to you."

Bobby sat back and crossed his arms over his chest, but did not say anything. He continued to listen. "We believe Isaac got his hands on the mother's will and destroyed it. So at this time, the father's will is the only one probated with the court. Your mother asked Cannon to investigate the Singleton family to ensure the will she received from Estelle was legit before sharing the information with you. Unfortunately, your mother died in the fire and her copy of the will was destroyed also. Because he did not want to interfere in your life, Cannon continued what your mother requested with the help of your sister Ericka." Vernon stopped. "Any questions so far?"

"Did Singleton kill my mother over this will?"

The question coming from Bobby surprised, but pleased Vernon. The man was not stupid. "That possibility exists. Since his mother and your mother died within days of each other, we believe the two deaths are related, but there is no proof."

"It's a hell of a coincidence don't you think? The two people with the last will dying that close together."

"I do." Vernon gave him a slight nod. "And I don't believe in coincidences."

"Neither do I," Bobby stated. "So why try to kill me? I have no knowledge of a will leaving anything to me."

"I think I'm at fault on that one. You see, I have this nasty habit of fighting back when attacked. See, William put a stipulation in his will. The firm had to locate the unknown grandchild and determine if said child was an upstanding citizen. If the child was, then Isaac would have to share the estate."

"And he doesn't want to share?" Bobby grinned.

"Right, so he set out to ruin my family's reputation in different ways."

"I've read about the trial with Nicole and Trish. Patrice is friends with both of them. I cheered for Nicole."

Vernon smiled. "Thank you. Trish made it an easy fight."

"She's a piece of work." Bobby grinned.

"Yesterday, I decided not to continue to play the game with Isaac. I filed an injunction to hold everything in abeyance until the court can determine the rightful heirs. I requested a full accounting, limiting his access to the family home and the headquarters building here in Virginia. I'm certain he is going to retaliate, so we put security on all the parties involved. Hence, the reason Agent Morgan was at your side today."

Bobby sighed, stood and walked over to the window in Vernon's office.

"It's a lot to take in," Vernon stated as he watched the man filter through all he had said.

Bobby turned to him in his black tee shirt that showed off the muscled arms of a man who worked for a living. "Vernon, I have a decent life. It's not your life, but I'm okay with it. I'm not sure I want or need Singleton's money."

"I thought that would be your reaction." Vernon walked over to stand next to Bobby. "I want you to ask yourself a question. "Why do you think, William nor Estelle wanted to leave the full estate to Isaac?"

"He doesn't seem like a very nice person."

"He's not," Vernon stated. "I believe the reason Estelle sought your mother out was to protect her husband's legacy. I think she wanted to put Singleton Enterprises in better hands, or at the very least someone who would hold Isaac accountable. I am certain she took the exact same steps I did and had you checked out thoroughly. She knew what kind of person you were before she approached your mother. What Isaac has done and is doing, is out of greed. What do you think the thousand employees at Singleton Enterprises will be in for under Isaac?"

"You really believe Isaac was in that car that tried to run me down?"

"I do." Vernon looked him directly in the eyes. "And I believe he will try again."

"Even though I want no parts of this?"

Vernon nodded. "I understand, I'm in the same position. I don't need and frankly don't have the time to run a company."

"Well, you can always put your management team in charge to run the company. You would need to ensure accountability is in place." Vernon watched as Bobby set things in motion in his mind. "But a monthly, or if the team is good, quarterly meetings would be sufficient to handle that." Bobby said all in a *'that's simple'* type tone.

"You already have it halfway figured out. I haven't had time to even consider all that would be entailed."

Bobby tilted his head. "You said there's over a thousand employees?"

That was Vernon's cue. He walked over to his computer and pulled up the information he was studying on Singleton Enterprises. "Here, take a look." He stepped back so Bobby could take his chair behind the desk. "I'm going to check on the food while you look that over."

Bobby nodded his head as he started scanning the report.

***

Isaac arrived at Constance's home in a bit of a huff. If any questions were asked, he would simply say he was here with her.

"Isaac," Constance kissed him the moment she opened the door. "I'm glad you came."

"I told you I would be here." He passed her.

She closed the door and followed him into the living room. "What's wrong?"

"What's wrong?" he yelled. "Your husband has blocked me from my business and my home. That's what's wrong."

"Vernon, why would he do that?"

Isaac gave her an incredulous look. "I'm with you Constance." He rubbed his hand over his greying hair. "He's punishing me because I'm in love with you." He sat as if he was frustrated.

She sat down next to him and hugged him. "I don't understand why he would, Vernon hasn't cared about me one way or another in years."

"He doesn't want you, but he doesn't want anyone else to have you. Can't you see that?"

He stood and walked over to stand by the fireplace. "He took B7Beats right from under my nose."

Constance jumped up nervously. "What do you mean he took it?"

"He got Pendleton to buy up all the shares in B7. I don't have the controlling interest in it anymore."

"What does that mean for Taylor's contract?"

Isaac gawked at her. "Is that all you can think about is Taylor's contract? This is my life your husband is messing with."

"I didn't mean it that way Isaac. I'm sorry he's doing this to you. If there was anything I could do to help, I would."

"Can you make him suffer like he's doing me?"

"I doubt it. I don't have the means to make Vernon hurt."

"Of course you do." Isaac shrugged his shoulders "Delay the divorce. Make him wait. That will ruffle his feathers a bit."

Constance walked over to the bar. She poured two drinks and gave one to him. She took a swallow. "The papers came in the mail today. He's supposed to drop by and pick them up."

"Don't sign them." Isaac took a sip of his drink. "Make him sign all rights to my company back over to me before you sign the papers."

"I can't do that." Constance smirked as she waved him off. "Vernon would cut me off without a dime and I will have nothing."

"Oh." Isaac sat his glass down. "This is about you. I thought it was about us."

"It is about us," Constance stammered. "But I don't know why you think I can get Vernon to do anything." Constance huffed. "The man hates me."

"So you are just going to let him walk all over you. Bring a new woman into your daughter's life and cast you aside like a piece of trash. I thought you were made of better stock than that Constance. The least you can do is make the man sweat. You've been eating the Brooks' shit long enough."

"You're right Isaac." She huffed. "Why should he have everything his way? I've lived through that crap with him way too long. I'll sign them when I'm ready. This is one time he is going to have to wait on me. She huffed as she took a seat on the sofa.

He picked up his drink and sat on the sofa beside her. "Where's Taylor?"

"I told you, she's in New York."

"She shouldn't be around ball players Constance." He chuckled. "Loose, women, drugs and alcohol. That's the kind of scene you want for your daughter?"

"You know I don't, but what can I do about it?"

Isaac put his arms around her and pulled her close. "I thought I read somewhere that the Whitfield kid had a girlfriend. Somebody from his hometown."

Constance sat up. "Taylor didn't mention anything about another girl."

"Maybe she doesn't know." Isaac shrugged, "Hey I lived the life. I had a different woman in every state there was a stadium."

"You think I should tell her?"

"That's your daughter. I don't want to interfere." He paused. "Sometimes a mother has to take certain situations under control to protect their children."

"What do you know about this girl?"

"I have no idea." He looked sideways at her. "I'm sure there is information on the Internet about her." Seeing she was thinking about it. He smiled and took another drink. "Hey I did not come here to discuss Taylor or that ex-husband of yours." He took her hands and pulled her off the sofa and into his arms. "I came so my lady could ease away the burdens of my day." He kissed her thinking, how to plant the information Cannon sent to his cell.

***

Vernon, Genesis and the police officers were standing near Geraldine's desk when Ericka, Nick and Cannon arrived. Patrice had stepped inside to feed Bobby, her words, and Genesis could not have been happier. Not only did the woman talk non-stop, she jumped from one topic to the next and expected people to keep up.

"Where's Bobby?" Ericka ran in, Nick at her side.

"He's in the office having dinner and looking over the Singleton report," Vernon replied.

"He wasn't hurt in the accident?" Vernon looked up at Nick. "Accident." He looked back at Ericka. "No, he wasn't hurt." The woman's face transformed from beautiful to exquisite when she smiled, Vernon noted.

"Did you tell him?"

"I did" — Vernon nodded, — "and he it took it all surprisingly well."

Ericka smiled. "Thank you, Vernon." She looked up at Nick. "Come on, I want you to meet my baby brother."

"Yes, Nick...by all means go meet the 'baby' brother." Vernon smirked. Nick narrowed his eyes wondering what that was about. Vernon glanced at Cannon. "Aren't you going in?"

"Yeah." He tilted his head. "Let me get a minute." They stepped to the side. "I got a call from Singleton asking for information on Jason Whitfield."

"Why?" Vernon frowned.

"Not sure, but I figure it might have something to do with your daughter."

"What did you send him?"

"Basic stuff off the internet."

Vernon nodded. "So he is still in the dark on you working with us."

"We want to keep it that way as long as we can." Cannon nodded.

"You go ahead in, I'll be there in a minute." Vernon pulled out his cell.

"Everything okay," Genesis asked.

"Checking in with Naverone." He held Genesis' eyes. "I told her about you and me in college."

"I know." Genesis exhaled.

"Everything okay with you two?" he asked.

"It will be."

"Hey." Vernon took a step away to speak into the phone. "Everything okay on that end?"

"Yes and no. Your wife just called insisting that Taylor comes home tonight. Claiming Jason has another girlfriend at home."

"Does he?" Vernon asked.

"Not according to his bodyman. There was the girlfriend from high school that's been trying to hang on, but he said Jason's been avoiding her since before Taylor."

"How is Taylor taking all of this?"

"She's pissed at her mother, but not blind enough not to be aware."

Vernon smiled. "Smart girl."

"She takes it from her dad." Naverone hesitated. "How are things on that end?"

"Progressing faster than we anticipated."

"Everything okay with Genesis."

"Yes, hold on, she's right here." He gave the phone to Genesis before either of them could protest. He had much respect for Genesis and was certain he was in love with Naverone. He was not going to be a point of dissension for them.

"Hey Boss. Close call." Genesis talked as Vernon walked back in the office.

"I think we have a starting point on Estelle's will," Cannon said as Vernon walked in.

"Bobby thinks that Mrs. Crabtree, our next door neighbor might help with information on our mom," Ericka explained.

"We talked about this before, but everything was happening so fast I did not have a chance to follow up," Cannon stated.

"If my mother shared anything with anyone it would have been Mrs. Crabtree," Bobby stated as Patrice held on to every word. "Anything that went on in the neighborhood, Mrs. Crabtree saw or was told about.

"I know the old bat told on me enough times," Ericka huffed.

"You were a problem child?" Nick raised an eyebrow.

"Bobby said she was the worst," Patrice laughed.

"You were," Bobby grinned at Ericka. "Not always, but that last year in high school you wore Mom out sneaking out that back window."

"Ahh, fun times at Ridgemount High," they laughed.

Patrice laughed. "You remember those days in ballet class, don't you Nick?"

Cannon and Bobby looked up at Nick as Vernon shook his head and coughed.

"I took ballet for coordination, thank you very much."

"Oh he was good at it too. All the girls wanted to dance with Nicolas."

"Is that so?" Ericka glanced at Nick with a smile.

"Don't sweat it man. I took wrestling to learn how to take those tight ends down better. We do what we must to improve our craft." Nick and Bobby bumped fists.

"That's right." Nick nodded in agreement. "Man, why don't you come stay with Ericka and me until this Singleton thing is over?"

"I have a home and a business here."

"And I'm here," Patrice added.

"Patrice can come to.... Right, Nick?" Ericka looked up to see a funny look come over Nick's face. Then she looked at Genesis who had just walked through the door and heard the invitation. And last at Vernon who was vigorously shaking his head no.

"I'm going to stay at Bobby's place tonight," Cannon offered, seeing the relieved look on Nick's face, he added, "That way I can go to see Mrs. Crabtree tomorrow."

"I'll go with you," Bobby offered.

"No," Vernon stated. "We need you to lay low for a day or two until we can get a good read on Singleton.

"I'll stay tonight, and I'll go with Cannon," Ericka offered. "You have a meeting in New York with Jason, tomorrow, right Nick."

"I do," Nick acknowledged.

"Good, then I'll stay with Bobby and Cannon. You go to New York and we'll meet up back at your house tomorrow night."

"Sounds like a plan," Nick replied as Ericka, Cannon and Bobby made plans for the night.

"Dodged a bullet with Patrice there, did we," Vernon whispered.

"Not funny," Nick replied. "How did the meeting with Crane go?"

"She talked, but everything is circumstantial. All these little pieces, but nothing solid to bring him down. It's as if he knows just how far to take things before they become more serious."

"You ever think about looking into that original murder case?"

Vernon nodded. "I had Geraldine contact the prosecutor in New York who handled the case. I need to interview him."

"I'll be there tomorrow. Give me the information and I'll check him out."

"Cool." Vernon retrieved the phone from Genesis. "Everything good?"

She nodded. "As long as you keep that woman away from me." She pointed to Patrice.

Vernon glanced at Nick. "Genesis thinks Patrice talks too much. She wants to shoot her."

"I can't imagine why." The two brothers looked at each other and laughed.

Chapter 16

Nick was in the hotel suite of Jason Whitfield by ten the next morning. It was not close to noon and they had just finished reviewing the endorsement deal when they heard a commotion outside the door. There was a woman's voice yelling with a lot of bumping against the door.

"Jason you better let me in there," the voice yelled out. "Or I'm going to bust this door down."

"Oh hell," Jason closed his eyes and let his head fall into his hands. "Why can't that girl just leave me alone?"

Nick raised an eyebrow. "Who is she?"

"Keisha, man. My girl from high school. I'm tired man, I'm just tired of going through the same old crap with her."

"What crap is that?" Nick asked in a much calmer voice then he felt inside.

There was now kicking at the door.

"Man," a frustrated Jason whined. "She keeps showing up doing stuff like this."

"When was the last time you talked to her?"

"Last week. I told her about fifty times this year that things were over. She just won't let go."

"Do you want me to handle it?"

Jason hesitated. "I don't want her to go to jail or anything, man I just want her to stop chasing me down and acting out like this." He looked at Nick as if he just remembered who he was talking to. He put his hands up to the ceiling. 'Man I swear I haven't been with her since way before Taylor. This is my hand to God I have not. And I don't play with him."

"Right now I'm your agent. We'll deal with Uncle Nick later. Do you want me to handle this?" Nick stood. "You need to know, once I handle this there is no going back. So do you want this girl out of your life?"

"Yes," Jason replied without any signs of hesitation.

"Okay." Nick sent a text, then hung up. "Let her in."

Jason glared at him. Nick motioned towards the door. Jason stood, huffed, then walked over and opened the door.

Keisha Jackson was dressed in a midriff top, short skirt and short-heeled boots. There was probably a pretty young lady under the massive hair and makeup. Nick thought as he watched the hurricane burst through the room.

"Why you let him hold me outside that door like dat...you got some stank bitch up in here?" She pushed him in the chest, then whirled past them, checking every room including the bathroom, the closets and under the bed. She came back out with her hands on her hips. "Who the hell are you?"

"Your worst nightmare," Nick replied as he stood with his hands in his pockets and a slight smile on his face.

Keisha's eyes narrowed as she turned on Nick with the sister-girl neck action. "Excuse you."

"Let's have a seat Ms. Jackson. Let's talk."

She walked towards Jason, but Nick blocked her way. Jason put his hands up and backed away.

She raised an eyebrow. "Jason, you tell him who he's dealing with."

"I think you...need to understand who you are now dealing with." Nick motioned to the bodyman. "Take Jason out for a walk."

"Jason ain't going nowhere until we talk," Keisha announce with pouted lips, neck action and finger pointing.

Nick turned and gave Jason a look. Jason walked away.

"Jason," she moved towards him. His bodyman blocked her way and pushed Jason out the door. Two women entered as they exited.

Nick waited until Keisha turned to him. "Who the hell are you?"

"My name is Nicolas Brooks." He took a piece of paper handed to him by one of the women from the New York office. "I am Jason's new Agent."

"Where's the Ty guy?"

"He's working on other things. I'm now the person you have to deal with." He looked down at the paper and nodded to the woman who handed it to him. She pushed the recording device on her phone.

"This is a restraining order against you on Jason Whitfield's behalf. It states that you are to stay one hundred feet away from Jason Whitfield, his home, or his workplace. As of this time and date all contact, whether it be by telephone, text messages, notes, mail, fax, email or delivery of flowers or gifts are prohibited. If you violate this order you will be arrested and prosecuted to the full extent of the law. Do you understand?

"I understand you have lost your damn mind thinking I'm gonna sign some shit like that." She huffed. "Jason thinks that now he's in the NBA he can just push me aside and lay up with some singing bitch he better think again. I was with him for three years in high school and two in college. He can't just walk away. He wants to get rid of me, he's going to have to pay."

Nick smiled. "What did you have in mind?"

"A million dollars" — she smirked,— "untaxed, cashier's check and another million when that one runs out."

Nick reached out. The woman gave him a pen. He placed it on the table next to the document. "Sign the document."

Keisha narrowed her eyes as they darted from the women to Nick. "Who are they?"

Before Nick could answer, the door opened. "Hey, I got your message and brought some real New York style pizza for your trip." Taylor turned with her hands filled with two pizza boxes. Naverone stood behind her holding the door. Both had surprised looks on their faces.

"Is this you?" Keisha had run across the room yelling, shoving a cell phone in Taylor's face.

"What?" Taylor stepped back.

"I said is this you all up in my man's face?" Keisha spat out.

Naverone quickly pushed Taylor behind her and confronted the woman. "Step back, please."

"Get the hell out of my way. Is you the reason Jason is doing this shit?"

"Doing what?" a stunned Taylor asked. "I don't even know who you are?"

"I'm Jason's girlfriend." She jumped, swinging at Taylor, but Naverone blocked her. "That's who I am. Who the hell are you?"

Jason and his bodyman were just returning when the commotion broke out. Jason jumped in pulling Taylor back out the door. Naverone turned to follow them.

"Jason, come back here." She jumped at the door. Jason's bodyman blocked her way and closed the door. "Get out of my way." Tears were now flowing down Keisha's face. "Just get out of my way," she choked out. "Get out of my way," she cried harder.

"Ms. Jackson," Nick spoke in a calm voice.

"Leave me alone," Keisha cried, covering her face with her hands.

It was clear to Nick, the young woman with all her big bark was hurt. However, it was her actions that brought the situation to this boiling point. "Ms. Jackson, let's complete this transaction so you can leave this place and move on."

"Give me my money and I'm out of here," she yelled out.

"I'm afraid that is not going to happen."

She turned and rolled her eyes up at him. "What the hell you mean that's not going to happen?"

Suddenly, the girl from the Exorcist appeared. "You asked earlier who these women were. Well, one is an associate of mine. The other is a New York City detective. They just heard your attempt to extort a million dollars from Mr. Whitfield. You now have a decision to make. You can sign the document or the detective can arrest you and charge you accordingly. He held the pen out. "What shall it be?"

An hour later, Keisha was gone. Escorted by the detective. Keisha had a ten thousand dollar check in her hand for her trouble and Nick had his signed restraining order and a very unhappy Jason was trying to explain Keisha Jackson to Taylor.

"I swear Taylor, I did not ask her to come here. I have no idea how she knew what hotel I was in. I swear Taylor. I didn't know."

"Jason, if she was here why, why did you send me the text to come over?"

"I didn't. I was meeting with Nick. I had no idea what time we were going to wrap." He pulled out his phone. "I swear look at my phone."

Naverone was getting tired of the discussion so she took the phone and checked the messages between him and Taylor. She held the phone up to Jason and pointed to a message. "Inappropriate." She then turned to Taylor. "The message didn't come from him."

"Of course it did," Taylor pulled out her cell and pulled up the message. She showed it to Naverone.

Naverone took the phone and read the message. It was in normal language, not today's text language. "You are going to have to apologize to him," she said to Taylor. "The message didn't come from him."

Naverone glanced up at Nick who had opted to stay out of the argument unless it was absolutely necessary for him to intercede. So far Jason had been holding his own. Taylor was giving him no slack and Nick was proud of her, too. "Someone is playing games with the kids." She pulled out her cell. "Hey can we trace a communication like a text?"

Genesis was on the other end of the call. "Give me the number." Naverone did. "Give me ten minutes."

"Thanks." Naverone turned and looked at the couple. Neither was happy. She hit Nick on the shoulder. "Do something."

Nick looked up at her from the chair. He stretched his neck and stood. "Taylor, let's take a walk."

Jason threw up his hands. Nick put his hand up indicating to just chill as he and Taylor walked out the door. Naverone felt bad for the kid. This time he really was innocent.

"She will be okay," Naverone said. "Taylor is not a Keisha Jackson. You can't play her like you do others, not if you want to keep her."

"She's not like the others. That's why I like her," Jason replied. The phone in the room sounded. He pushed the speaker button.

"Team loading up in twenty."

Jason huffed. "Awe man. I'll never get this straight."

Naverone's cell rang. She answered and listened. "Thanks for the info. Check to see what other messages were sent from that number in the last twenty-four." She frowned like she could hit something.

Jason looked at her. "Whatever it is, I didn't do it." He walked into the bedroom.

Nick and Taylor walked back through the door. Naverone looked at them. "The text came from your mother."

"My mother?" Taylor frowned. "Why would my mother send me a text from Jason?"

"Oh, I don't know." Nick smirked. "To cause trouble between you two. I'm just thinking out loud."

Naverone smiled at Taylor. "He's pulling out in twenty minutes."

Taylor sighed, then turned and walked in the bedroom.

Nick picked up the paperwork he was working on. "Constance is going to end up pushing that girl away."

"I'm not touching that one." Naverone walked over to the door and waited.

Nick looked at her and laughed. "If it's any consolation, I haven't seen my brother this happy in years. Whatever you are doing, please don't stop."

The kids walked out hand in hand and smiles on their faces. That, in turn made

Naverone smile and Nick frown. They walked Jason to his bus, waved at a few of the other players and like that, the bus was rolling.

"You flying back to Virginia with me?" Naverone asked Nick.

"No, I have another meeting in Manhattan. I'm catching a commercial flight later."

"I'm flying back with you," Taylor announced. "It's time I had a talk with my mother."

***

The prosecutor on the Terrell Bell case was more than willing to discuss Isaac Singleton. After telling Nick about the fact that he believed Singleton lured Bell to the club for the sole purpose of killing him, he shared a few other tidbits that intrigued Nick.

"I'm always fascinated by the calls I get on Singleton," Dominique Drummond stated from behind his desk at his new practice. "He's a slippery son of a bitch who still has not faced justice." He's the reason I left the prosecutor's office. I figured if we were going to let murderers go I might as well get paid for it."

"I can understand that." Nick nodded and smiled with the man. "You received other calls about Singleton?"

Drummond nodded. "Sure did." He walked over to a file cabinet, then came back with a folder. He opened it. "From a detective in Fredericksburg, Virginia. Said he wanted to do a background investigation on Singleton. They were looking at the accidental death of his mother." Drummond said, "Imagine that, being a suspect in your own mother's death. Don't that beat all?"

"Yes, imagine that," Nick said as facts started swimming around in his head. "Would you happen to have any notes from that time?"

Drummond looked at Nick. "Are you going to go after that son-of-a-bitch?"

"That's my plan."

He took the entire file and slid it over to him. "Bring him to justice."

Nick took the file. "I'll keep you in the loop."

Nick walked out of the office and hailed a cab. He immediately started skimming the file. By the time he reached the airport, he knew with the information they had on Felicia Kennedy and the information in his hands they could bring the situation with Isaac to an end. He smiled knowing he and Ericka were on the verge of having the life they wanted.

***

Vernon had just finished a call from Naverone telling him what occurred with Taylor. He wasn't sure if he was more pissed with Jason or Constance. False, he knew exactly who he was more pissed at. He picked up his phone and dialed the number.

"Are the papers signed?"

"No," Constance replied

"Why?"

"I haven't felt like signing them."

That reply pissed Vernon off. He sat up at his desk. "Constance, listen to me very carefully. If you ever do anything to my daughter to cause her a single tear, you will pay for it with your life. You have until midnight to sign the papers." He disconnected the call.

Chapter 17

Cannon and Ericka stood at the door as they waited for Mrs. Crabtree to answer.

"You better be right about this. This old bat never liked me and believe me the feeling was mutual."

"Yes," an elderly lady dressed in an old housecoat and slippers answered the door.

"Mrs. Crabtree, you may not remember me, but I used to live next door. I'm Ericka, Felicia's daughter."

"I remember you. You're that fast-tail gal who used to climb out the window at night. What you doing here?"

"Mrs. Crabtree." Cannon stepped in front of Ericka sensing a few choice words were about to explode out of her mouth. "I'm Felicia's nephew, Cannon McNally."

"I know who you are, too. I have seen you come over from time to time before Felicia died."

"Yes, ma'am. May we come in?"

Mrs. Crabtree looked the two over, then turned leaving the door open. "I guess it can't hurt nothing."

They followed her inside. Ericka glanced around the modest home before taking a seat on the sofa. Cannon sat next to her as Mrs. Crabtree sat in the chair in front of the television. She turned down her television show, then stared at Ericka.

"You straightened up your life yet?"

Ericka bit the inside of her lip to keep from cursing the old bat out. Bigger picture, as Cannon kept saying, the bigger picture. "Yes, ma'am. I'm working on it."

"You should be more like your brother." Mrs. Crabtree huffed. "That boy made sure his mother was okay, every day. He came by, like clockwork, just to say hello and eat dinner with her from time to time. You," she snarled, left her and never as much as gave your mother a call."

"So how are your children? Do you see them often?" Ericka asked knowing they had moved miles away.

"They are doing fine, missy."

"Mrs. Crabtree," Cannon interrupted before things went down the wrong side of the road. "We are trying to get some information regarding the fire at my aunt's house. Were you home that night?"

"Of course I was home. I was the one to call the fire department."

"You saw the smoke coming from my mother's house?"

Mrs. Crabtree started to answer, then paused. "Not exactly."

"Why did you call the fire department?" Cannon asked.

"It was a few years ago. Let me get my thoughts together. Oh yes, I called the police first. See it was late and I had fallen asleep in my chair looking at the television. The sound of the window woke me up."

"What window?" Ericka asked.

"You know what window. The one you always climbed out of at night." She frowned. "That noise would wake me from a sound sleep every time you snuck out."

"You heard the window go up?"

"That's what I said, isn't it."

"You heard it go up the night of the fire?" Cannon asked.

"That's what woke me up. My first thought was you. I couldn't imagine why you would be coming out of the house through that window, so I called the police."

Ericka and Cannon shared a quick glance. "What did the police say when they came?" Cannon questioned.

"They didn't come. It's not like the old days when they cared about people around here. Times have changed you know. The police don't come like they used to."

"Did you see anything when you went to the window?" Ericka asked, knowing the nosy woman looked out."

"No." Mrs. Crabtree was melancholy for a moment. "My eyesight isn't what it used to be and it was dark. I wish I had stayed at that window. But I...turned the television off and crawled into bed. It was an hour or so later I could smell the smoke coming through my window. That's when I called the fire department."

"Did you tell the police about the window?"

"They didn't ask me," Mrs. Crabtree replied.

"That never stopped you from telling on me."

Mrs. Crabtree cut her eyes on Ericka. "Your mother asked me to watch that window. She knew what kind of gal you were."

"Mrs. Crabtree," Cannon interrupted again. "Did Aunt Felicia say anything to you about any trouble she was having, or someone causing her problems during that time?"

"No. Felicia was a good woman. She didn't have any problems with anyone. Other than Bobby, her card games and church activities, she mostly stayed to herself."

Cannon started to rise, but Ericka put her hand on his knee. "Mrs. Crabtree, my mother didn't talk to a lot of people. But she did with you. I remember seeing you two taking in the backyard over the fence many days, especially during the summer." She sat forward. "If anything was going on with her, you are the only person I could think of she would have told. Is there anything about my mother during that time that was unusual, or out of the norm for her?"

Mrs. Crabtree's eyes narrowed. "You're talking about the will?"

Cannon and Ericka both asked. "What will?"

"The one the Singleton woman gave her?"

The jolt hit both of them. Cannon pushed forward as his pulse quickened. "Estelle Singleton?"

"The one and the same. Do you know she died a few days after Felecia? It's a shame." Mrs. Crabtree said as she shook her head.

"What is?" Ericka asked.

Mrs. Crabtree looked incredulous. "The situation with Bobby."

"Situation?" Cannon raised an eyebrow.

"Yes." Mrs. Crabtree nodded. "A few more days and Bobby would have had what was due to him."

"How so?" Cannon sat forward.

"Well, the will," Mrs. Crabtree exclaimed. "The will would have been signed and taken to the court. You see. The son promised he would make sure Bobby had what was coming to him."

"What son?" Ericka asked.

"The Singleton's son," Mrs. Crabtree replied as she stood. "Girl if you had called your mother once in a while you would known this stuff." She walked out of the room leaving Ericka and Cannon wondering. She returned with an envelope and handed it to Cannon as she sat back down. "Felecia gave me a copy of that to keep in my safe. See, mine is fire and waterproof." She nodded, proudly.

Cannon opened the envelope and pulled the document out. It was a copy of the will his Aunt Felecia showed him. He wanted to shout. Instead he gave the document to Ericka. While she read, Mrs. Crabtree continued to talk.

"It's a shame the boy didn't get a chance to change the will. See that one right there only gave Bobby one third of the estate. The boy was going to change it so Bobby gets one half of the estate. But, then Felecia died and old lady Singleton died a few days later."

Cannon frowned. "Do you know who the boy was?"

"Why yes. It was that basketball player that got in trouble a few years back. Seen him at Felecia's with my own eyes. Good looking young man." Mrs. Crabtree nodded as she smiled. "Felecia came right over when he left her house to tell me what he was going to do for Bobby. Yes, she was right happy." Her smile faded. "Then the house caught on fire and well, that was that."

"May I have a copy of this?" Cannon asked.

"Hell, you can keep it. One less piece of paper I have to store."

"Mrs. Crabtree." Seething, Ericka was doing all she could to keep her temper in check as the implications behind the story she just heard began to take root. "Did you ever think to tell Bobby, or me or the police about any of this? It's been two years."

Mrs. Crabtree rolled her eyes at Ericka. "Nobody asked. Besides, I just told you."

Cannon had barely gotten Ericka outside the door before she exploded.

"That bastard killed my mother." She almost doubled over in pain. She clutched her stomach. "He killed her. Oh my God, he killed her."

Cannon was doing all he could to keep her upright. He gave in, picked her up and put her in the car.

"I need you to listen." He glanced over at a distraught Ericka as he pulled off. "We don't have any proof that he killed Aunt Felecia. Mrs. Crabtree did give us something to go on. Do you think it's a coincidence that Isaac's mother died within the same week as Aunt Felecia?" He looked out of the driver's window, then back to the front. "Is it possible that Isaac killed Aunt Felecia, and his mother?"

"Of course he did," Ericka cried out. "He did it to hide the will. You know it and I know it, too. He took my mother's life for the damn money." She angrily wiped the tears from her cheek. "I'm going to make sure Bobby gets his and then I'm going to kill Singleton."

***

The moment she walked into the house, Ericka knew what she had to do. Cannon was right. They had no proof that Singleton killed her mother. If it was proof they needed, that's what she was going to get. She pulled out her cell phone and dialed a number.

"Mr. Singleton please."

"I'm sorry, Mr. Singleton is not in the office today. May I help you with something?"

"Yes, I have a report that was due to him, like yesterday. Could you tell me where I can find him?"

"Certainly. He is at the Fredericksburg location all week."

Ericka smiled. "Thank you." Back in the day when she was allowing men to call the shots, Ericka had one lover that wasn't necessarily on the right side of the law. He taught her a few things about firearms. One was if you ever want to make someone talk, put a gun in their face. Don't go with the single action, too much work. Get a fully automatic or a semi. It lets people know you didn't come to play. You plan to take them down. She walked over to Nick's nightstand, opened the bottom drawer and picked up his SIG. There were a few things she loved about her mild-mannered Nick. He had a kick-ass attitude whenever you pissed him off. His weapon of choice was another example. She checked the mag to make sure it was fully loaded. Nodding her head, she walked out of the room, through the hallway, grabbed her purse and dropped the pistol inside. As she started the car she cleared her mind of murdering Isaac Singleton. For she knew the first thing prosecutors would look for was intent.

"What was your intent when you took the fully loaded weapon to Mr. Singleton's place of employment?"

"My intent was to scare Mr. Singleton into telling me the truth about my mother's death, then call the police."

"Why was the weapon loaded if you only wanted to frighten him?"

"I've never handled a weapon before. I had no idea it was loaded."

On the drive over, Ericka played the conversation over and over again in her mind until she knew exactly how to handle the situation.

"Good evening, I'm Ericka Kennedy. I have a report due to Mr. Singleton. Is he in the office?" Ericka smiled as she spoke with the receptionist. "The man hates late reports and I'm six hours overdue."

The receptionist nodded her head in understanding. "You don't have to tell me. It's the reason I'm out here at the receptionist desk."

"Late reporting to him?" Ericka chatted.

"Yep. Let me see if I can locate him for you." The receptionist dialed a number and asked a series of questions. "He's in the conference room on the third floor. Good luck."

Ericka shrugged. "I may be replacing you at that desk."

"I don't wish this on anyone." The receptionist spoke to herself for Ericka had walked away, and was on the elevator moving upwards to the third floor. Her cell phone chimed. She didn't have to look. It was a text from Nick. If she spoke to him, she would have to tell him what was happening in her mind. He would talk her down and she didn't want that. There were a lot of things she'd done in her life that weren't right. Most of them were for selfish reasons. This time it was about justice for her mother. Isaac Singleton could kill his mother, but he had no right to kill hers. She would have to ask for Nick's forgiveness for yet another infraction to his trust.

The elevator chimed. Ericka stepped out into an open area with cubicles and offices around the wall. Most of the employees were gone for the day it seemed, but there were still a few.

"Excuse me. Could you tell me where the conference room is located?" she asked a young man.

He pointed. "Down the hall to your right."

"Thank you," Ericka smiled, then followed the directions.

When she reached the room, the door was open. There was a long conference table that seated about twenty-four. Glass floor to ceiling windows made up the outside wall. The opposite wall was lined with pictures. On the wall near the door she walked through was a television monitor, and a podium in front with a microphone on a small stage. At the far end of the room, with a painting of William Singleton on the wall behind him, sat Isaac Singleton with his head down reading and a pen in his hand.

Ericka realized he did not hear her come in. She would change that. She reached behind her and closed the door.

"Mr. Singleton." The voice was not calm. Deadly calm as she placed her purse on the podium and leaned across it. "There comes a time in every person's life when they have to atone for their sins. Would you agree?"

Isaac looked up. It took a minute for recognition to hit. Then he sat back wondering why in the hell she was in his building.

He shrugged his shoulder. "You would know better than me. You're the whore. How many destroyed marriages do you have to atone for?"

Ericka laughed as she reached inside of her purse, hit the record on her phone, then pulled the gun out and released the safety. "Now...is not the time to insult me Mr. Singleton." She stepped from behind the podium and pulled out a chair at the table. She sat on the end of the table and put her feet in the chair. Isaac started to stand. Ericka pointed the gun at him. "Math quiz. There are thirty-two rounds in a semi-automatic." She tilted her head. "How many do you think I can pop off on your ass before you reach the door?" She smirked at him.

Isaac narrowed his eyes. He knew guns. Learned a lot about them when he was on trial for killing the son of a bitch who stepped on his shoes in the club. She was holding a semi-automatic SIG. If the mag was full and he pissed her off to the point that she squeezed that trigger he would be a dead man. "What is it that you want? Did Cannon cheat you out of your money? What?"

"Have a seat." She swung the gun towards the chair behind him. "We're going to have a conversation." Isaac started to put his hands in his pockets. "Keep your hands where I can see them. I'm a little shaky right now. My finger might twitch in a moment. Now that wouldn't be good for you." Isaac sat down and placed his hands palm down on the table. "Thank you." Erica smiled as she glanced at her watch. "I figure we have a good ten minutes before anyone comes in here so let me tell you what I need." She sat in the chair and placed the gun on the table. "You killed a woman name Felecia Kennedy. I want you to tell me how and why?"

"I have no idea what you are talking about," Isaac lied without hesitation.

Ericka sighed. She picked up the gun, checked the mag then replaced it and walked to where Isaac was sitting. She shoved the weapon at Isaac's balls causing his chair to roll backwards until it hit the wall. "Let's try that again."

"All right!" Isaac squealed as he cuffed his hands to the fire now between his legs. "Who in the hell are you?"

"I'm the whore you hired to steal from Nicolas Brooks. Don't you remember?" She sat back against the table with both hands holding the gun, which was now pointed at Isaac's head. "Why?"

"All right." Isaac held one hand up blocking his face and the other was still clutching his balls. "She had an affair with my father."

"I don't have time for the fillers. Get to the point. Why did you kill Felicia Kennedy?"

Isaac's mind was clearing after the shock from her blow to his balls. He shook his head and began snickering. "When you hold a gun on someone you better be ready to use it. I don't think you have the nerve."

"You want to try me?"

"Who the hell are you? Why do you care about Felecia Kennedy?"

"I care about her son. You know him. His name is Bobby Singleton Kennedy. Everyone calls him Bobby Singleton because his mother always called him that. So it stuck."

Isaac glared at her when she mentioned the Singleton boy. She knows about the will. How could she? He destroyed all copies with the mention of the boy. "How do you know the woman? Do they hold history lessons on gold diggers? Was she a case study?"

Ericka learned to mask her feelings a long time ago. To date the only person able to cut through was Nick. But damn if Isaac wasn't pushing some buttons.

"Our time is running out. I'm going to ask you one more time," She waved the gun up and down as she spoke. "Why did you kill Felecia Kennedy?"

There was a sound outside the door that caused Ericka to take her eyes from Isaac for a split second. That was all he needed. He grabbed her hands pushing them and the gun upwards as he pushed her backwards on the table and grabbed her throat. He brought the gun down and pointed it to her temple.

With jaws clenched and a tick in his eye, he shoved the gun so hard against her temple it made an indent. "I don't know how you know. But there was no way in hell I was going to let a whore's son have one third of MY inheritance," he snarled. "Now, here's what's going to happen." Ericka struggled beneath him as she pulled at his hand around her throat. He shoved his leg between her thighs and tightened the hold. "You made an advance. I turned you down. You shot yourself." He grinned. "When you want to kill someone you don't talk. You simply pull the trigger.

He pulled the trigger, heard the click but nothing happened. The door opened. Isaac stood, releasing Ericka and putting the gun behind his back.

The janitor looked up. "Mr. Singleton. I'm sorry sir. I thought the room was empty. "I can come back."

"No." Ericka jumped up and quickly walked to the other end of the table. She grabbed her purse. "I guess we'll have to finish this another day, Mr. Singleton." She turned and quickly walked out of the room.

"Mr. Singleton, sir, my apology," the janitor said again.

Isaac put the gun in his waistband behind his back. "It's not an issue," he bit out as he gathered his things and walked out of the room. He walked into his office and picked his cell phone up from the desk. He dialed Cannon's number.

"Cannon who in the hell is the woman you used for Brooks?"

Cannon clinched the phone in his hand. "Nicolas Brooks?"

"Get me all the information you have on her...NOW!"

Cannon ended the call and wanted to throw the phone. He sat back in the chair frustrated. "Ericka, what have you done?"

Chapter 18

The moment Isaac ended the call with Cannon his cell phone rang. "What?"

"Isaac? It's Constance. We need to talk."

Isaac hung his head. He was tired of dealing with bitches. Every one of them was always trying to take something from him, one way or another. First it was the bitches on the rope line. They wanted a piece of him because his tax return said professional basketball player on the occupation line. Then it was his mother always telling him to make something of his life. Then it was the Kennedy woman trying to take his inheritance to give to her son, the woman tonight who was trying to get information from him. And now, Constance. It's time to take the bitches out of their own misery.

"Yeah baby, what's up?"

"Isaac, we need to talk. I have done everything you asked of me. I gave up my husband, and the life I was living for you. I've broken my daughter's heart by setting up some boy I don't even know and now my daughter won't talk to me. I need you Isaac. I need you," she cried into the phone.

"I'll be right there to ease your pain, Constance. I'm going to take all the misery away."

***

Constance couldn't believe what was happening. One minute he was hugging her and in the next Isaac had a gun to her had. "Isaac, I don't understand. You're scaring me?"

"Good," Isaac replied as he kicked the door closed behind him. He pushed the pistol against Constance's forehead and she walked backwards into the house. "Isaac please," she cried out.

"You know, I completely understand why Vernon turned to other women. You are an annoying bitch."

A shocked Constance finally saw the light. "They were right. You used me to get to Vernon." Tears ran down her cheeks. "You never cared about me or my daughter one way or another, did you?"

"Oh I did." Isaac nodded his head. "I cared that you did what I told you to do when I said do it. And you did it. It didn't matter if it was against your husband or your child. You did it. That's what I call a weak-ass woman."

Constance held her head up. "So what are you going to do, Isaac," she snarled. "Shoot me because I fell for all the crap you fed me for almost two years?"

"No, I have one more thing I need you to do."

"What makes you think after this that I would do anything else for you?"

"Because I have a gun to your head and after I shoot you I will find that little bitch you call a daughter and shoot her, too. Now pick up the phone and call your husband."

"For what? You would kill your own son?"

"If he got in my way, you damn right I would. Now dial the number."

Constance sniffed. "No. If you are going to kill me, then do it. I'm not calling Vernon over here."

"Okay," Isaac said as he pulled out his cell phone. He pushed a button. "Taylor, it's Isaac. I know you're angry with me, but I really need your help. Your mother is acting...well a little crazy."

"Don't believe him Taylor," Constance yelled into the telephone.

Isaac hit her across the cheek with the butt of the gun. "See what I mean. Taylor you have to come. I'm afraid she might hurt herself. She has a gun."

"All right, all right, I'll call Vernon. Just let me speak to Taylor."

"Hold on Taylor. Maybe you can talk her down."

"Taylor listen to me," Constance cried as she thought of words to say to her daughter. "I love you Taylor. Nothing in this world is more important to me than you." It was then she heard the beep indicating she had ran out of time. She looked at the phone in her hand and swung at Isaac. "You son of a bitch."

Isaac hit her again. "Yes, I am. Now call your husband. Tell him you are ready to sign the papers. Convince him to come over and get them now before you change your mind."

Constance got up off the floor wiping the blood from her mouth. She picked up her cell phone and dialed Vernon's number. For the first time in a long time she prayed. She prayed that Taylor would find love and happiness. She prayed her parents would one day know how much she loved them and last she prayed Vernon would not pick up the phone.

"Yes, Constance."

Her prayers were not going to be answered tonight. "Vernon, I've signed the papers. Come and pick them up before I burn them. Remember to kiss Taylor for me." She ended the call before Vernon could respond.

"That was sweet, Connie."

"My name is Constance Marie Abernathy-Brooks," she said with a strength she didn't feel. "Since it seems I'm going to die this night. Would you tell me why you did all of this?"

Isaac thought for a moment. "Why not. It's about to come to an end and I've been dying to tell someone about this." He laughed. "My parents would have been proud to know just what a freakin' genius I turned out to be." He bent down in front of her with the gun in his hand as if he was telling a child a story. "See, my parents were disappointed in the way I turned out. They came to the realization that I don't have a caring bone in my body about anything or anyone except myself. Well, they created me. You know what I'm saying. I am a product of my environment. You know that woman you call mother–in-law? Well," he wiped at his nose. "I was in love with her. Yeah it was puppy love, but I loved me some Gwen Spivey, yes I did," he said as if thinking back to that time. "But then she got pregnant, I was seventeen, she was sixteen and my parents." He chuckled. "God rest their souls, said nothing was more important than their son having a life. So you see, it was them who made me believe that nothing in life was more important than me. I was sent off to college, early admission and all. And Gwen, well she ended up married to her best friend, who I always thought, was a pussy. Always talking about saving African Americans from oppression. I wasn't oppressed. My parents had money you see. And when you have money, Black or White, you dance to the beat of your own drum. And I did. Someone step on my shoe and make a mark, I kill them. Got away with it, that's what money can do. I don't have to tell you. That's why you got pregnant on purpose so you could marry into the money, so I know you understand." He held his hands out wide. "Anyway, my father decided to buy penance before he met his maker and put my son, the child he took from me, in his will. To add insult to injury, I found out my father had another son who my mother decided deserved a share in my inheritance, as well. Can you believe they had the gall to expect me to share my inheritance with anyone..." He scratched the back of his head. "You know that was not going to happen, so I went to see the woman my father had the bastard son by. She showed me the hand-written will my mother gave her.

I told her not to do anything with it because I felt her son deserved half of the estate instead of one third as the will indicated. She was greedy and did exactly as I expected, she held out for more money for her son. I went back to her house one night, found the will and burned it and her down. But I knew my mother had a copy of that will. One day I went by there to get it out of the safe. She caught me coming out of the room. We had words and she fell down the grand stairway to her death." He shrugged. "With both wills in my possession the estate was mine...or so I thought. It seemed my father added an amendment to his original will. The law firm was to locate the child he forbid me to have anything to do with. If said child was of moral standing he would get a portion of my inheritance. You can't imagine how pissed I was when they read that little tidbit. I couldn't change or destroy that document so I had to destroy the Brooks. Make Vernon as big of an ass in the eyes of the public as me. I knew how protective he was about family, so I started destroying their reputations, one by one. But those damn Brooks are worse than the damn energizer bunny. They keep going and going and going. Nothing I had my team do would stick. I had a woman embezzle funds from one of Nick Brooks' clients and the public never got wind of it. That damn Whitfield boy did not press charges or go public with the information. I'm sure it was because of that daughter of yours. Then I put a woman out to take down Nicole Brooks, well that didn't work. Used another woman to take down Avery and that didn't stick." He shook his head disgusted.

Constance stared at Isaac as if he were losing his mind. "Like it or not. The Brooks are blessed people. You did all of this just to make them look bad. Do you have any idea how crazy this all is?"

The gunshot sounded and Constance Marie Abernathy-Brooks fell to the floor. Isaac stood over her. "Yes, I do. But I didn't need you to tell me that."

***

Vernon pulled out his cell phone and called Naverone. "Rene, pack a bag. We're going to Vegas."

"Okay, we can go to Vegas. You should know the "what happens in Vegas stays in Vegas thing don't work with me."

Vernon laughed. "You are so hard on me. Did you treat all your men like this?"

"No, just you."

"Them I must be blessed."

"What is up with you?"

"Constance just called. She signed the papers I'm on my way over to pick them up."

Naverone stood to her feet. "Just like that, she signed the papers."

"According to her." Vernon laughed. "We're getting married in Vegas first thing in the morning. Then I'm going to wear your little ass out."

She smiled at the thought, but her spiddy sense was sounding off big time. "Babe how far away are you from her place?"

"I'm at the house. About twenty minutes away."

"How about if I meet you there?" Naverone was strapping her gun to her thigh as she spoke.

"That may be problematic. I don't want anything to piss her off. I've waited long enough for these papers and you. I want you in my life Rene."

She loved it when he called her Rene. "I want this too, but I want you safe more." I'm in route," she said as she climbed into her SUV. I'll meet you there. Tell me, how did she sound? Was she sincere?"

"Come to think of it she sounded a little melancholy. Told me to kiss Taylor for her."

Naverone paused before she pulled off. "That didn't sound weird to you?" Her phone beeped. "Hold on babe." She clicked over. "Taylor, hey what's up?"

"Naverone, I have a weird message on my phone from my mother. When I called her back I'm not getting an answer. As pissed as I am with her, I'm a little worried."

"Where are you?"

"On my way to my mother's place."

"So am I and your Dad. We'll meet you there."

"Is everything okay? Why is my Dad going to see my mother?"

"She called him to come by."

"Oh," Taylor hesitated. "This could be one of her tricks to get me to come over. Maybe I'm worried for no reason."

"If your gut tells you something isn't right. Go with it. Your Dad is on the other line. Let me tell him what's going on."

"Don't tell him what my mother did. That will just make matters worse."

"I gave you my word, I would not mention it to him. I'll see you in a few." She clicked back over to Vernon. "That was Taylor. She said she received a weird call from her mother, too. Vernon, I don't have a good feeling about this."

Vernon hesitated. "What? You think she might hurt herself?"

"It's not out of the realm of possibilities. She's been through quite a lot the last few months."

"I'm pulling up in front of the house now," Vernon said as he looked around the premises. "Everything looks in place. Her car is here."

"Don't go in until I get there."

"Naverone, I'm going to get those signed papers." He disconnected the call and stepped out of the car. As a precaution, he turned on the recording device on his phone and walked towards the door. "Oh hell, the front door is open." Vernon hesitated. The memory of his clients in this same type of situation played in his mind. He stopped the recording and dialed the police.

"My name is Vernon Brooks. I'm at my estranged wife's home. Her front door is open. Please send a patrol car to 7423 Cox Road. I'm going inside."

"Affirmative. A car is in route."

Vernon put the recorder back on and called out, "Constance, it's Vernon. I'm coming in." He pushed the door open with the ball of his hands, then stepped into the foyer. "Connie? Are you here?" He walked further in, turned left to look into the dining room, then he turned right and froze. "Connie," he said with a sadness as he sighed. "Connie's body is lying in the living room in a pool of blood. I'm going to check her pulse. Vernon hesitated, then walked and bent down next to Connie. He saw the gun on the other side of her body near her hand. Her face was turned away from the door and her eyes were open. There was a sound behind Vernon he recognized all too well. It was the cock of a gun. Vernon didn't think, he grabbed the gun next to Connie and fired in the direction of the sound.

"Daddy?" Taylor called out when she ran into the house. Vernon turned towards her with the gun still in his hands. Naverone ran in with her weapon drawn followed by two police officers.

"Drop the gun," they yelled as they pulled their weapons.

Vernon bent and placed the weapon on the floor. "I'm the person who called you. Someone is in this house. "

One officer cuffed Vernon, while the other searched the house.

"Taylor, I didn't do this," Vernon held his daughter's eyes. "I didn't do this." He looked up at Naverone, shaking his head. "I didn't..."

She walked over to him. "Don't say anything."

"I'm standing here in handcuffs in front of my daughter. Of course I'm going to say something."

"Daddy, what would you tell your client?" Taylor came and stood next to him. That's when she saw her mother's body. "Mother?" She reached out, but the officer stopped her from touching the body. "Mother!" she screamed.

Vernon stepped towards her to comfort her, but his hands were cuffed. Naverone stepped between Taylor and her mother's dead body. "Taylor, lets' wait outside."

Taylor looked up at her father with tears streaming down her face. "Daddy?"

"I'm going to be okay, you go with Naverone."

Naverone turned sharply towards him. "Not a word." She then took Taylor from the room.

The other officer came back into the room. "No one's in the house."

"Secure the premises and call it in," the officer said as he moved Vernon into the foyer. "You're Vernon Brooks."

"Yes, I'm the person who called you prior to coming into the house."

"Tell me what happened."

"I can do better. When I saw the door was open, I recorded my every movement on my cell phone. It's in my pocket."

The officer reached in and pulled the cell phone out. It was still recording. "Officer Jamison, badge number 1556. It is nine-forty-two pm. I am turning the recording device off."

Chapter 19

Ericka walked into the house with tears streaming down her face. She had been so determined to get to Isaac Singleton that she never stopped to think what she could lose. Everything that Nick saw in their future she now realized was what she wanted.

She put her purse on the table, then walked over to the piano and sat. It was the place in the house where she felt the closest to him. *I want forever*. The words sounded as if they echoed through the house. The tears flowed, but they weren't sad tears. They were cleansing tears. She cried for the baby she had to give up and never had the opportunity to hold. She cried for the lost time with her mother. Never having the chance to say I love you Mommy. Then she cried for herself. All the years she was searching for something to fulfill her life. Money wasn't the answer. Her cell phone rang.

She reached in her pocket and pulled it out. She wiped the tears and began to laugh.

"Did you feel me thinking of you?"

"I was about to ask you the same question," Nick replied. "I have a few minutes before we take off and I could not think of a better way to spend my time."

"Nick, I did something foolish today," she looked down. "I almost ruined our future, but you know I think God interceded and despite all my efforts he brought me out of the situation so I could spend the rest of my life with you."

"Whatever you did doesn't matter. I'm coming home with information that is going to free your mind. We can let go of the past and begin our lives together. Maybe have a few babies, two or three."

Ericka laughed out loud, with tears flowing. "That would be wonderful, because Nicolas Brooks, I'm done. My fatal mistake was falling in love with you. My life is irrevocably changed forever."

"I am so happy to hear that." He laughed. "They are calling my flight. Will you remember where we left off so we can pick up once I get home?"

"I'll remember that and more."

"I love you Nick."

"I love you more." The call disconnected.

***

James sat in the office of the Chief of Staff, Calvin Johnson with President Harrison. It was a very seldom moment of a quiet evening, with 'no end of the world' crisis happening. It was actually the first time in a while they had to sit back, have a drink and shoot the breeze in a while. Suddenly Secret Service rushed in the room.

"Mr. President the building is crashed. Please step into the Oval Office."

This was not an unusual situation. The men calmly stood and walked through the breezeway connecting the two offices. "This should only take a moment Sir."

"What's happening out there?" JD asked.

"A plane has entered the restricted airspace."

The men glanced at each other knowing their moment of peace had ended.

"All clear," an agent announced.

Brian Thompson entered. "There's an unconfirmed report that a plane went down in the Potomac River."

"Private plane?" JD asked.

"No sir," Brian replied. "It seems the plane originated in New York. More information is being assembled."

"Keep me posted," JD replied as James' phone vibrated.

He stepped away and answered. "Hey Pop."

"Son, you need to come home."

"What's wrong Pop?"

"Your brother is being held for questioning in the death of Constance."

"Constance is dead?"

JD and Calvin turned towards James' raised voice.

"She was shot and Vernon was found standing over her bloody body."

James hung up the phone and turned to JD. "Constance is dead and Vernon is being questioned in her death." He turned and walked into Calvin's office to get his suit coat. He was about to walk out the door when JD called him back. He held a document in his hand.

"What is it?" James asked, clearly in a hurry to leave.

"You need to take a look at this?" JD stated.

"It can wait..."

"No, look now." JD ordered.

James took the document from him then glanced down at it. "A manifest for a flight?" He shrugged his shoulder.

"James, look at the name at seat 1A."

He looked down and his knees almost buckled.

***

Ericka had fallen asleep waiting for Nick. She was jarred awake by something on the television. She glanced at it and saw it was a special report. She reached on the nightstand for the remote control and turned the volume up.

"We are still awaiting information on the number of passengers aboard Flight 1556. What we do know is the flight took off from JFK airport at seven-o-five p.m. with one stop at Dulles International. It was scheduled to land at Richmond International at nine p.m.. More at eleven."

Startled, Ericka picked up her cell and dialed Nick's number.

"You've reached Nicolas Brooks. I'm unable to take your call. Please leave your name and a brief message."

Ericka was about to panic when the house telephone rang. "Hello."

"Ericka, I've sent a car to get you to the airport. The plane will be waiting for you."

"Nikki," her voice was weak and questioning.

"We don't know anything at this point. I have to go." The phone went dead just as there was a knock at the door.

***

Ericka rushed through the emergency doors at the hospital where an administrator greeted her. "Are you Ericka Kennedy?"

"Yes," she walked quickly, to where she did not know.

"The Brooks asked that I direct you to where the family is waiting."

She stopped. "Where is Nicolas?"

"I have no information ma'am. I'll take you to the family."

"Okay, okay." Ericka looked around. "Where to?"

"This way."

Ericka followed the man. They walked by people in tears, hugging each other. There were groups talking to doctors. She didn't see anyone she recognized. Then they came to a closed door. Her heart sank. "Why are they behind closed doors?"

The man opened the door. Inside were Nicole, Xavier, Naverone and a group of other people she did not know. "Ericka." Nicole stood.

She looked at Nicole with tears on the brims of her eyelids; looked at all of them, she saw nothing. Her head was shaking back and forth.

Not again, she thought. This can't be happening to her again.

"He's alive Ericka." Nicole caught her as she bent over crying out as if in pain. Vernon, who was standing behind the door with Taylor, picked her up and carried her to the sofa. He placed her down, positioning the pillow under her head.

Gwen sat next to her. "Have the staff to bring in a cold cup of water," she ordered. "Take this pillow and place it under her feet." Nicole removed her shoes and started rubbing her feet.

Ericka was trying hard to control all the emotions flowing through her. The heat from her feet was building to a point of being unbearable. She pulled her feet away and tried to sit up.

"Stay down."

"I have to get to Nick. I have to...."

"No dear. Right now you have to sit here and breathe. Short breaths"

Ericka followed the instructions as she breathed in and out, slowly.

Once her breathing was under control, Gwen helped her to sit up. "Drink this." She held a cup of water out for Ericka.

She took the cup and then took a sip. She gave the cup back to the woman. "Thank you." She inhaled. "Where is Nick?" the fear was in her voice.

"He is in intensive care. He has a broken leg, some cuts and bruises and a slight concussion. He is not out of danger," her voice broke. "But he is better than those who did not survive."

Ericka took her hand. "Nick would tell me to pray. That's what I think I will do." She looked at the woman. "Do you pray?"

"For my husband and my children every day."

"I don't have any children," she cried. "I only have Nick." She closed her eyes. "We talked about it, but...."

The woman squeezed her hand. "You and Nick will have plenty of time to give me grandchildren."

Ericka nodded her head, then she stopped. She looked around the room.

Nicole stood next to her. "Ericka," she cleared her throat. "My father, Avery Brooks."

Avery stood. "Hello dear."

"My brother, James and you know Vernon. That's his daughter Taylor. And this is my mother, Gwen."

Ericka looked at the woman holding her hand. "You're Nick's mother."

"I am and I am telling you, Nick isn't going anywhere. So you wipe those tears." She used a napkin to touch Ericka's face.

A doctor walked into the room. Xavier put his arms around Nicole. Avery stood and took Gwen's hand. Vernon and James came to attention as they all faced the doctor eagerly waiting for him to speak.

"Who is the lovely Ericka?"

She turned to face the doctor. "Yes."

"Nicolas is asking for you. Nicole?"

"Yes."

"He indicates his leg hurts like hell. Can you use the twin telepathy and pull some of pain away?"

Nicole laughed as tears ran down her face. Xavier held her tight as she turned and cried into his chest.

Gwen took Ericka's hand. "Please tell him we are here and we love him."

"You should see him."

"He needs to see you, dear." She kissed Ericka's temple and gave her a sad smile.

Ericka nodded and followed the doctor.

Gwen turned, then took Taylor in her arms.

James turned to Vernon. "Talk to me."

"I did not..."

"That I know. Give me details."

"She called stating the divorce papers were signed. I went there to pick them up. The door was open I walked in she was on the floor dead."

"Constance dead, Nick in a plane crash. What's next?" Nicole sighed.

Epilogue

His eyes were puffy. There were cuts on his face. His left leg was broken and God knows what else, but Nick was a wonderful sight. Ericka bent down and kissed his cheek. A tear dropped from her eyelids to his cheek. She sniffed and wiped the other tears away, then took his hand.

"Marry me?"

She whispered in his ear with a loud hiccup of a cry. "Yes."

"Now."

She smiled. "You have to wait until you can get on one knee and ask me properly.

"It's a date," he closed his eyes and slept.

Ericka walked out the door to get Nick's mother when she saw the officers and a man in a suit walk in the room. She stood behind them.

"Vernon Brooks?"

Vernon stood facing the men, he looked over his shoulder at James. "You're on."

Taylor pulled away from her grandmother and stood next to her father. Naverone held his hand. Vernon squeezed her hand as James spoke to the officer.

"Captain, James Brooks, I'm his attorney. Is this something that has to be done here...now?"

"Mr. Brooks, I have a dead body and a witness who indicates your brother shot and killed his wife."

James looked over his shoulder at Vernon, then turned back to the officers. "There is a witness to the shooting?"

"No, we received a call from a..." he looked at his notes. "Isaac Singleton stating he heard Mr. Brooks threatening his wife tonight. We have to take him in."

An officer stood behind Vernon, placing handcuffs on his wrist. "Vernon Brooks, you are being arrested for the murder of Constance Brooks. You have the right to remain silent. Anything that you say can be used against you in a court of law. Do you understand these rights as they have been read to you?"

"Yes," Vernon replied.

The officer took Vernon by the arm and led him out of the room. Vernon looked over his shoulder to see Naverone taking every step he took. The people in the waiting room staring at him as he took what was referred to, as the perp walk did not concern him for Rene Naverone had his back. He knew there was a light at the end of the road.

Beacon of Love
Prologue

Vernon Eugene Brooks was a wealthy man in many ways. With a successful legal practice, a loving family, a talented daughter and a beautiful woman by the name of Rene Naverone, at his side, one would think he had it made. Wrong.

"Next case," the judge called out.

"The Commonwealth of Virginia vs. Vernon Brooks."

The judge's head flew up with startled eyes. "Mr. Brooks, I must say I'm somewhat surprised," he said in a voice filled with confusion.

"I am somewhat perplexed myself, Your Honor," the six-two, one hundred ninety-five pounds, Vernon Brooks stood at the defense table. The statement was not frivolous. He honestly was at a loss as to why he was placed under arrest for the murder of his estranged wife, Constance Brooks.

Close to twenty-four hours ago, he walked into his wife's condominium to find her lying in a pool of blood and a gun inches from her hand. At first sight, it looked as if she had shot herself. However, moments after discovering her body, Vernon heard the click of a gun being cocked behind him. He grabbed the gun off the floor, swung around, and fired. Seconds later, two police officers burst through the door. They found him standing over a dead body that had a gunshot wound, holding a gun. The logical conclusion was he was the person who fired the weapon. While being questioned, Vernon revealed that his cell phone had been recording from the moment he stepped out of his car until he entered the house. The recording supported his statement and he had been released. Now he was standing in arraignment court answering to the charge of First Degree Murder.

"What do we have, Mr. Murdock?" The judge asked the prosecutor.

"Bruce Murdock for the people, Your Honor." The prosecutor pulled open the folder and read from the police report. "Mr. Brooks was found standing over the dead body of his estranged wife who he had threatened earlier in the day. We are asking he be held without bond."

The judge stared in dismay at the prosecutor. "Are you certain those charges, are against Mr. Brooks and not his client, Mr. Murdock?"

Sensing something was amiss the young prosecutor reread the charges, then looked at the judge. "That's what it reads here, Your Honor." He then looked at the man standing at the defense table.

"Vernon," the judge looked at him questioning, filled with concern.

"Not guilty, Your Honor, " Vernon stated.

"James Brooks for the defense, Your Honor."

"It's a family affair, I see," the judge stated. "Tell me this is some type of a joke, Mr. Brooks." The judge spoke as the clerk handed him the file.

"I concur, Your Honor." James nodded. "However, technically the statement is correct. As to bail..."

"A moment, Your Honor."

Everyone turned to see the familiar face of District Attorney Neal Kirkland, dressed in his thousand dollar suit, walk through the entrance with a television camera and reporter behind him.

"D. A. Kirkland what is the meaning of this?" He pointed to the reporter. "The press is not allowed in my courtroom. "

"Your Honor, they are working on a documentary. The True Defenders of Justice. They follow me twenty-four seven."

"Not in my courtroom, they don't. Bailiff." The judge pointed to the door. "State your business, Mr. Kirkland."

Neal Kirkland with his blonde hair, blue eyes, and all-American charm, handed a document to the bailiff. "The people are submitting a motion requesting this arraignment be moved for disposition."

The judge read the document. "On what grounds?" he asked, clearly perturbed by the request.

"Mr. Brooks is well known by the courts and the people believe an impartial judge should preside over all aspects of this case, including the arraignment."

The judge glared at Kirkland for a long hard moment.

"Your Honor," James and Vernon, called out simultaneously.

"I'm with you, Mr. Brooks." James shot Vernon a look as the judge continued.

"Mr. Kirkland, this court is not going to allow you to run ram-shackle on this case if it gets anywhere near a court. You are insinuating this court cannot be impartial."

"Your Honor, there is no question as to this court's integrity. Vernon Brooks makes his living in these courts."

"As well as many others," James interrupted. "Is it D.A. Kirkland's intention to move this case out of the country?"

Kirkland looked up to see the two Brooks brothers standing side-by-side staring at him. It was an unsettling feeling. It was one thing to bring down Vernon, quite another when it came to James Brooks. What the hell. If he chooses to stick by his brother on this, he would bring him down as well. If a blemish hit the White House in its wake, all the better. "Mr. Brooks. It is an honor to have the advisor to the President with us. I am certain we can find a court here to serve our needs."

James noticed the smug look on Kirkland's face as Vernon whispered in his ear. James nodded. "We have no objections to changing courts, Your Honor."

"Very well. Approach the bench. Bailiff give me the list of available courts."

James, Vernon, Kirkland and Murdock gathered at the bench. The judge looked at the calendar. After glancing through, he looked up. "Your request is granted Mr. Kirkland. However, the defense gets to select which court." He glared at the D.A. as he turned the tablet towards James and Vernon.

Vernon pointed to a name on the list. James nodded, then advised the judge.

"Bailiff, contact Judge Silvio. Advise her she has a case coming over. Step back gentlemen."

"Your Honor," Kirkland interrupted. "I'm not certain I agree with the defense having a choice. After all..."

"Put on your big girl panties, Neal" Vernon sneered. "You're in the big leagues now."

"Your Honor!"

"Be careful what you ask for Mr. Kirkland."

"It's D.A. Kirkland."

"Earn it." The judge replied without looking up. "Mr. Murdock, I take it you are handling the next case. It's not big enough for Mr. Kirkland to soil his hands. No media potential." The judge's gavel came down on the desk. "Next case."

Vernon and James turned to the people in the courtroom as they stepped from the defense table. Rene Naverone, the five-eight, one hundred and twenty pound ex-Secret Service agent who had captured Vernon's attention a few months ago and James' protection detail walked with them out the door.   A police officer took Vernon by the elbow.

James held up his hand. "Would you give us a minute?"

The officer looked to his partner and nodded. They took a step back giving the group a little space.

Vernon took a deep breath. "From the top attorney in the country to this."

"You think a bit much of yourself, don't you?" James who was taller than his older brother teased as they stood in a moment of discomfort. He looked away, then back to

Vernon. "The police had to make the arrest based on the evidence at the crime scene. Do they still have your cell phone?"

"Yes." Vernon replied as he thought. "We need to get that back as soon as possible."

"Anything on there they can use against you?"

"If they knew what they were looking at, or for, it could make things interesting."

Rene Naverone who was leaning against the wall as the brothers talked, stepped forward. "I'll take care of it." She walked off as Vernon watched.

"You can't do that."

Vernon glanced at James, then back at Naverone. "Those jeans, the leather jacket and the spike heels turn me on."

"They can also be the motive the D.A. needs to put you behind bars."

"It's not going to happen." Vernon smiled at his brother.

"How can you be certain about that?"

He shrugged his shoulders. "For one, I didn't kill her. And two, my brother is defending me."

"Why isn't this man in handcuffs?" Kirkland yelled at the officers as he walked towards them with the reporter and cameraman in tow.

Vernon and James turned towards him as the Secret Service agents held the reporter and cameraman back.

"I don't see him trying to escape," the officer replied.

"He is a man under arrest for murder," Kirkland countered as he stopped in front of

Vernon. "There will be no special favors because your last name happens to be Brooks."

"Neal Kirkland, the District Attorney himself. You contradict yourself. I am indeed getting the special treatment, for you came to the dungeon from your palace on the hill just to see me."

"I came to finally ensure you are put where those animals you set free should be. I am going to go for the maximum on you Brooks. And make no mistake, I will see you under a jail."

"So much for seeking justice which is supported by truth."

"Truth." Kirkland laughed. "When did you become interested in truth?" He laughed sarcastically. "You, the attorney to the stars who defiles the truth at will just to line your pockets."

Vernon took a step forward getting into Kirkland's personal space. "It is your responsibility to prove beyond a reasonable doubt, to convict. Don't blame me because you and your team fall short." He looked the man up and down. "Try getting your suits tailored rather than off the rack at the warehouse, it helps with confidence."

"Handcuff him!" Kirkland growled.

"For what? Because he wears better suits than you do?"

Kirkland slowly turned to the officer with a glare that would burn most people. "Do it or turn in your resignation."

James stepped between Vernon and Kirkland. "He will not be handcuffed during these procedures. If you have an issue with that, talk to your boss, the Attorney General of The United States." He looked from Vernon to Kirkland. "If you are finish posing for the camera, let's get this hearing over with so my brother can mourn the death of his wife and see to her burial." James and Vernon walked off as Kirkland stood there watching.

"Make that the last time you grandstand with Kirkland," James said to Vernon.

"He's an asshole."

"I don't disagree. But he is the asshole who will gain political ground and personal satisfaction in seeing you behind bars." He stopped. "He's going to throw everything he has at you."

"You scared?"

James stared at his brother. "Hell, no. I'm a Brooks. We eat assholes like him for breakfast."

***

Judge Madeline Silvio looked around her courtroom. To her right at the prosecutor's table, she had a D.A. with political aspirations and on her left the top advisor to the President of the United States. All she had to do was dispense of this situation with all due haste, and pray this case did not show up on her docket. "District Attorney Kirkland, you called for this special hearing."

"Yes, Your Honor," Neal Kirkland stood, with the pompousness of a king sitting on a throne, a staff of approximately ten surrounding him. "Vernon Brooks is a man of significant means. He has clients here in the United States as well as overseas, who will go to any means necessary to keep him from the arms of justice. Not to mention his connection to the President of the United States. I request...no demand that he be held without bond."

"I take it you are not inferring the president would assist in an attempt to have this man escape your capable hands of justice?" Judge Silvio questioned.

"Your Honor. Mr. Brooks has significant ties to the community. He has never been arrested for any offenses and to my knowledge never received as much as a traffic violation. He wants this matter dispensed of in all due haste."

"Mr. Brooks in all your wisdom you are not standing in my court comparing the murder of your sister-in-law to a traffic ticket."

"No, Your Honor."

"Good. Let's set some rules gentlemen. "District Attorney Kirkland, there will be no cameras in my courtroom and you will limit the merry-men of your staff to three. If you need more assistance than that, then you should assign someone else to this case." She turned to James. "Mr. Brooks, Vernon Brooks. I will not have your infamous antics in my courtroom. I will have no issue with removing you. You will then have to follow the procedures from closed circuit television and allow your brother to proceed solo. Are we clear?"

"Yes, Your Honor."

"Good. Bail is set at five million dollars."

"Your Honor that is pocket change to the Brooks."

Judge Maggie, as she liked to be called, looked up from the document she was about to sign. "You have issues with the amount of bail?"

"I most certainly do."

"Oh, okay then, let's make it two-point-five million." Kirkland started to speak. "One more word and he will be walking out on his own recognizance." She held his surprised glare.

"If you so much as snicker, Mr. Brooks, you will he held." She finally turned from Kirkland. "Is it clear who is in charge of this courtroom?"

"Yes, Your Honor," both Kirkland and James replied.

"Good." The judge hit the bench with the gavel. "Court's dismissed." She left the bench.

James turned to Vernon as the officers guided him to the back. "This is going to be fun."

Vernon smiled. "The Brooks boys against them." He tilted his head towards Kirkland and his staff.

James glanced across his shoulder then shrugged as he grinned up at his brother. "I'll take the Brooks family every time."

Made in the USA
Middletown, DE
08 March 2024

51029292R00166